The Wisdom of

Water

T0131375

The Wisdom of

Water

Karen Hood-Caddy

RENDEZVOUS
PRESS

Le Conseil des Arts du Canada DEPUIS 1957 | The Canada Council for the Arts SINCE 1957

Napoleon Publishing gratefully acknowledges the support of the Canada Council for our publishing program

We acknowledge the support of the Government of Ontario through the Ontario Media Development Corporation's Ontario Book Initiative

Published by RendezVous Press
a division of Transmedia Enterprises Inc.
Toronto, Ontario, Canada   www.rendezvouspress.com

Printed in Canada

07 06 05 04 03   5 4 3 2 1

National Library of Canada Cataloguing in Publication

Hood-Caddy, Karen, date
        The wisdom of water / Karen Hood-Caddy.

ISBN 0-929141-09-1

I. Title.

PS8565.06514W58 2003   C813'.54   C2002-906129-6
PR9199.3.H5918W58 2003

To my brother Jim

Acknowledgments

Warm-hearted appreciations to Wade Oliver, Chief Operator for Port Carling Water and Sewage, for his kindness and time in helping me understand water treatment processes in Muskoka, and to Pauline Shirt and Paul Shilling for explaining Native traditions—*miigwech!*

And for other research: Judy Brouse, Don Currie, Randy French, Randy Gardner, Neil Hutchinson, Peter Jekel, Neil Johnson, Bev Middleton, Scott Northmore, John Oldham and Hilary Rollingson.

Gratitudes also to: Cheryl Cooper, Melissa Gray, Jack Hodgins, Jim Hood, Stewart Katz, Sylvia McConnell, Jim McMahon, Mel Malton, Theresa Sansome, Allister Thompson and Andrew Wagner-Chazalon for commenting on the manuscript at various stages of its evolution.

Special thanks to Ken Black and all those on the Muskoka Watershed Council and its committees.

Finally, hearty appreciations to all of my writer friends in the Muskoka Ink Writers' Guild.

Although this book is set in Muskoka, where Port Carling, Gravenhurst and Bracebridge are real towns, the people and events are entirely fictional.

Chapter 1

The weight of water. Jessie felt it against her paddle as she pulled it through the lake. The surface of the water dimpled and the blue kayak shot forward. She lifted her paddle and waited until the boat skimmed to stillness, then let it float. There was something sacred about a body of water first thing in the morning. The peace of it seemed to radiate out like the smile on a big-faced buddha.

The phone broke into her dream, ringing and ringing.

Jessie groaned as her kayak dream disintegrated from her awareness. She peeked at the bedroom clock. At this hour of the morning, the ringing phone could only mean one thing: a bird or animal in trouble.

Harley stretched over her and picked up the phone. "Hello."

His body was pressed over hers, and she could feel the vibration of his voice deep in his chest.

"Blood on the road?"

Jessie whispered. "Tell them to call the bird refuge." The answering machine at the refuge gave out all the emergency numbers.

Harley leaned further across her, and she heard the drawer of the night table sliding open, then the sound of a pencil scribbling.

She was remembering the warmth of the sun as it

hugged her body in the dream when her side of the mattress lowered.

Harley was standing now. "Keep the bed warm," he said, leaning over to kiss her forehead.

She had planned to get out of bed and go with him. If it was a large animal, he might need help lifting it. Blood on the road. It did not sound good.

"Who was it that called?"

As she listened for his answer, she heard his truck starting, then going down the road. She felt guilty about not going with him but told herself that if Harley had needed her, he would have said so. She snuggled under the covers and tried to find the dream again, but it had sunk down into a part of her that was no longer accessible. She lay awake, listening to the rhythmic rippling of the water lapping against the shore, then flung the covers aside and stood up.

The silver blue lake filled the window.

"God, you're beautiful," she said to it. She pulled on some shorts and a sweatshirt and headed down to the floating dock. Why dream about a paddle on the lake when she could have one?

She slid the narrow nose of the boat into the water and paddled out until the cottages looked like little coloured dots against the deep green forest. Way out here, the cottages didn't seem to take over the lake as much as they did up close. And at this time of day, there were no boats. The surface of the lake was as calm and solemn as a hymn.

Resting the paddle for a moment, she slipped her fingers over the side of the kayak. The lake slithered over and around her skin. The water felt silky and tingled against her hand as if in greeting. She swirled her fingers around in a return "hello" and brought her wet hand to her face, anointing her forehead and cheeks with the cool water.

If she were a beaver, she might be able to smell all the places this water had been before arriving at this part of the lake. She imagined a storm in Algonquin Park and saw rain sliding off some otter's back, rain that trickled into a stream merging with one of the rushing river-veins traversing the great husky chest of the Canadian Shield. From there, this little handful of water would have flowed from lake to river to lake until meeting her hands here. And now it would continue its journey. She imagined it going down the Moon River and out to Georgian Bay, then streaming through the Great Lakes and the St. Lawrence River as it made its way home to its mother, the ocean.

Water was always on the move. Like any wild thing, it was happiest when it was free to go where it needed to go. Contain it, put it in a cup or bucket for a day, and you could practically feel it sulk.

And when it moved, it always took the path of least resistance, flowing with the pull of gravity and changing its shape as the terrain required. Yet, despite every change, it remained relentlessly itself. She could learn a lot from water.

Jessie had never been easy when it came to change. She didn't like that about herself, but it was true. Harley, on the other hand, paddled towards new things as if they were adventures. No wonder it was easier for him to think about leaving Muskoka. Last weekend, however, when the lake had become a hornet's nest of buzzing boats, she had told herself that leaving such noise wouldn't be so bad. Although she hadn't said so to Harley.

"If people like being on the water so much, how come

they're so eager to get to the other side of it," Harley had grumped a few days ago as two neon-yellow jet skis chased each other up the lake.

The May long weekend was always crazy, she thought. "It will be over by Monday."

Harley had frowned. "People come here for the wilderness, then chase it away." Shaking his head, he'd lumbered off to his leather-craft studio like a bear retreating to his den.

She'd watched him go. There was something essentially untamed about Harley. She'd known that the moment she'd seen his long, raven-feather hair. But, as much as she'd loved his untamed spirit, he needed wilderness and lots of it. And he said he couldn't find enough of it in Muskoka any more.

It grieved Jessie to think this might be true. Ever since she'd been little, she'd always thought of Muskoka as the epitome of wildness. She remembered the drives up here from the city, when she'd roll down the window and pull the air into her lungs. Just north of Barrie, it began smelling of water-washed rocks, pine needles and wet moss. Even the texture of the air became different, feeling thick and moist as fur.

Back then, Muskoka had seemed so big, bigger than her, bigger than the town, as big as all of Canada. But in the last few years, even she had to admit that Muskoka's wildness was becoming emaciated somehow and, like some endangered animal in search of survival, seemed to be leaving the area and heading north. How could she blame Harley for wanting to follow?

It wasn't as if he'd said for sure he wanted to leave. For all she knew, this talk about making a foray north to look for property might just be spring talking. At this time of year, Harley was as restless as a moose tied to a tree. Whether this was due to his half Ojibway, or Anishinaabe origins, she didn't know, but every spring, his need for wilderness strained against the tether of his life here in Muskoka.

A dark shadow sailed across the bow of her kayak, and she looked up. The broad black wings of a turkey vulture spread above her, regal and resolute. She sighed. Because of global warming, turkey vultures were becoming common in Muskoka now. They were easy to recognize, because they flew as if the air were their servant, ready to carry them wherever they wanted to go. And carry them the air did—the vulture was barely moving its wings.

Brushing a strand of her long hair away from her face, Jessie lifted the binoculars and examined the wrinkled red cowl around the vulture's neck. Was it true turkey vultures could smell? A birder friend had told her that since turkey vultures ate only dead things, they needed the sense of smell to locate rotting carcasses.

Jessie moved the field glasses down so she could pan along the shore. There, nestled in the midst of some huge hundred-year-old pines, was the forest green boathouse of Wildwood. The geraniums in the window boxes looked like red and pink balls suspended in the air. The official name of the lodge had been changed to The Wildwood Nature Reserve, and in the last year, over three hundred school children had taken part in workshops that took place there. All the workshops centred on teaching kids about wild things and about being in tune with nature. Although Alex, their first director, and a woman at that, had made most of it happen, Jessie was proud to be a part of it. But lately, Alex had become a part of a new project, one that would take her attention away from Wildwood. What would happen to the Reserve then? "More change, that's what," Jessie said quietly.

Moving the binoculars along, Jessie's eyes collided against the next cottage like a bird against a window. No matter how many times she saw this cottage, she could never get used to it. The place had two, no three, turrets and looked as fanciful as a castle in a Disney movie. All it needed was a few Daffy Ducks or Larry Loons and the scene would be complete. She counted the boat slips. There were five. Five!

A "For Sale" sign had been nailed to the front of it. Jessie knew from reading the real estate section of the paper that it was listed for 3.5 million dollars. And what made it worth such an astronomical price? The water. It all came back to water.

It scared her to think about what was happening to the lakes south of here.

Lake Ontario was the worst example. Harley had once told her that the word "Ontario" came from the Huron Indians and meant "beautiful sparkling water". What a joke that was now.

In the last decade or so, lake pollution seemed to be moving north like a flu virus, infecting lake after lake. Apparently, Lake Simcoe was all but dead, although she'd heard that steps were being taken to revive it. She hoped it wasn't too late. And what about the lakes in Muskoka? Maybe she should get the Grannies together and start a water awareness group. The Grannies hadn't taken on any environmental campaigns in a while.

The Grannies, or the Guerrilla Grannies, as they formally called themselves, had banded together a few years before to stand up for the environment. They figured there was already so much weight on the development side of things that it was crucial to add some poundage to nature's side of the scale. Over the years, this group had saved a stand of hundred-year-old trees, stopped some of the more irresponsible development projects and raised enough money to keep the bird refuge from closing down. Even though Jessie was not a grandmother and was at least a decade younger than the youngest in the group, she'd been made an honourary member.

Although it gave her hope that there were others who felt as she did about the environment, it was tiring being continually on guard, fighting to save trees, animal habitat and wilderness. Would it be so awful to leave her beloved Muskoka and move further north, where nature wasn't under such constant siege? Harley didn't think so.

His talk about leaving had started after a gambling casino had been approved for the Rama Reservation just south of there. A huge complex employing thousands of people, Casino Rama had been built on Indian land, after much debate. Good had come from it—Harley was the first to admit that. The money from the casino proceeds had brought important services to native communities. Nonetheless, Harley couldn't reconcile his heart to its existence.

"I know the land where they built it," he said. "One of my favourite bird watching trees was there. Now instead of warblers, all I can hear is slot machines. Ka-ching. Ka-ching..."

Jessie paddled on. Above her, another bird caught her eye. She didn't have to raise her binoculars to know it was a cormorant. Cormorants always flapped their wings as if they were trying to shake off something stuck to the end of their feathers. She followed its flight path and saw that it was heading right for a small house with natural wood siding that was just visible in a nest of trees. This was where she and Harley lived. Harley would say this was a sign, a message telling her to go home. But Harley couldn't be home this soon, could he?

As she paddled past Wildwood, she wondered whether she should pull in. After all, she was due there shortly to help Alex pack things for their first eco-tour. Alex had become involved in an eco-tourism business, and she and Jake, her pilot business partner, were about to fly their first group of business executives up north to Temagami.

As tempting as it was to go in, Jessie headed back home. She wanted to have breakfast with Harley. If he wasn't back, she could at least leave some breakfast out for him. Harley liked eating breakfast, and it would be a small way to make up to him for not going along earlier.

Back at the dock, she tied the boat in a loose chain knot and trudged up to the house. She found Harley sitting in the kitchen, grimly hunched over a beer mug full of tea.

Gently, she went over and wrapped her arms around his wide, generous shoulders. "That bad, eh?" She could feel his emotions swelling up though the fullness of his body.

"Don't know why anyone called me. There was nothing I could do." He paused. "The wolf's guts were smeared all over the road." He raised his hand and touched her arm. "The guy who hit it didn't even stop. It was some other guy who phoned."

"It was a wolf?"

"*Was* is the right word, all right." He sipped his tea.

"There was a collar around its neck saying 'Wolfy'."

Jessie squeezed him hard. She hated it when someone made a wild animal like a wolf into a pet. Or tried to. In a way, she could understand. Wolves, like all animals, were adorable as babies, and sometimes people attempted to domesticate them. But wolves were wild, and when they reached maturity, that wildness usually showed up like a set of newly grown incisors, scaring the owners enough to set such animals loose. Unfortunately, by that time, these animals didn't belong anywhere—they were too wild for the human world and too tame for the world of their siblings. Familiar with both people and cars, they often went to places that they shouldn't go.

"There's an Anishinaabe prophesy about wolves," Harley said.

"Tell me."

Harley was half white and half Ojibway, but because his mother was native and he'd spent his first nine months swimming in an Anishinaabe womb, he'd always maintained that native ways were more a part of him. Lately, he'd been reading and talking a lot more about his Ojibway traditions, and Jessie was eager to know more about them.

Harley reached across the table for some strands of sweetgrass and put a match to them. A musky, sensual smell filled the kitchen.

"When the Creator made the first Anishinaabe, He gave him a brother, Maegun, the wolf. The Creator said that whatever happened to Maegun would also happen to the Anishinaabe. That's turned out to be true. Both the Anishinaabe and the wolf mate for life, they both live in clans, both have had their land taken away, and both have been hunted for their hair. And now both are facing extinction."

Jessie wished she could think of something comforting to say, but sometimes words seemed like such small baskets to carry the largeness of the emotion she felt. She moved his long hair to the side of his neck, eased back the collar of his black shirt and kissed his skin.

Harley blew on the sweetgrass, and smoke billowed up towards them. He encouraged the smoke towards his chest and face with his hands. This was "smudging", a purification ritual, and Jessie knew he would feel better after doing it.

She smudged herself with some of the smoke too, just because she liked the smell of it on her body. Then she moved over to the counter to make more tea. As she waited for the water to boil, she put some bread in the toaster and watered the huge spider plant in the window. Outside she could hear the gentle tinkling of wind chimes.

A few minutes later, she moved aside some of Harley's beads and leather scraps and put a large round teapot on the round oak table. Beside it, she placed a large platter of whole-wheat toast. Harley picked up one of the wedges and slathered it with honey he'd collected from their own bee hives the previous summer. He sucked the dripping honey from his fingers.

She smiled. "You sure you're not half bear?"

He looked at her for the first time since she'd arrived home. His eyes were as dark as the woods. "I'm going north."

Her throat narrowed. "When?"

"Soon." He watched her face.

"How long will you be away?"

He shrugged.

Jessie frowned. She hated it when he was vague like this. Knowing him, he'd just see where things took him. Harley was good at following the compass of his intuition.

"Will you call?" The topic of phoning had often been tricky for them. To her, "calling" meant phoning every day, or every other day. But Harley was as comfortable with the phone as a caribou with a computer.

Harley looked at her tenderly, then pulled her onto his lap.

"I just worry, that's all," she said, nuzzling her head into the muscular pad of his shoulder. She reached through the buttons of his shirt. His chest felt as smooth as the skin of a tree with the bark peeled off.

"I wish I had your ability to cope with the unknown," she said. "You have so much faith."

"It's not faith," he said. "It's trust." He touched her temple. "Faith lives up here, in the head." He moved his hand along her chest and torso, towards her legs. "Trust lives in your body."

His hand stopped on the mound between the tops of her thighs. She knew he hadn't intended to stop there, but he had.

Jessie chuckled. Sensuality had always been their refuge. Despite all the years they'd been together, this had never changed. "And what lives there?"

Deep in his chest, laughter stirred. When he spoke, his voice was softer, less burdened. He shook his head as if there were no words to describe what she was asking him to describe.

"What?" She was smiling now.

He moved his hand between her legs, and his tongue

moved along his lower lip. "You want to be careful with what lives there."

"Is that right…"

He began stroking her. "What lives there is wild. Crazy wild."

The heat of his palm radiated into her. "She likes you…"

He nodded slowly, adamantly. "That's because I give her what she wants."

"Really."

"And when she gets what she wants, she starts to sing like a cat at the moon." He continued stroking her. "She's starting to sing now. Can you hear?"

Her voice was wide with pleasure. "Uh-huh."

"She's getting louder…"

Jessie checked the clock and winced. "I'm due at Wildwood in ten minutes."

He began undoing her blouse. "Call. Say something unexpected has…come up."

Laughing at his choice of words, she tried to imagine the consequences of being late. Alex was in a flap trying to get everything ready for the twelve financial guys she and Jake Corbett were flying to a remote fishing retreat tomorrow. Alex would be in no mood to wait for anybody. "Alex's knickers are already in a knot."

Abruptly, but firmly, Harley eased her off his lap and stood up.

Before she could stop him, he strode outside, shutting the door behind him.

Jessie reached out her hand, then felt it sink down through the empty air. What was going on? It wasn't like Harley to get upset about a lost sexual moment.

She went to the window. Outside, Harley's battered black pickup was pulling away at a funereal pace. A wolf leg stuck up into the air. Anyone else would have left the wolf's carcass by the side of the road, but Harley must have picked it up. He was probably going to go off and find it a final resting place. No wonder he was grouchy.

As the truck disappeared, she mouthed a kiss into the air and sent it off to him.

Chapter 2

Dan Gorman picked up the silver trophy and chucked it into the garbage. He and the other guys at the water treatment plant had won it in last winter's Old Timers hockey tournament, but he wasn't going to lug a trophy from some rinky-dink league full of guys who were over the hill all the way up north to Muskoka. He stared down at it. Was that his only accomplishment last year?

Thank frigging Christ, in a few days he'd be out of here. Out of this job, out of this city and out of a few sticky situations he'd stupidly got himself into. He was going to have a new start, in a new town. From what he'd seen, Muskoka was the playground of the rich and famous. Although he was still recovering from the gut-wrenching financial hit his reserves had taken in the divorce, he was climbing back. And Muskoka was the perfect place to begin his ascent.

In Muskoka, he'd be hobnobbing with some major players. Like Meat. The brother of Dan's best friend in high school, Meat was one of those naturally talented kids who had shot into hockey fame like a puck into the net. Dan's father was always going on about him, how famous the guy was now, the gazillions of bucks the guy made every year, the incredible goals he scored. Meat was everything Dan's father had wanted him to be.

It wasn't that Dan hadn't tried. He'd spent hours skating on the rink his dad had made in the backyard, practising his slap shot until his arm ached, but he'd never excelled. Now, if someone had asked him to draw a caricature of any of the players, he would have been able to do that, no problem. In fact, he had such a talent that the other kids at school were always pushing a pencil into his hand and asking him to draw things. But not his father. The only piece of wood his father wanted him to hold was a hockey stick.

Meat, however, being the hotshot hockey player that he was, had all the toys, including a two million dollar "cottage" in Muskoka that came equipped with an antique launch, a ski boat and two jet skis. Dan was waiting to hear if he could crash there for a few weeks. Just until he found a place he could afford.

Pulling another beer from the cooler, Dan sat back in the vinyl-covered swivel chair. It was Sunday, so he didn't have to worry about anyone seeing him drinking. In Muskoka, his dad kept beer in the little fridge at the back of his office. There would be advantages to living out in the boonies.

From the sound of things, his father had built quite a little fortress for himself up there in Bracebridge. Dan was grateful he wasn't going to have to work in the same building. He'd never survive that. His father had a way of pulling people in close around him, as if to increase his own bulk and substantiveness. As if he weren't substantial enough. His father weighed at least 250 pounds.

Dan looked down at what he'd drawn on a pad of paper: a worried looking man stared back at him. Dan threw aside his pen. One of these days he was going to break this stupid doodling habit. He scrunched up the piece of paper and picked up a large, silver-framed photograph that had been lying face down in the bottom drawer of his desk. The photograph, taken two years ago, included himself, his ex-wife, Barb, his kids, Franny and Claire, and his parents. Although the photographer had tried to tuck his father in behind everyone, it was like trying to tuck in a bull. Not that his father ever seemed to mind his size. Dan secretly suspected he rather liked having so much weight to throw around.

Dan scanned his own body in the picture. How much thinner he had been then. He looked down at the burp of blubber that now extended over his belt. He sucked in his gut sharply. He was going to have to start cutting back on his beer. Fat chance of that, he thought, given the drinks his father was always pressing on him. He was not an easy man to say no to.

"He bullies you," Barb used to say.

Dan looked cautiously at Barb in the photograph, as if she might lunge out at him. She had worn her blonde hair long then, the way he liked it. He had been so in love with her. How had it all gone so wrong?

A year ago, Barb had met someone else and told him to move out. At first, he saw the kids a lot. But Barb kept them continually busy, and seeing them became an organizational nightmare. When he did manage to see them, he had to face Jerry, Barb's new man. The last time he'd gone to get them, Jerry and Barb and the kids had all been snuggling on the couch watching TV. The thought of it made his bones burn. He took a long guzzle of beer, as if to soothe the heat.

"You should have listened to me," his father had told

him. "A woman like that wants to be boss. She'll try to be the balls in the family."

Although he hated to admit it, his father had been right. The moment he'd put a ring on Barb's finger, she'd inserted a larger one in his nose. When she'd wanted kids, they'd had kids. When she'd wanted a big house in the suburbs, they'd bought a big house in the suburbs. I want, I want, I want. That's all he'd ever heard from Barb. Even in bed. He cringed, remembering the final year of their marriage. During the last few months, he hadn't been able to perform at all. Not even when she took him in her hand and pumped him. Thinking about it made his palms sweat.

Dan moved his hand across the faces of his two little girls. The glass clouded from the moistness of his fingers, but he could still see their pink skin and eager eyes. A wave of yearning rose up in his chest as he leaned towards the photo. According to the divorce agreement, he was supposed to have regular access, but every time he called, they were busy. Franny went to gymnastics, Girl Guides and swimming. Barb had Claire signed up for piano, skating and ballet. He was glad they were active, but what about him? Why did he have to make an appointment to see them?

He wiped his eyes with his sleeve, chugged the rest of his beer and opened another. He'd told himself he was only going to have one beer today, but packing up was proving to be more of an ordeal than he'd imagined. He would cut back as soon as he was settled in Port Carling. He'd have more motivation then. Besides, it wasn't as if all women found his belly unattractive. Christie had kissed it several times. Christie. She had kissed him everywhere. And when she did, his body had worked the way it was supposed to. At least some of the time.

It had all gone so well at the beginning. Compared to Barb, who was so sharp and full of corners, Christie was round and easy and uncomplicated. She had a plump, generous body, and snuggling into it had felt like falling into a deep feather bed. Which was nice at first, but after a while, he found her softness irritating. Getting away from her was like trying to stand up in a pile of pillows.

Just thinking about her made his legs twitch. Two months ago, he'd told her he needed space. It was a partial truth, but all he was capable of at the time. Somehow he'd convinced himself that telling her the truth would have been too hurtful. But he could see now that although it would have hurt, it would have been a quick hurt and a clean one. The way he'd done it, bit by bit, made him feel as if he'd hacked away at her with a dull knife, until he'd made even more of a bloody mess.

He guessed that even now she was hoping that if she gave him "space", he'd start missing her and call, but whenever he thought about calling, he felt pressure. He was never good under pressure.

If only she'd agreed to have the abortion. He was way too old to father another baby. It wasn't that he didn't like kids; he did. If she'd had a five-year-old, he wouldn't have minded, but the idea of diapers and night feedings—it was all too much. Besides, he already had kids. Holding Franny and Claire as newborns had been one of the biggest thrills of his life, but that time in his life was over.

What if Christie had a boy? He'd always wanted a boy. He imagined tossing a ball to a small replica of himself, then erased the picture from his mind. Unconsciously, he picked up his pen and began doodling once again.

Chapter 3

Jessie paddled with purposeful strokes to Wildwood and thought about Harley. It wasn't often he was unhappy with her, and it made her feel unsettled. A remembrance bloomed into her awareness. Wasn't this the time of year when Harley's mother had died? Yes, it was. Was he aware of that? Even if he wasn't, his body might be. The body had a way of remembering these anniversaries, even when the mind didn't.

Harley had been close to his mother, close in the unique way a son becomes when he has to fend off a father's abuse. Not that his father was always abusive. At first, it had only been on Saturday nights after a drink-up at the bar. When his father began spending weeknights drinking too, the abuse became more frequent. And more brutal. By the time Harley was a teenager, the abuse was regular and violent enough to have his mother bouncing between a women's shelter and a mental institution.

Unfortunately, according to Harley, the mental institution was as crazy-making for her as her husband.

"The drugs turned her mind to mush," Harley told Jessie once. "Made it so nothing mattered. Even living." Harley had been the one to cut her swinging body down.

After that, Harley's father had taken off and had never been heard from since. But he'd left some muddy footprints in Harley's emotional life. When Jessie tried to get him to talk about his feelings for his father, he wouldn't.

"The past is over," he always said.

The forcefulness of his voice told her more than the words. It was like someone saying, "I'm *not* angry." Unfortunately, wanting one's past to be over didn't make it so.

Jessie sighed and wondered what it would take for Harley to make peace with his past. If it were important for him to do that, the great teacher of Life would create a situation that forced him to do it. Until then, there was nothing to be done.

She paddled further up the lake and in a few minutes was close enough to see the totem pole that stood in front of Wildwood. The faces on the pole were like ancient ancestors guarding the lodge, and she was grateful for them. Closer now, she noticed that a pair of mirrored sunglasses had been arranged on one of the lower faces. She smiled. Kids!

These days they came by the busload from schools and towns across the province. Ever since Alex had moved here two years ago to be Wildwood's director, she'd made the place bustle with activities. Who was going to handle all that if Alex kept on with this eco-tourism business? City people, Jessie thought. They moved up here because they wanted a slower, more humane pace, but they couldn't give up their hustling. Alex was always thinking up something new. And why shouldn't she? a voice inside her countered. Alex had every right to create her life as she wanted. Things would still work out. They always did.

She tied up the kayak and sat for a moment in one of the Muskoka chairs. Muskoka chairs were so seductive. "Let go," every slanting slat of its structure coaxed. She lay back and relaxed.

The sun felt warm on her face, and she could smell the sun roasted wood of the dock. She breathed into her shoulders but couldn't get her muscles to let go of their grip on her bones. If Harley found a place and wanted to leave Muskoka, would she go with him? What about her friends? What about her work? Hadn't she made enough changes in her life already?

The first big change had come when she'd decided to retrain as a psychotherapist. Although she only did counselling half time now because of her environmental work, that change had been for the best, hadn't it? The next change had been to take on the running of the bird refuge—that had brought her many joys too. What made her think that whatever changes she made now wouldn't also be good?

She looked out over the lake. In nature, change was everywhere. The landscape she was staring at now, for example, had once been part of a mountain range as high as the Rockies. Later, this same area had been submerged under a large sea. At another time, it had been under hundreds of feet of glacial ice—ice that gouged the basin for the lake that shimmered in front of her now. The last glacier had left 10,000 years ago, which was an eon in human terms, but a mere blink in the planet's schedule.

It was thanks to the glacier that the earth had so much water. It was remarkable, really—given the lack of water on other planets. Although she'd read that Mars might have had water once too. Perhaps Mars had lakes and forests and animals at one time as well. Had the Martians burned holes in the ozone and caused their planet to be dried up by the sun?

She sighed. She wished she had time to go swimming. She would have loved to dive into that cool water and wash away all her thoughts. There was nothing that could change her state faster than a swim.

Promising herself she'd have a swim later, she carried her shoes up the path that went around the side of the building. She liked the feeling of the cool, bare ground against her toes. In shoes, her feet sometimes felt like stumps at the end of her legs, but when she went barefoot, she felt as though she almost had another pair of hands.

At the top of the steps, she could see the bird refuge nestled into the woods a few hundred yards behind the lodge. She and Harley had moved the refuge here when there were too many birds for them to handle at home. In the woods surrounding the building, a thousand trillium heads peeked up from the lush green undercover. Jessie considered taking a stroll through them, but she knew Alex would be waiting for her, so she turned and climbed the sun warmed steps of the main lodge.

Smoke? Was that smoke she smelled? She moved quickly around the corner of the wraparound verandah.

"Alex!"

Alex stubbed a cigarette out. "Don't say anything!"

Jessie nodded. "I thought you gave up smoking when you moved here from Toronto."

"I thought you weren't going to say anything."

"It's just opening night jitters," Jessie said and moved behind Alex. She put her hands on Alex's shoulders and started kneading the rigid muscles. Wisps of Alex's Chanel #5 perfume wafted towards her. Jessie smiled. You could take a woman out of the city, but you couldn't take the city out of a woman.

Jessie always found it interesting watching someone adjust to living away from the big city. When Alex had first moved here from Toronto, she had been a burnt-out executive in her early forties. Not surprisingly, she'd thought Muskoka was the most relaxing place in the world. But she was learning, like all newcomers, that Muskoka could be busy too, if you made it that way.

"I wish Harley was coming," Alex said.

"No doubt." Not only did Harley know about birds and animals, he had a calming effect on everyone around him. "Did you ask him?"

"Uh-huh."

"What did he say?"

"That men with money calling him Tonto didn't interest him."

Jessie suppressed a smile.

Alex stretched her arms up. "That feels better. Now, let's get at it, or I'll be tense again in two minutes."

They went out to the storage room and, for the next two hours, checked off supply lists and loaded boxes into the truck. The work took them most of the morning, and they were recuperating on the porch when they heard the screen door whack.

Alex's eyes went to Jessie. "Elfy?"

Jessie looked at Alex. "Know anyone else that can whack a screen door that loud?"

"She sure can make a lot of noise for someone so little," Alex said, lowering her voice.

"Think mosquito," Jessie said.

Elfy appeared around the corner of the porch, and Jessie smiled at her fondly. The old woman was wearing black pants and a bright yellow-striped top.

"Given what she's wearing, I'm thinking 'hornet'," Alex said.

Jessie laughed. Elfy was the oldest Guerrilla Granny, but when she got what she called "her dander up", you could almost hear her buzzing.

"I feel like a hornet." Elfy forked her wrinkled hands through her ginger hair. "I've already had a bird die, and I haven't even had breakfast."

"Die? How come?" Jessie asked, not without alarm.

"Botulism. Looks like. Probably some malfunctioning septic near where the bird was feeding. Who knows? Not the government, that's for sure."

A year ago, the government had slashed the wrists of The Ministry of the Environment and drained the blood out of the province's chief ecological protection agency. As a result, water wasn't being tested properly, septic systems weren't being monitored and other crucial programs that ensured the health of the lakes and forests had been seriously compromised.

Elfy swiped at the tears in the corners of her eyes.

Jessie passed her a cup of tea and put her arm around the old woman. Elfy felt so small, far smaller than one would imagine from the bluster of her personality.

"Maybe we should get the Grannies together," Elfy said.

Jessie nodded. "I don't like hearing about birds dying of botulism." She thought for a moment. "Maybe it's time we did a kind of environmental check-up."

Elfy jutted her thumbs in the air. "Now you're cooking with gas!"

"As if you guys don't have enough to do." Alex tossed her coffee back like a shot of whiskey. "Speaking of—I'd better get my ass in gear." She waved and was off.

Jessie sipped the last of her tea.

"I don't envy that lake," Elfy said.

"What lake?"

"The one Alex is taking all those money men to. By this time tomorrow, they'll probably be peeing in it. And in a year, one of them will build some new-fangled lodge, and there will be even less places for the animals to go."

Jessie looked at Elfy's tired face. It was easy to get discouraged when it came to how people treated the environment. The news was full of stories of man's mistreatment of nature. But people who worked in animal rehabilitation were hit particularly hard. Seeing something on television was difficult enough, but when you had to hold a baby frog that had multiple cancers all over its body because some company couldn't afford to detoxify its emissions, that was something else. And this morning, Elfy'd had to deal with a dead bird.

"The idea was to give people a wilderness experience so they would be more likely to understand the importance of wild places," Jessie said. People had to get their craving for wilderness met somehow. And buying an SUV, despite what the ads said, was just not going to do it. "Besides, who knows, one of their group might just come back and make a big donation to the bird refuge."

"Yeah, and I could sprout wings." Elfy downed the rest of her tea. "Hey, don't you have that talk at the lake association today?"

Jessie nodded as she made her way down to her office. She turned on the computer and waited for it to boot up. On the wall above the desk were photographs of Sushi and Gumption, two loons the bird refuge had helped return to the wild. It always filled her with warmth to think about them. Neither loon had been expected to live. In fact, when these loons had first been found, bird experts had suggested euthanizing them. Luckily, she and Harley and Elfy hadn't listened.

It had been a lot of work, but both loons had survived. And thrived. Since no loons had ever survived in captivity before, this had been quite an accomplishment.

Sushi, bless him, had ended up migrating south. Gumption's plight had been more difficult. Having had one of his feet severed by a propeller, his ability to balance had been damaged, which had made his chances of flying almost impossible. She winced, remembering all the times she'd watched him fling his flight-craved body into the air. One time, however, through the sheer force of his determination, he'd been able to get a grip on the wind and pull himself into the air. She could have sworn from the airy feeling in her chest that her heart had gone on that flight with him.

Turning back to the computer, she was about to click on the notes for her talk, but typed "botulism" into the search engine instead. As she scanned the entries, various articles came up on water pollution, which led to other articles on snow machines and boats.

A flash of indignant heat swept across her chest. She called out to Elfy, "Did you know that two-stroke engines dump a third of their fuel, unburned, directly into the water?"

Elfy appeared in the office doorway. "I knew it was bad, but I didn't know it was that bad."

Jessie scanned down the page. "It says here that one day of driving a two-stroke engine boat produces the same amount of pollution as a car driven 160,000 kilometres. Yikes!"

The lines on Elfy's face deepened until they looked like gashes. "That's scary."

Jessie read from the text on her screen. "That's the equivalent of dumping fifteen two-litre jugs of gas into the water." She put her hand to her chest. Pollution from cars she could understand. People had to get to work. But polluting to have fun?

"When I was a kid," Elfy said, "we used to drink the water right out of Lake Joe."

Jessie slumped back in the chair.

"You should take some of that stuff to your cottage association meeting," Elfy said.

She should. "But you know what? People want to know how they're polluting, but they also don't want to know."

"They don't want to know because that might make it more difficult to keep doing what they're doing."

"Basically." Jessie pressed "print". The light on the printer flashed orange. "Damn, it's out of ink." Mentally, she added it to her list of things to get in town when she went in before her meeting.

She finished some tasks and, heading out the door, found Elfy dragging some garbage bags out from the kitchen. Jessie grabbed one and put it in the back of the old Toyota station wagon. They threw in some other bags as well as the Blue Box for the recycled items.

"I'll ride down with you," Elfy said. "Help you unload."

Jessie drove down the dappled lane. The garbage bins were out by the main road.

"Oh, for crying out loud!"

Jessie stopped the car. Garbage was strewn all over the road around the big metal container with the sign above it that said "For Wildwood Garbage Only".

"That bonehead cottager still hasn't learned to read!" Elfy said.

They suspected a cottager, because the garbage was left out on a Sunday night, the night most tourists returned to the city. And it was a city way of thinking to be unaware of the invitation it posed to animals.

"This is becoming a regular occurrence," Jessie said, getting out of the car. She kicked a tomato juice can towards the bin. She hated other people's garbage.

"Yuck," Elfy said, trying to shove a half-eaten chicken carcass over to the side of the road with her shoe. She picked up a stick and began pushing the cans, milk cartons and food refuse into a pile.

Going back to the car, Jessie pulled out two pairs of rubber gloves from the bird refuge supply bag and tossed a pair to Elfy. She pulled the latex over her hands and picked up the chicken bones. "This stuff stinks!"

"Can't smell it," Elfy said. "My sniffer never did work so well."

Jessie picked up a Smirnoff bottle and threw it into the recycling box.

Elfy held up a tin. "Look what the bozo's tossing out with the regular garbage—varnish! I'll have to take this back and put it with the other toxic waste stuff." She took it over to the car.

Meanwhile, Jessie prodded something with a stick.

"What the heck is that?" Elfy craned forward for a better look.

Jessie harpooned what looked like a withered cellophane tube. "You'll be glad to know someone's having safe sex."

"Why does that fail to raise me to the heights of ecstasy?" Elfy held out the garbage bag, and Jessie flicked the stick so the condom jumped off.

They piled more of the garbage in the big green bag.

"If I knew where to find this guy," Elfy said, "I'd take this over to his place and dump it on his front lawn."

They were almost finished clearing up when Elfy spied something. Using her latexed thumb and forefinger as pincers, she picked up a rumpled sheaf of yellow paper. "Methinks we have a clue." She unfurled the credit card receipt and held it about an inch from her eyes. "Can you make out the signature?"

Jessie shook her head. "Too much of a tomato stain."

Elfy shook off the tomato seeds and folded the slip of paper carefully. "I think I'll just take this clue home. Put it under a magnifying glass and see if I can track this idiot down."

"I wouldn't want to be in his shoes if you do track him down."

"Oh, I'll track him down all right. Don't you worry your pretty little head about that," Elfy said. "And when I do, he'll wish his father had used a condom."

Jessie let the top of the bin drop to a close. It made a loud bang, like an exclamation mark.

Chapter 4

Dan closed the cardboard top of the packing box and took it out to his black Jeep. When he came back in, the drawers of his desk were hanging open. It looked odd seeing them all askew like that. It was just how he felt lately—empty and exposed. He closed the drawers firmly. It was time to pull himself together and mobilize his energy for a new start.

What he had to do next was call Barb and tell her he was leaving. He'd meant to tell her ages ago, during one of his pick-up-the-kids times, but he hadn't seen his daughters in a few weeks. Should he call Christie as well? He liked the idea of hearing her voice, but if he called, he might get roped in. Knowing his own feelings were as dangerous as anything else, he decided not to risk it. He was going to have to show some self-discipline. If he'd done that in the beginning, he wouldn't be in this mess.

The affair with Christie had started a few weeks before last Christmas. It had been his first Christmas by himself, and during the weeks leading up to the big day, his loneliness had pushed him around like a thug, dragging him out of his cold house to cruise the streets, even hauling him into bars where women danced on tables. A few times he'd thought about propositioning one of the dancers and buying himself some sex. Whether he was scared of picking up a disease, or too frightened to face the possibility that he might humiliate himself by being flaccid, he didn't know. All he knew was that he couldn't do it.

By the time the Christmas party at the office came around, his craving for touch had devoured the last of his caution, and he found himself hungrily eyeing one of the secretaries. Christie was a bit pudgy for his usual interest, but in the blur of five rum and cokes, she'd looked as voluptuous as a movie star. When she'd responded to his attentions, he'd asked if he could take her home. He started kissing her in the back of the cab, and when she didn't resist, he just kept pushing the possibilities.

It wasn't as if he hadn't used birth control. He'd used a condom. Every time. In spite of the fact that she'd told him she didn't think she could have kids. Or was that just some bullshit line? For all he knew, the child might not even be his. That's what his father thought.

His father had sighed long and loud when Dan told him. It sounded as if the last of his father's hope was leaking out, like air from a punctured tire.

"Why is it son, that you don't see things until they hit you smack-dab in the face?"

"She's going to have an abortion," he had told his father. It wasn't exactly a lie, because when he'd said it, that's what he was hoping she would do, but he hadn't been able to convince her.

His father never asked about Christie again, but a few weeks later Dan was offered a job in a treatment plant in Muskoka. Although nothing was said between them, Dan knew his father had arranged it. Just as he'd tossed out every other life rope Dan had grabbed on to when he fell into water over his head.

In a way, Dan was grateful. He'd been wanting to leave his present job for a while, and running the treatment plant in Port Carling was a wonderful opportunity. But moving to Muskoka meant living closer to his father. That made him nervous. And he felt guilty about being nervous. After all, his father cared about him a great deal. But sometimes that caring seemed like more than Dan could handle. Like everything else about his father, his voice, opinions, even his love took up so much room, coming towards him like a fat man down a narrow hall.

"Stay away from her now," were his father's only words on the situation with Christie. "And watch where you point that thing."

As Dan remembered all this, he stared down at his blotter. It was covered in drawings. Or "scribbles", as his dad would have said. Miss Emmett, Dan's Grade Seven art teacher, had dignified them by calling his drawings "cartoons". Dan smiled. Miss Emmett had believed in his talent, so much so that she had even looked up colleges he could attend to learn how to become a professional cartoonist.

According to Dan's mother, he'd been born with a pencil in his hand. The first time she'd arranged his pudgy baby fingers around a Crayola, he'd gurgled with delight and started scribbling. His scribbles soon turned into faces, then animals and birds. His mother got so tired of washing the walls that she finally taped huge pieces of paper along the sides of his room.

When Miss Emmett encouraged him to try his hand at a full-fledged comic strip, Dan drew with excitement. Every time he lifted his pen, it was like picking up a magic wand. He felt like a god, being able to create whatever he wanted. Monsters or heroes appeared at the stroke of his pen.

Then one day, InkBoy had swooped onto a page of white paper and changed everything.

Big and black, InkBoy had thighs the size of fire hydrants. The muscles in his arms were as hard as bowling balls. Because he was made of ink, he could do anything that ink could do. He could elongate himself into rope and rescue someone from the top of a mountain, he could draw wings on his back and fly at supersonic speeds, he could become a huge fist and bash some evildoer into submission.

Like all heroes, InkBoy had one archenemy: The Invader. The Invader was a gargantuan monster that could stick invisible tentacles into someone's brain and suck the person's personality right out of them. Only InkBoy was able to stop him. If InkBoy saw what The Invader was up to, he could draw a protective shield around the proposed victim, but sometimes, InkBoy actually had to retrieve the personality. When he did, there was always some beautiful girl hugging him in appreciation at the end of the episode.

Dan submitted the cartoon to the high school newspaper, and the editor liked it so much that he asked Dan to contribute weekly. The strip became popular, and Dan decided to print his own comic book. He bought a second-hand printing machine and put it in the basement. He told his parents it was for a school project and only used it when neither of them were home. He felt guilty doing something behind his father's back, but not guilty enough to stop.

When the first edition of *The Adventures of InkBoy* came off the press, an ecstatic feeling filled Dan's bones, and he thought he might actually float up to heaven. But there was a frightened feeling too, the kind he got when he was up high and was worried about falling. He resolved to make sure his father never saw the comic book.

The comic book sold out of its first five editions, and Dan began to think he just might become a professional cartoonist after all. Was it really possible to do something he loved and get paid for it? He could see from various newspapers and magazines that others were making a living at cartooning. Why not him?

He told his parents he was thinking about going to Art College. His father had transferred him out of art class. Dan begged his mother to intervene, but she wouldn't.

"Your father knows best," she said as she always did when there was a disagreement in the family.

Did his father know best? With his father so adamant about what Dan should and shouldn't do, it was difficult to follow his own sense of things. In the comic strip, however, InkBoy followed his own instincts. He did what he wanted, without a concern about what anyone else thought. Dan jumped over tall buildings with him, flew through space faster than an airplane and caught robbers and thugs.

The only thing neither Dan nor InkBoy could do was destroy The Invader. Episode by episode, InkBoy battled The Invader, but he could never eradicate him. Which was fine with Dan, because it gave him endless episodes to write about. The neverending battle made him money, and lots of it.

One day when Dan was heading home, a wad of bills in his jeans, he saw his father's truck in the driveway. Dan slowed his pace. Sometimes his father came home early, but there was something about the way the truck was parked in the driveway that disturbed Dan. He went inside. His comic book was lying on the kitchen table, his father's fist set on top of it like a gavel.

"Bring me the printing press," his father said.

For months now, in his comic strip, Dan had known what it was like to make his own decisions and do what he thought was right. The comic book had been wildly successful, and he didn't want to give it up. Besides, if InkBoy could stand up for what he believed, so could he.

He tried to speak, but fear clutched his throat, allowing no words to escape. He shook his head instead.

His father exploded out of the chair and pounded down the narrow, wooden steps to the basement. The thumping reverberated through Dan's entire body as he followed his father.

Helplessly, Dan watched as his father wrapped his huge arms around the heavy printing press and lifted it. He grunted. Exertion forced blood into his face, turning it red. The colour changed to a deep, bruised purple, then drained from his face as he collapsed to the ground.

Dan stood immobilized as the ambulance came and took his father away. Over the next few weeks, he didn't know whether his father would survive. Slowly, however, he recovered and when he was well enough to leave the hospital, Dan became his constant helpmate, bringing him meals, getting the mail, doing whatever his father needed.

When his father went back to work several weeks later, the newspaper asked Dan to carry on with his comic strip. Dan picked up his drawing pen, but it felt strangely empty in his hand—as if the ink had drained out of it. Just like the blood had been flushed out of his father's face the day of the heart attack.

He resigned from the paper and applied himself with more fervour to sports. His dad liked it when he reported about the games he played. And the two of them often watched games on TV together.

His hand continued to draw things, but what he drew had no meaning. From time to time, he scribbled a few funny ducks or some cute little animals to impress a girl, but he didn't draw anything that mattered. Once, when he'd had a lot to drink, he'd done some drawing for Christie. Like his art teacher, Miss Emmett, she'd been enthralled and had begged him to draw more. He'd almost told her about InkBoy but caught himself just in time. InkBoy meant trouble, and he'd had enough of that.

Still in his office, Dan stared down at the scribbles on his blotter. He pulled off the paper and tore it in half. He kept tearing and tearing until the blotter was a heap of black and green shreds. With a sweep of his arm, he brushed it into the wastepaper basket.

He was getting ready to leave when he remembered to call Barb. There was no one home. Or if they were there, no one was answering. He imagined them all sitting at the table, laughing and playing cards.

Very slowly, he put the phone down, locked the office and began the drive home. Home. It was a funny word, a word that had no meaning for him any more. When he and Barb had separated, he'd expected to be seeing a lot of the kids, so he'd taken a small apartment not far from his old house. That meant that each and every day he had to drive the old route and be reminded of his loss. He wished now that he'd stuck to his guns and stayed in the house himself. Barb was the one who wanted to separate, she should have been the one to leave. He had let her push him out.

On impulse, he turned down his old street. Maybe the

kids were outside playing. He had to take the chance. He swung into his old driveway and caught sight of Barb trimming a tree with the pruning shears. He was so preoccupied watching her dismember the tree that he didn't see Claire's bike until it was too late. Why was it that the minute he got near Barb he went into screw-up mode?

Barb came over with a scowl on her face and lifted up the bike. The wheel was bent. Her face said, "Now look what you've done!"

His eyes stung. "Is Claire here?" He would take her to the store right now, buy her another bike. One she could be really proud of.

Barb shook her head and nodded to the bike. "Jerry can put on a new tire. He's good at stuff like that."

Dan felt a pain in his chest. He saw himself falling forward, felt his head bash into the steering wheel. Is that what would happen if he had a heart attack right now? He imagined his daughters staring down at him, their eyes full of worry and concern.

Where are they? he wanted to ask. How are they doing? He was hungry for information about them, but asking would make him feel like a beggar.

"I'm taking a job up north." Her eyes jumped on him. "I'm leaving this week."

She hoisted her eyes up as if trying to raise them over the heap of his ineptitude. "Thanks for the notice."

"Some guy quit up north, and they needed a replacement right away," he said, lying. He couldn't remember if he'd lied much before knowing Barb, but he'd certainly perfected the habit since. When you lived with an emotional sniper, you learned to dodge bullets any way you could.

"The kids will be back any minute," she said now. "They're off with Jerry."

Dan felt breathless. Anxious now to get away, he decided he'd call Claire later and apologize for the bike. He sped out of the driveway. Did he ever want a beer. He was tempted to pull over and grab one from the back of the Jeep. He needed to numb himself to the awful feelings he had in his body.

No, he'd wait until he got back to his apartment. But then he was going to let himself drink as much as he wanted. And he was going to watch his favourite movie. *Fantasia.* Fuck the packing.

He was imagining the taste of the beer when he saw Jerry's Mustang. The convertible top was down, and he could see Franny in the front, Claire in the back. As they passed, he could have reached out and touched them.

His fingers tightened on the steering wheel as if around Jerry's neck. His heart flip-flopped again. When the light-headedness didn't go away after a few blocks, he pulled over. It scared him when his heart did this. He threw his head back against the seat and tried to calm down. Was he going to have a heart attack now like his father? Die right here on the side of the road like a dog? If a person could die of a broken heart, he thought that very likely.

Chapter 5

It was almost eight o'clock by the time Jessie returned from making her presentation to the cottage association. It had gone well. Sometimes such meetings were taken over by people angry at the town about exorbitant taxes, but this group had been pleasant and receptive. A few had even asked questions about the bird refuge's pamphlet that she'd handed out, *Top Ten Things Cottagers Can Do For Birds.*

As she pulled up to the house, she was disappointed to see that Harley's truck wasn't in the driveway. Sometimes when he didn't come home for dinner, it was because he was having supper down at the Rama Reserve with One Eye, his grandmother. If so, she wished he'd waited until she could have gone too.

Jessie slumped against the seat. One Eye was one of her favourite people. A true kindred spirit. If it hadn't been for One Eye, Jessie never would have fought so many environmental campaigns. One Eye had taught her to be spiritually ferocious in going after what she believed in. Jessie felt grateful to her for that. And grateful for the fact that One Eye never made her feel second best for being white. That wasn't always the case with others from the reserve.

Some First Nations people applauded any white person who wanted to know about their ways. Others were derisive, calling such a person a Wannabe. The term infuriated Jessie. What was wrong with a white person wanting to know Native ways? Most Native cultures still had a path cleared to the heart of Mother Nature. Whites may have had the Garden of Eden at one time, but there was no way to access it now. Given that, it wasn't surprising white people tried to follow the footprints that another culture had made. Besides, wasn't the point to get more people in tune with Mother Earth, rather than worry about what colour they were?

Jessie got out of the car and dragged herself into the house. As soon as she was inside the door, she saw the flashing light of her office answering machine. Damn. She didn't feel like responding to anyone right now. The machine was just flashing once, so, thinking that she could call whoever it was back later, she made herself listen to it.

The almost inaudible voice sounded exhausted.

"Jessie, it's Lyn. I need to talk."

Lyn Appleton? It had to be, but goodness, Lyn Appleton was a young, vibrant woman. From the sound of her voice, something was wrong, very wrong.

The caller paused, gave a phone number, corrected that number, apologized again, gave another number and hung up, making Jessie even more concerned.

Jessie had worked with Lyn many years ago, helping the young woman recover from a relationship break-up. When Jessie had first met Lyn, she'd found her to be a classic "sensitive". Jessie had always been interested in "sensitive" people, partly because she considered herself to be in that category as well. When she was doing her thesis years ago, she'd done some research on the topic and had been pleased to learn that there actually was a small portion of the population which was not only more affected by such physical things as bright lights and noises, but was also more vulnerable to the psychological vicissitudes of ordinary life.

Lyn was definitely one such person. Nevertheless, Lyn had been eager to grow, and it hadn't taken Jessie many sessions to help her heal the wounds she'd sustained during the break-up and develop some strategies for coping with her sensitivities. It had been a few years now since Lyn had said a grateful goodbye, and Jessie had assumed all was going well. Last summer, she'd met Lyn at a garden centre. There had been a warm exchange between them, and Lyn had seemed fine. So, what was up now?

Jessie was standing by the phone, debating whether to call back now or leave it until later, when she saw a flower on the floor. How had a flower got there, she wondered as she bent over. The flower was in the shape of a small, delicate bugle and was impossibly yellow. Like all trout lilies, it had a fine spray of crimson dots decorating its throat. In her hands, it felt both fresh and fragile. Like love, she thought.

She saw another flower, then another. A whole line of them was arranged on the floor. Like a path. She went from one to the next, until she was in the kitchen. The last flower was on the countertop, lying beside a piece of birch bark. On the birch bark was a crude drawing of a beaver and two, round, smiling faces. The only printed word was, "Come."

So Harley hadn't gone to the reserve after all. He'd gone to the beaver pond. Lately, he'd been telling her about a beaver he'd made friends with, and she'd been asking to be taken along. Here was her invitation. The thought of being out in the woods with Harley gave her a light, airy feeling, and she went off to change. She'd call Lyn later.

She was scampering down the steps, ready to head out the door, when she stopped.

"All right," she said aloud, "but I'm keeping it short." If she didn't call Lyn, she'd feel guilty for the rest of the day.

She dialled the number. The phone was picked up on the first ring. "Lyn? Is that you?" It didn't sound like her. "It's Jessie." Jessie pressed the phone harder to her ear. "Lyn, can you speak up? I can hardly hear you."

With great effort, the woman seemed to throw her voice into the phone. "I'm sick, Jess."

"Sick? What kind of sick?"

"Headaches. Nausea. I'm getting these weird nosebleeds." Lyn's voice faded, and she strained to talk louder. "I'm tired all the time. Some days I can hardly get out of bed. I have this weird itching too, at the roof of my mouth and in my nose."

"Have you been to the doctor?"

"I've been poked and prodded and punctured. He thinks it's all in my head."

Jessie grimaced. This didn't sound good. She reminded herself that Lyn, being a sensitive, was going to experience her symptoms more acutely than the average person.

"I can't stand fumes, fluorescent lights give me headaches, certain foods make me throw up. It's like I'm allergic to the world!" Lyn said. "I feel like I'm going crazy!"

Jessie took a deep breath. She didn't want to deal with this now and felt guilty that she didn't. "We better get you in here," she said and checked her appointment book. There were no available times. Normally, she didn't allow herself to write in extra appointments, but she made an exception and booked the appointment anyway. Jessie spent a few more minutes empathizing with Lyn and ended the call.

The poor woman, Jessie thought as she drove along the country roads. It was early evening now, and the butter-yellow sun was low in the sky. Everything was bathed in its golden light. She loved this time of day in the spring. The world was shining like a face in front of a candle.

Yet, despite the incredible beauty, someone was suffering. It was always this way. One of her clients might be in the rapture of having a baby, or feeling the high of a new love, while another was in the depth of a depression or illness.

Suddenly an SUV zoomed past. She caught a glimpse of a single man, hunched over the wheel as he went past. She imagined the driver was a city person intent on getting to the cottage a few minutes earlier. Was that worth risking life and limb? She rolled up her window to keep the exhaust fumes out.

Lyn had said "fumes" were getting to her. Isn't that what Warren, one of her favourite colleagues, had said his sister had complained of when her sickness had started? Yes! She remembered now. Warren's sister had something he called Environmental Illness, or E.I. Warren had sent her an article about it a few months ago. It was one of those new syndromes that still hadn't settled on a name for itself. Jessie had also heard it called Multiple Chemical Sensitivity and Twentieth Century Disease. Whatever it was called, like so many modern illnesses, it was polysymptomatic, with sufferers reporting a heightened sensitivity to all chemicals and chemical fumes. Even household cleaning products could cause headache, dizziness, confusion and sometimes paralysis.

Could Lyn have E.I.? Deciding that it was far too early to speculate, Jessie made a mental note to call Warren as soon as she got back. She returned her focus to the road and saw Harley's truck. She pulled over and looked for a pathway into the forest. It always amazed her that a substantial man like Harley could slip into the woods and leave no sign. Searching around, Jessie finally found a piece of birch bark positioned in the crook of a maple branch. There was an arrow on it. From there, she followed the clues he'd left: branches snapped off at the ends, pinecones arranged in the shape of an arrow, clumps of leaves positioned as a happy face.

The leaves of the trees brushed against her as she walked. It felt reassuring to have them so close. When she was farther in, she stopped and took a deep breath. The cool aliveness of the air pressed against the inside of her lungs. Around her, the air felt supercharged with the energy of spring. She smiled. If the woods could sing, she'd be in the middle of an opera.

She walked on and soon saw the whitish haze of the swamp ahead. As she moved closer, she could almost feel its hushed sanctity. In the middle of a round pool of unrippled water, hundreds of heron-grey trees stood. They looked as if the sun had sucked the marrow of colour right out of their innards. The stillness of it was breathtaking.

A few decades ago, this area would have been a thriving wood, full of healthy trees, but a beaver had come along and chomped a tree down. Then he'd felled other trees and woven them into a barricade-like dam until the flow of the stream had completely stopped. Slowly, the trees had all died, creating the scene she was seeing now.

But she knew the pedal of nature wouldn't stop here.

The cycle of life would continue to move forward, and in a few more years, this scene would look different again. The drowned trees would eventually disintegrate and topple into the water. When that happened, and there was nothing more to eat, the beavers would abandon the dam and move on. After a while, the stick and twig blockade would collapse, and the water would drain. The pond would dry out, leaving a nutrient-rich meadow that would soon be full of saplings. Those saplings would multiply and mature until there was another forest of lush, leafy trees. Until another beaver came by and said, "Hmm. Look at those tasty trees." And toppled one across a stream.

Birth, growth, old age, death. It was the ever-turning circle of life. Ponds and lakes were not different. They were born, they matured and had a time to die. And beavers were the midwives of that process. No wonder these animals created such controversy. A single beaver could change the landscape faster than any other animal. If someone had just spent two million dollars on a cottage, he wasn't going to be happy about a beaver eating its way through half his trees.

But beavers weren't stupid. Like all the species on the planet, they had their particular strand of wisdom. When their strand was woven in with the others, the combination formed the weft and weave of a huge environmental tapestry. A tapestry so large and spanning such a long period of time, it was hard to grasp the totality of it. How could a human with a life span of eighty years understand a beach that was a thousand years old? Or a mountain many millions of years old?

Yet, despite their limited point of view, humans had somehow begun to think their particular "strand" was more important. How had this happened? The Bible talked about man having dominion. Is that how people began justifying their dominance over other species? Beavers, for example, were often called "nuisance" animals and could be killed at whim, by anyone, for any reason. That was not only unconscionable, but dangerous. If any species was silenced, its thread of wisdom was lost. The web of life needed all its threads.

She was at the edge of the beaver dam now, and balancing herself carefully, she stepped up on to the rim of it. About three feet high and a few hundred feet long, the dam was an intricate weave of sticks and rocks and clumps of mud. Although most of the twigs were no bigger than her wrist, some of the rocks looked to be about twenty or thirty pounds. How could such a small animal move something so heavy?

Up ahead she saw something pink and plastic wedged into the thatch of twigs and mud. A hula hoop? How had a hula hoop gotten way out here? She was musing over this when she saw Harley ahead and moved quickly towards him. When she was close to him, he took her hand. That's what he always did, touched her at the first opportunity. It was as if he trusted his hands more than his eyes.

"See over there?" He pointed to the side of the stream that led into the pond.

Jessie looked a few hundred yards downstream. She saw the stick moving before she saw the beaver carrying it. Although she knew that underwater, his paws and tail were making powerful motions, other than a thin arrow of water that spread behind the beaver's head, the surface of the water stayed mirror smooth.

When Harley made a special sound in the back of his

throat, the beaver changed direction and came towards them. In sleek silence, he pulled his glistening dark-rust body up into the shore grasses nearby.

"Hey, buddy, how's it going?" Harley held out some yams he'd pulled from his pocket.

The beaver's hands were coal black and his fingers were small and slender. Using his ping-pong paddle tail as a prop, he set himself up on his haunches and took the yams that Harley offered. As he ate, he made happy little grunting noises.

"He's beautiful," Jessie said. She looked at Harley, who grinned at her. His face was plump with happiness.

"He's really gotten bigger in the last few weeks," Harley said. "He must be over twenty pounds."

Jessie chuckled. "No wonder, with the room service you're giving him."

"I saw one granddaddy a few years ago who must have weighed over fifty," Harley said.

Tentatively, she reached out and lightly touched the beaver's fur. It felt bristly like a toothbrush. She felt privileged to be touching it.

"You haven't named him yet, right?"

Harley shook his head. Jessie knew he liked to wait until an animal told him its name.

"But his mate has a name. Willow," Harley said.

Jessie remembered now. He had nicknamed her Willow because of her fondness for willow branches.

"She kicked him out," Harley said.

Jessie had an inkling of what that might mean. In some species, the female kicked the male out just before giving birth. "Are there going to be babies?"

Harley was smiling at her excitement. "Follow me."

Moving slowly so they could go quietly, they made their way through the marsh. It wasn't long before Jessie saw a huge dome of sticks.

"Wow," she whispered, as they got closer. "I wonder how long it took them to make that."

"Not long. A beaver can cut through a five-inch tree in three minutes."

They were close to the lodge now, and hearing what sounded like soft mewing, Jessie caught her breath and listened. There was a contented snuffling sound, the kind all babies make, regardless of their species, when their noses are nuzzling a mother's breast.

In slow motion now, Jessie inched forward until she could peek into the air hole at the top of the hut. There was Willow, lying on her side, suckling three tiny babies. The babies looked like small, furry balloons of milk. One was clutching Willow's teat. This one had its eyes open. Jessie put her hand on her heart.

"Oh, goodness."

Harley squeezed her shoulders. Jessie could feel the elation in his hands. Would he still want to go away now? Maybe the baby beavers would make him want to stay. She put her own hands up and covered his, grateful to be sharing the moment.

"Those babies will be swimming tomorrow," Harley whispered.

Jessie nodded. In the animal world, survival depended on agility. "I could stay here for hours," she said.

"I know. I've been here most of the day. But it's getting dark. We can come back tomorrow. By then, our little yam-eater will be back on the scene, giving them all a swimming lesson."

Reluctantly, Jessie pulled back from the hut. "Beaver kits stick around for a long time, don't they, before going off on their own?"

"Two years," Harley said.

The sun had gone down now, and the light was dimming as they headed out of the more open marsh area and into the woods. It was darker in the trees, but Harley walked as if it were broad daylight. They had walked for a while before Jessie realized they weren't going back the way she had come. She was wondering where Harley was taking her when she saw the campsite. There was a still-smouldering fire with a blackened pot set over it, and pine boughs had been arranged on the ground around it, a sleeping bag spread over top. Her sleeping bag.

"We're staying the night?" It was a ritual for them to spend a night in the woods before the bugs made it impossible, but as yet, they hadn't found the time to do it.

"If you want."

"I want!"

She saw his face flush and was pleased. She sat down, leaned against a tree and watched Harley get the fire going again. He sorted through various pieces of wood for the fire, assessing each stick for weight and moisture. She loved the way he imbued every action with respect. He never treated an object as a "thing" but touched it as if it were a living entity in its own right, something that contained an innate intelligence that deserved his respect.

A crowd of feelings gathered in her chest. Sometimes she loved him so much she could hardly stand the intensity of it.

When the fire was lit, Harley gave the contents of the billycan a stir. As he waited for the contents to heat up, he took some strands of sweetgrass and began to braid them together.

"What's sweetgrass called again?" She still had trouble remembering the Ojibway names.

"*Weskwumashkoseh.*"

"Long name," she said.

"Long grass."

She ran her fingers through some of the honey-coloured strands. "Why is it always braided?"

Harley touched the sweetgrass gently. "Sweetgrass is like the hair of Mother Earth. It's braided in her honour." Harley stirred the pot of food, amusement pulling one side of his mouth. "Want some Muskoka Moosaka?"

She laughed. Harley's concoction wasn't really moussaka, at least not the kind one would find in Greece. But because his had been made from moose meat, he had given it that nickname. He spooned some onto two tin plates, and they began to eat.

"Saw a bunch of buffleheads this morning," she told him.

"On their way north," he said. "They'll be gone by the end of the month."

"Then the mergansers will be here."

"I untied fishing line from three last summer. Buried two from lead poisoning."

They were at it again, her trying to provide irrefutable evidence that there was still wilderness in Muskoka and him shooting down her every example. Deciding she didn't want to play this game with him tonight, she finished her stew and lay back. A lovely moon had risen above the trees.

"Goose moon," Harley said.

"What's a goose moon?"

"The first full moon in the spring when the geese come back. Sometimes it was the geese coming back that saved a tribe from starvation. The sight of them meant food and a celebration."

The celebration reminded him of something, and he put his mouth on hers.

Jessie could hear the even, deep pull of his breathing as the warmth of his mouth moved around her face and throat. Planting kiss after kiss, he made his way to her chest, then pressed his mouth over her heart and held it there. He had told her once that he always like to kiss her heart, because she had a good one.

Tears came to her eyes. There were so many levels to lovemaking with Harley. There was his body feasting on hers and her body feasting on his. That was delicious and delightful in itself, but with Harley, the experience involved pleasures of the heart and spirit as well. It was as if his mind, body and soul were meeting her mind, body and soul.

Harley brought his face to hers and licked the tears away. She wrapped her arms around him and pulled him tighter. He moved down her body again, sowing kisses into her skin, then buried his face in the delicate folds of her womanness. She spread her arms and legs wide, feeling as swollen and luminous as the moon above.

Chapter 6

Dan didn't know it, but when he turned north on Highway 400 and felt a sense of relief, he was acting like a true Muskokan. The back of the Jeep was stuffed with his possessions. When he and Barb had separated, he'd left all the furniture with her, partly because he didn't want to disrupt the children's lives, but also because he knew it would remind him of his failed marriage. He didn't need any more reminders of his fuck-ups. After moving out, he'd rented a furnished apartment, and now that he'd let that go, there wasn't much to take with him.

It was just after dawn, but already there was traffic. As he sped by the transport trucks and delivery vans, he felt excited about getting out of the city. After he'd driven for about an hour, he started to smell water. Taking a few furtive glances out his right window, he saw lakes and more lakes. Water, water, everywhere, but not a drop to drink. What the hell had made him think of that line? Wasn't that from some poem he'd learned in high school? Damned if he could remember. All he'd done during English class was draw cartoons.

He took note of what was around him as he got closer to Muskoka: junkeroos with cheap fridges and bikes heaped on the cement out front, ice cream places and fast food joints. One hamburger place, Webers, had some antique railway cars for people to sit in. Webers wasn't open yet, so he stopped at a Tim Hortons and had muffins and coffee.

A little way up the road, he saw the exit for Gravenhurst and, thinking it would be fun to drive through it before heading to Bracebridge, where he was meeting his father, he turned off. He followed a bus that had Chinese writing on the side through the big square arch that said "Welcome To Gravenhurst, Gateway to the North" at the south end of town. Dan smiled. How many towns took the time to welcome visitors? Except he wasn't arriving as a visitor to the area now. He was arriving as a resident. A resident who was about to make a new life for himself. It was the spring of the new millennium, he had a new job and he was going to be a new man.

In the bright early morning light, Gravenhurst looked charming. The bus pulled over in front of the Opera House on the main street, and Dan watched as Chinese people streamed out, cameras at the ready. A teenager ran to pose in front of the sculpture of Dr. Norman Bethune that stood near the entrance.

Dan drove on. It seemed odd to him that such a small, conservative town like Gravenhurst would celebrate a Chinese Communist, but Bethune had been born in Gravenhurst, so the town had dedicated a statue and a museum to the man. Bet that's brought them a tourist dollar or two, he thought.

Dan stopped at the lights at the crossroads of the main streets. On the far right corner was the local B&B, or Beer and Babes place, as Dan's dad usually called such establishments. Every town had one, but it made Dan smile to see that Gravenhurst had its B&B smack-dab in the middle of town. No doubt the place would be hopping on a Friday night. Not that it was the kind of place he would frequent. No, if he were going to hang out anywhere, it would be at the resorts.

His father always grumbled about the tourists, but Dan liked the idea of summer people. In truth, he was a little worried that the local women were going to be back-to-the-woods types, with hairy legs and not much interest in a man who wasn't handy with a chainsaw. Cottage women, however, might be eager for the company of a city-smart guy like him. Provided all his body parts worked. But he'd been able to get it on with Christie, hadn't he?

Before he knew it, he was back out on Highway 11 again, going north. Now that's what I call a small town, he thought. Port Carling, the town he was going to be living in, was even smaller. What if his father was wrong? What if small town life bored him to tears? Your father knows best, his mother's voice repeated.

His father was certain this was the right move for him. Dan, having botched his marriage and made a mess of things with Christie, had lost faith in his own ability to make decisions, so he'd let his father's assuredness lead him forward. It just seemed easier.

He took the first entrance to Bracebridge and followed the road as it swung into the south end of town, then turned left on Beaumont. He was driving away from the downtown now, following the river out to the treatment plant. When the road forked, he went to the left. He could see a wide line of blue at the end of it: Lake Muskoka.

Just as it looked as if the road were going to drive straight into the water, there was a sharp turn to the right, which led down to the marinas. He turned left instead, heading towards a large modern building that was set a few hundred yards back from the water. Jutting out of the far end of the building was a long intake pipe, set like a straw in the mouth of the lake. With such a resource to draw from, there would be no problem in supplying Bracebridge with all the water it could ever need, Dan thought. What had his father said, that this plant could process ten million litres a day? That was one hell of a whack-load of water.

As Dan drove in, he could see his father's maroon, four-wheel-drive Ram pickup truck. It wasn't parked in any of the designated spaces but was right by the door, as if the building were his personal residence. His father never did like walking.

Dan pulled into a parking space beside another truck. This one had the words Ministry of the Environment on the side, printed in what his father would have called "tree-hugger green". His father would not be pleased to have the government guys, the "suits", descending on him. Was this a routine inspection, or was something up?

Dan went through the double set of glass doors. The building was constructed of thousands of pounds of concrete, and he felt the weight of it pressing down on him. He felt as if he were stepping into a crypt. He checked his father's office but, except for a stack of sandwiches sitting in the middle of his desk, there was no sign of him. Dan winced. That poor government guy. Interrupting his father while he was having his lunch was not a fortuitous thing.

Dan scouted around and found his father giving a young woman the tour. The woman was wearing a shirt with the official emblem of the Ministry of the Environment on the front.

"Miss Hadley, this is my son, Dan," Frank said. "He's going to be handling the plant in Port Carling."

"Ms. Hadley," she corrected, giving Dan a no-nonsense handshake.

"Ms. Hadley doesn't like how I'm doing things around here," Frank said.

Ms. Hadley flushed furiously at his exaggeration and tried to explain. "It's your reports, Mr. Gorman."

Dan knew what his father was doing. Getting her off balance so she'd feel defensive and have to explain herself.

Frank looked at Dan. "You know these university types. They like their paperwork. And most of them don't know much about how these places really run, so I thought I'd offer a tour."

As usual, his father was taking charge. Dan could tell Ms. Hadley wasn't pleased, but like most people, she was no match for his father.

Frank put the palm of his pudgy hand on a huge water pipe as tenderly as another man might touch a woman's thigh. "Some plants have to pump their water in from the lake—that's what Dan will have to do up in Port—but my water comes in on its own. Right through this pipe." He patted it gently. "After we get it, we shoot some alum and lime into it, inject it with some carbon dioxide and chlorine, and pump it upstairs."

Dan walked behind them up the steps. The MOE inspector was slim, but she looked even slimmer beside his father's vast body. Yet, despite his bulk, Frank moved forcefully up the steps to the upper level. There, in a cavernous room, were several rectangular vats arranged in the floor like small swimming pools. Dan was familiar with the process. When the water was pumped up from downstairs, already prepped with lime and carbon dioxide, it went to the first pool, where it was mixed with more alum. The alum helped separate out the particles in the water. Then it was moved on to the next set of tanks, called the floctation tanks, where the particles congealed so they could be removed. Dan looked down and could see that particles, or "floc", was already forming.

"Looks like spit, don't it?" Frank said to Ms. Hadley and laughed.

As his father explained more of the process, Dan wandered to the next set of tanks, which took the separated floc, or sludge as it was called now, out of the water. This sludge would be collected and sent to the local sewage plant. The departicalized water went on to a final stage of purification, which involved a filtering system that pushed the water through various layers of anthracite, sand, gravel and stones. Once it had passed through the last filter, it would go to every home and business in Bracebridge, filling thousands of toilet bowls every day, cooking the suppers for every man, woman and child in town.

Dan peered into the dark water of the final tank. Shouldn't there be some sort of cap on the tank, or plastic sheeting? He knew no such covering was required, but the water seemed so exposed somehow. All some crazy person would have to do was slip a vial of poison into the water, and Bracebridge would be no more.

But for that to happen, a stranger would first have to get in here, and he had to admit, the place didn't exactly invite visitors. Besides, his father patrolled it like a troll.

Dan turned and saw Ms. Hadley stroll near one of the

empty sludge tanks. Dan, who was afraid of heights, usually stayed well away from the empty vats. When a tank didn't have anything in it, it could look pretty scary, like a huge concrete coffin. Besides, an empty tank went down a long way and could give a person a feeling of vertigo if he stood too close.

Ms. Hadley seemed to sense the danger and, keeping well back, stretched her torso forward to get a better look. Dan could tell she didn't hear Frank come up behind her. He barely nudged her, but she cried out.

Frank laughed. "You think I was going to push you in?" He turned to Dan, inviting him to share in the humour. "You'd think these ivory tower people would be used to heights."

If the woman hadn't regretted her visit yet, she did now. She looked pale, and Dan shook his head, thinking how lucky they were that she hadn't chucked her breakfast.

The three of them went downstairs, and Dan occupied himself in the office while his father and Ms. Hadley talked in the hall. She had a hard, official tone in her voice as she emphasized the importance of chlorination.

When she was gone, his father sank down into his chair and grabbed a sandwich. He nodded down at the pile of thick-cut bread slices that were oozing with curls of turkey meat.

"No, no, thanks," Dan said.

Frank took a huge bite of his sandwich but continued talking. "I've been drinking this water all my life, and it's never hurt me."

"What does she want the water to taste like—a swimming pool?" He chewed some more. "A little bacteria isn't going to kill nobody. Bacteria's in everything."

Dan wanted to argue with him, wanted to tell him that the woman was just doing her job, but he said nothing.

Another worker came in and Frank said, "Dan, this is Pete. Pete, Dan."

Pete put some water samples on the table.

"You get these from all the right places?"

Pete winked at Dan. "'Course, boss." He coughed. The phlegm in his lungs made a sound like a shovel full of gravel landing on cement. He rolled a cigarette and stepped outside to smoke it.

"Probably took it from the donut shop," Frank said.

It was common knowledge that sometimes the men in water treatment plants didn't make the rounds to the various places they were supposed to and just took water from whatever taps were handy.

Frank took one of the bottles, poured some into a thumb-sized jar and put it in the turbidity machine. "Says 0.5. Just like it's supposed to." He looked at Dan. "You'll do a lot of your own water testing in Port too. But, like us, you'll still have to send in stuff to the lab every week. The good news is, because of the cutbacks, the results get sent back to us now, not to the health unit, so if there's a problem, you can get to it without the MOE breathing down your neck."

Frank carried on talking, and Dan tried to listen. Suddenly he felt his father's iron grip on his hand.

"You're scribbling again."

Dan yanked his hand away, and Frank snatched the paper Dan had been doodling on and scrunched it up.

Dan saw a fist whiz through the air and hit his father. It wasn't his fist, it was a cartoon fist. The kind one might see in a comic book. Then a white balloon appeared with the word "Bam!" inside it.

Dan stood up. He didn't like it when cartoons started happening in his brain like this. That was what used to happen before.

"I gotta go," he said. "I've got to get the key from Meat. And I don't want to keep him waiting."

"Thought you were staying with us tonight?"

Dan tensed. Had he said anything about staying with his parents? That was the problem with lying, you had to keep track of what you'd said to whom.

"Meat wants me stay at his place," he said. "To keep an eye out. Apparently there's been a bunch of break-ins."

Lies. It was all lies. They seemed to slip out of his mouth so easily, before he could stop them.

His father looked at him uncertainly, but as Dan suspected, the mention of the hockey hero had the intended effect.

"See his goal in the game against the Red Wings?" Frank asked. "That puck must have been going faster than the speed of light."

Dan nodded. He hadn't seen it, but he didn't want his father knowing that. Besides, all Meat's goals were amazing.

"Go on with you, then," Frank said, scrunching the foil around the last remaining sandwich and pushing it at Dan. On the way into town, Dan ate it, even though he wasn't hungry.

Chapter 7

The baby beavers were slipping in and out of the water hole the next morning when Jessie and Harley went to see them.

"I'm in love," Jessie said. They'd been watching the beavers for over an hour. Her back ached from leaning forward, but she didn't care.

"That makes two of us," Harley said.

The male beaver was back in the hut now and had positioned himself by the swimming platform to help the babies climb back up after diving into the water, which was about every two minutes.

When it was time to go, Harley left a pile of yam slices by the side of the hut, and they made their way back to where they'd camped. Jessie hated to leave the beavers and was already planning how she could come and visit them again. It felt like such an honour to have this opportunity.

They had packed up the foodstuffs and Jessie was about to roll up the sleeping bag when Harley sprawled out beside her.

"Give me ten minutes of shuteye, will you?" he said, yawning as he rested his hand on her thigh. "Someone kept me up late last night."

Jessie smiled and lay back as he curled into her. There

was a rope of sweetgrass on the blanket beside her, and she could smell the aroma. Reaching over, she moved her fingers along the flowing curves of the braid and closed her eyes. Above her, the wind gusted, filling the air with bursts of rustling leaves. If trees could laugh, she thought, that would be the sound.

The warmth from Harley's body swelled towards her, and she felt a wave of sleepiness wash over her.

She was descending into it when a colossal rumbling exploded up through the ground beneath her. An earthquake? Thinking she was having a nightmare, she was about to turn over, when an obliterating sound, jagged and horrible, jolted her into complete and utter wakefulness. She yanked her eyes open as Harley scrambled to his feet and broke into a run.

Even in her dazed state, Jessie knew that if Harley was running, she should be running too. But it was hard to get her legs to move when she felt so frightened. She forced her body forward, stumbling over rocks and branches. Harley was far ahead of her, and she pushed herself on, trying to move faster. Something terrible had happened, that she knew, but where were they running to? And why?

Determined to keep Harley in view, she ran and ran and ran. She kept tripping on sticks. Sticks that had pointed ends, like the ones she'd seen yesterday. Why were they littered all over the ground like this? And what was that awful burnt smell?

Breathless with fear, she finally caught up with Harley. His eyes were wild, and his chest was pumping hard from running. Jessie's eyes ransacked the scene around them, looking for something that would tell her where they were and what had happened. They were in a clearing, a very boggy clearing, similar to where they'd been yesterday, except she couldn't see the beaver dam. All she could see was a jumble of sticks and logs and rivulets of water streaming through them.

The beaver dam had been dynamited!

Harley began to paw through the tangle of mud and sticks. Jessie knew he was looking for the beavers, hoping against hope that they had survived. Given the devastation she was seeing, she couldn't imagine how any living thing could have survived. She helped him search anyway, terrified of what she might find.

After what seemed like hours, she sat on a rock, her body wet with sweat, her hands black with char. She was too exhausted to search any more. Whoever had done this terrible thing had done a good job of it. Not only had the lodge and dam been obliterated, she couldn't even tell where it had been. She put her head in her hands. In a way, she was hoping they wouldn't find the bodies. She didn't think she could stand to see them. It would hurt too much. Besides, if she saw them, the horror of their burned little bodies would be in her memory forever.

But Harley wouldn't be continuing to look if he didn't have some strong feeling that one of the beavers was alive. That idea gave her strength, and she pulled herself up to continue searching through the rubble. When she came upon a piece of burned hula hoop, she wept.

Ahead of her, Harley stopped and stood perfectly still. Seeing that his eyes were fixed on something, she watched as he reached down and cleared some debris. His hands moved as slowly as if he were easing back the hair from around a loved one's face. He lifted what he found, held it to his chest and began rocking it. Whether he was mourning a dead body or cradling a living beaver, Jessie couldn't tell.

Feeling as if she were a hundred years old, she made her way through the charred sticks towards them.

Chapter 8

Dan climbed into the shiny Ford pickup and drove the big, muscular truck out of his Medora Street office. Not bad, he thought, heading into Port Carling. The truck was full-sized, and it held him up high over the road. He liked looking down at everything. He also liked the fact that the truck came as one of the perks of the job.

He flipped on the air conditioning, just because he could, and revelled in the cool air that blasted his face. Then, deciding he'd rather have the day as it was, he turned off the air-conditioning and rolled down the window. He snapped on the radio and began drumming his fingers on the side of the truck in rhythm with the music.

He was listening to The Moose, the radio station everyone listened to up here. The name was a bit hokey, but hey, this was cottage country, not the big city—it was supposed to be hokey.

"It's going to be hot, hot, HOT!" the disc jockey was saying. "Hot all weekend, folks, with highs in the thirties and no rain in sight."

Dan grinned as he swung into the parking lot of the liquor store. Muskoka was putting on its best weather, just for him.

The woman who was walking ahead of him was wearing designer jeans. Other people in the store looked classy too, even though they were dressed in casual clothes. They all had an air of confidence, the kind of confidence that only money and power could buy. One of these days, he was going to have that kind of confidence too.

Peering outside, he saw a long, fibreglass boat pull up. A woman in skimpy white shorts leaned over to tie up her boat, displaying her snooker-ball rump to the world. Once she'd tied up, she adjusted the strap of her orange bikini top and strode into the store as if it were her personal pantry. She left her sunglasses on. Was she a movie star? Dan had already heard about all the famous people who came to Muskoka.

With a box of light beer on the passenger seat beside him, Dan drove through town, over the swing bridge, up the little hill and turned left on Reservation Road. Part way down, he turned into a narrow driveway and parked in front of a square box of a building not much bigger than a fishing hut. This was the water treatment plant. When Sean, the guy he was replacing, had showed it to him yesterday, he'd almost laughed aloud. This was what he was in charge of?

The reason the building was small, he soon learned, was because almost nothing happened there. The pump drew water from the Rosseau side of the Indian River, held it long enough for the system to inject some chlorine into it, and sent it out again, to every sink and bathtub in Port Carling. It was so Mickey Mouse that running it wasn't even considered a full time job. That's why Dan, as Chief Operator, would be responsible for both water treatment and sewage treatment.

"Showers and shit" had been his father's way of putting it.

Dan frowned. Showers and shit. He didn't like the idea of that at all. Hopefully, he would soon be expanding his horizons. He would have left water treatment years ago if it hadn't been for Barb always being on him about the security of government jobs. But he was in Muskoka now and rubbing elbows with the rich and famous. A new opportunity was bound to come his way.

What he had to do was get out and meet people. He'd already decided to scout around the various resorts for a golf course to join. From what he'd heard, Muskoka had golf courses coming out the ying-yang. He hadn't played golf in a while, but at one time, he'd been rather good. He needed to feel good at something again.

Dan parked in front of the small building and walked down to the water. Just in front of him, a few hundred yards away, was an island. If he remembered correctly, the island had a museum on it. To the left, further downstream, was a set of locks that led to Lake Muskoka. These were smaller than the main locks located on the other side of the island.

He stared out at the open water between the island and the mainland. Sean had told him that it was in this narrow, shallow bit of water that the pipe for the town's water supply was situated. The pipe was in a crib no more than ten feet down. There was something not quite right about that, Dan thought. It was in too open a place. Dan shook his head and walked back to the building.

He unlocked the door and went inside. His eyes went to the meter on the far wall first. It gave a chlorine reading of 1.3 parts per million. Good. That was where the chlorine level should be. He checked the sodium hypochlorite supply next. Because of the small space, they used the liquid form and had it delivered in six hundred-litre tanks. Sean had told him they'd go through that every few months, depending on the time of year.

Sitting on top of the tank that held the sodium hypochlorite was a yellow piston pump. The pump was responsible for dispensing chlorine into the water after it was drawn in from the lake. Sean thought it needed replacing and had even showed Dan where the new one was stored.

Dan checked his watch. If he started the job now, he could have the new pump in by dinner time. The problem was, he didn't feel like starting it now. He examined the pump more closely. Sure, it looked old, but it seemed to be functioning all right. Even if it did stop working, and the chlorine levels got low, the automatic alarm would go off, and Dan would be notified. Dan felt for the little plastic box on his belt. As long as he had his pager, there was nothing to worry about.

When the new treatment plant on Ferndale Road was up and running, he wouldn't have to worry about old equipment like this at all. Sean said the new plant had all kinds of "new-fangled" technology. He told Dan he'd be able to manage the place from the golf course. Dan doubted that, but it was a nice idea.

Dan spent a few moments making a list of other improvements he wanted to make. The place needed a coat of paint for one thing. Sean had told him the inside of the water tower might need painting too. Which meant Dan was going to have to drain the sucker and climb up into it.

That thought gave him the creeps. He hated heights, and he hated enclosed spaces, and the idea of having to deal with both fears at the same time made his clothes feel sticky. He checked his watch. He'd worked late last night, so he wasn't going to overdo things today. Besides, it was summer. And hot. And the weekend. Time for a beer. He hadn't had one in days, and he deserved a little pleasure. In fact, he might even go to some resort, sit out on the deck and have one there. With that thought, he wiped the sweat from his forehead and left the building.

Chapter 9

The stench of burned flesh filled the kitchen, pressing against the walls and ceiling like a dark and evil force. It had been like this for days now. Even though she had the windows open, the smell seemed to saturate everything, making her continually nauseated. In a way, she wished she could be sick, but she knew that even if she could empty out her stomach, she would not be able to rid herself of the bellyful of anger.

She turned and looked again at the beavers lying on the kitchen table. She knew she should be glad that any of them were alive, but at the moment, she could summon no gladness. Willow was dead and two of her three babies had been roasted alive. The one baby that was still breathing had severe burns all over its small body, and it seemed like an injustice to wish him life.

The adult male, Harley's buddy and friend, the one she and Harley had fed yams to such a short while ago, had burns all over his belly. Harley was treating the burns now, gently brushing fresh aloe juice over the seared flesh. As sickening as the smell was, and it was certainly sickening, it was the sight of the beaver's burned fur and the raw, bloody patches on its skin that made her want to retch.

She wished that the man who had blown up the dam could know the suffering he had caused, but she doubted whether a person capable of such an act would even care. Or perhaps he told himself that he'd done the world a favour by getting rid of a bunch of "nuisance" animals. Jessie sighed. She needed to stop thinking about who had done it, push away her anger over the three beavers that were dead and focus all her attention on the two still living.

It really was a miracle that any of the beavers were alive at all. The baby must have been thrown clear and the other one, Harley's friend, must have been away from the lodge, gathering food, when the dynamite had blasted everything apart.

Jessie passed Harley some fresh aloe. It was getting dark in the kitchen now and more difficult to see. The darkness told her that another day had gone by. In a way, it seemed like only seconds had passed since the explosion, but that was because her mind kept replaying it. She didn't know if she'd ever get the memory of the horrible sound out of her ears.

She lit a candle. Beavers were used to darkness, and she knew it would be stressful for them if she put on the overhead light. Even in the dim candlelight, Jessie could still see the patches of black all over the beaver's body where his fur and skin had been burned. She turned away and busied herself filling another hot water bottle, which she then slipped under the towelling beneath the beaver. She didn't want the beaver having to use any of its valuable energy maintaining body heat, so she was trying to keep it warm by other means. It was a small thing, but her work with birds had made her all too aware of how thin the thread was between life and death. The slightest weight could cause the thread to break.

The outside door opened, and Jessie turned to see Elfy

come in with some supplies from the bird refuge. The old woman moved slowly through the shadows, as if she were walking uphill.

"Powdered milk," Elfy said, putting a bag on the counter. Her voice had a closed sound to it, like a shut door. "And more syringes."

Jessie nodded. Closer to Elfy now, she could feel the old woman's exhaustion. When had Elfy last slept? When had any of them slept? The beavers needed constant attention, so the three of them had been catching naps here and there, but the lack of sleep was beginning to get to them all.

She touched Elfy's arm. "Somebody's going to have to function in the morning. Why don't you get some sleep?"

Wearily, Elfy let her head drop against Jessie's shoulder. "Don't think I could sleep."

Jessie put her arm around the old woman. Her shoulders were all bones. "Even so, rest."

For a moment, Jessie thought Elfy had fallen asleep standing against her, but the old woman pulled away. "Maybe I'll just lie on the couch for a bit. Wake me if you need me, okay?"

When Elfy disappeared into the dark living room, Jessie slumped against the counter. Her head felt like a bag of wet sand. Her eyes were full of grit. Deciding she needed something to help her stay awake, she opened a tin, and the rich smell of coffee bloomed up into her face. She spooned some into the filter and poured in boiling water, watching as it dripped through. The smell of it fortified her, penetrating her discouragement and offering a whiff of sanity from a former life.

When the coffee was gone, she went to the phone. She

hesitated before dialling. She didn't like cancelling clients and never did so easily, but she would be too exhausted to see clients tomorrow.

The first client Jessie called accepted the cancellation easily and rebooked.

Jessie hung up and called her second client, Lyn. Although she knew it was being chicken-hearted, she hoped the answering machine would get it.

Bill, Lyn's boyfriend, answered.

"Lyn's sleeping," he told Jessie.

"Can you tell her I'm sorry, very sorry, but I'm going to have to rearrange our appointment?"

"You're cancelling?"

Something hot and angry shot up Jessie's throat. She should tell him about the explosion and the stench in her kitchen and the death of the beavers. She should tell him that she hadn't slept in two nights. But what was the point? He was probably overwhelmed too with all that was happening to Lyn.

She made herself take a breath, then, keeping her voice neutral, apologized once again. She gave Bill a possible appointment time for Lyn next week, asked him to tell Lyn to confirm it and ended the call.

When she got off the phone, it was time to feed the baby beaver again. Taking a fresh syringe from the bag, she removed the needle and disposed of it. The hole at the end of the syringe was bigger now, and she nosed it into a dish of formula and pulled back the plunger so the clear plastic tube filled. She took the syringe over to Harley and the baby beaver.

As gently as if he were touching a flower, Harley pressed the baby's mouth so it opened. Beavers have flaps of skin that cover their throats so water can't enter when they're swimming, so Jessie was careful to slip the syringe in behind this covering so the food could get into its throat. Then she slowly pushed her thumb down on the plunger and injected the formula. She felt as if she were injecting all her yearning for the beaver to live along with the food.

She refilled the syringe, and Harley positioned his fingers to open the baby beaver's mouth again. Its tiny head suddenly flopped over. Harley closed his eyes, and Jessie stared out the window into the dark night. Death could be so stealthy. Like a robber, it had a way of slipping in and stealing life so silently, you only knew of its presence after it had done its deed.

Harley pulled the towelling over the baby's inert body and lifted his face to look at her. "*This is why I want to leave,*" his eyes said.

Jessie put her head down on the table. She couldn't take much more of this.

The phone rang, and she dragged herself up to see who it was. She had placed a call to one of the other wildlife centres earlier to see if she could get any other ideas about how to help the beavers. This was someone from the centre calling back.

A few minutes later, she returned to where Harley was and slumped down in the chair.

"That was Brad from The Haven," she said. "He doesn't think the beavers have a hope in hell of living."

The beaver that was still alive made a weak, murmuring sound.

Harley leaned closer as if to listen to a child whispering. He spoke softly. "What do you think, buddy?

Do you think you have a hope in hell of living?"

The beaver made another sound.

"I think he likes that name," Harley said.

He took some fresh aloe and began spreading it gently over the beaver's burned paw. He spoke gently to the beaver as he worked. "All right, my friend, if you're going to be a Hope-in-Hell, you're going to have to start acting like one and get better." He paused and eased the towel around so he could work on the lower part of the beaver's body. "Start thinking about swimming and the feel of water on your skin. And think about the stars and the warmth of the moon. And the sweetness of a new summer morning..."

As Harley spoke, Jessie closed her eyes. His voice was strong and rich, and it soothed her tiredness and discouragement.

She didn't know how long she slept, but when she awoke, Harley was asleep too, his head resting on his arms, his fingers just touching Hope-in-Hell. At the far end of the table was the inert body of the kit that had died. She picked it up. It fit into the palm of her hand.

Moving slowly and steadily through the darkness, she carried it down to the boathouse. There she found a piece of birch bark and laid the baby beaver's body on it. She carried the little birch bark boat to the end of the dock and set it down on the surface of the black water. The waves, like tiny little hands, drew the bark sarcophagus out into the lake.

When the eye of dawn opened, the seagulls and turkey vultures would spot this breakfast offering and have a feast. As tired as she was, this thought made her smile. It was part of nature's code for an animal to offer its body for the nourishment of others. Even in death, a contribution was made to life and its continuance.

She wrapped an old fishing jacket around herself and watched until the night had swallowed the boat in its dark mouth. Too tired to get up, she lay on her back and listened to the lake water lapping. It was such an ancient sound, a sound that had washed through millions of lives over millions of years. This sound knew about life and knew about death. It soothed her and rocked her in its rhythmic wisdom, and she let it carry her away from a world she didn't want to be a part of.

Chapter 10

Over the next while, Dan visited several resorts. There were dozens to choose from. Some were huge complexes with world-class golf courses, tennis courts, swimming pools and four-star restaurants. Others were like glorified summer camps and had cabins nestled into the woods, ping-pong tables and old-fashioned fieldstone fireplaces.

Although Dan liked staying at Meat's, it did him good to get out and meet people. Hanging out at resorts afforded him the perfect opportunity. If the weather was good, he'd order a beer and sit out on the deck and chat with the other guests. He knew others assumed he was a guest too, and he liked that. One day, perhaps he would be. Or, maybe one day, he would even own one. He couldn't imagine a better job than running a resort.

Today he'd decided to visit a resort called Carlingview, and as he approached it, the road wound its way through the spacious greens of an eighteen-hole golf course. The main lodge was an older, wooden building, freshly painted white. The gardens surrounding it were full of yellow and pink snapdragons and white daisies. Some of the resorts had gardens with formal, geometric arrangements of flowers, but the gardens here had a sort of triumphant largesse, spilling out everywhere.

He wandered down to the water, passing behind a line

of brightly coloured Muskoka chairs. There was a sandy beach area off to the side, and Dan walked along it.

"Hey, mister, you're stepping on my dinosaur."

Dan looked up and saw a small boy running down the beach in his bare feet. He had a stick in his hand. Looking down, Dan saw what the boy was referring to. There, sketched in the sand, was the outline of a dinosaur. Dan's feet were standing on its head.

"Sorry," he said, stepping aside.

The boy, who had reddish-gold hair and freckles the size of snowflakes, pulled his mouth to one side in disappointment. Dan picked up another stick and repaired the lines his feet had blurred. Then, to make up for his transgression, he added something to the drawing: a boy on top of the dinosaur's back. A boy that looked like the one beside him.

"Is that me?" the boy asked with shrill enthusiasm.

Dan smiled, adding a burst of fire coming out the dinosaur's mouth.

The boy could hardly contain his glee. "More. Draw more!"

"Sonny, don't plague the nice man!"

Dan turned, and there she was. The sun was behind her, making a sort of halo of her strawberry-blonde hair. When she smiled at him, he could feel the warmth of it hurtling through the air towards him and thunking into his chest like an arrow into a board. It was all he could do not to step back from its impact.

How could a man tell one woman he wasn't ready for a relationship, then immediately fall in love with another? Dan had no idea, yet knew that was exactly what was happening.

"Draw my mommy," Sonny said.

Happy to have a reason to look at her, Dan did exactly that. Everything about her delighted him: her freckles, her girlish face, her sturdy, capable and curvaceous hips. He held his breath as he searched out her left hand. When he saw no ring there, he let his breath out again.

"You make me look like a goddess," she said.

"I draw what I see."

She laughed. It was a light, youthful laugh, and Dan felt himself tumbling through it. He held out his hand. "I'm Dan."

"I'm Megan."

Dan repeated her name to himself. Megan. He had never known a Megan before. He liked that. It gave him a fresh feeling. He turned to the boy and, hamming it up, bowed and gave him his hand. The boy giggled with pleasure.

"I can draw a bird," Sonny said, wielding the long stick with his thin arms. "Watch me."

Dan watched, then drew one beside it.

Sonny drew a grasshopper.

Dan drew one beside it.

Sonny drew an airplane. In the cockpit, was a stick man, waving. "That's my dad," he said.

Dan kept his drawing stick still.

"He doesn't live with us any more."

"I don't live with my two kids either," Dan said. Before he could stop himself, he said, "I miss them."

The boy's eyes settled on his for a moment, then he began drawing again. Dan drew alongside him. Soon the two of them had the beach covered in prehistoric animals and aircraft. When there wasn't any sand left to draw on, Sonny turned to his mother, who had been watching.

"Mommy, can Dan come out in the boat with us?"

Megan blushed. "Sonny, I'm sure Dan has other things to do with his afternoon."

"I don't, actually," Dan confessed. "But I don't want to impose."

Sonny began pulling his arm. "The boat's really big. Come see."

Dan allowed himself to be pulled down to the dock where a pontoon boat with the word Carlingview on the side was tied up.

"You're welcome to join us," Megan said.

Dan couldn't hide his delight and hopped on. Soon he was steering the boat out into the waves.

"How long are you staying at the resort?" she asked.

He tensed. "Oh, I'm just here checking it out for some friends of mine. I stay at a cottage just around the corner." He'd tell her the cottage wasn't his later. "How about you?" If she was only going to be at the resort for a few days, he needed to know so he could figure out how he was going to see her again.

"I live here," she said. "My brother and I own the resort." She smiled. "Or at least the bank does, and we manage it for them."

Dan felt as if someone had just turned a heater on in his chest. "Lucky you." Then he added, "I've been wondering about getting into the resort business for myself."

"You should talk to my brother, Wayne."

"I'd like that."

She nodded, and Dan grinned so widely he could feel his ears move. Happily, he steered the boat out into the lake. Another boat passed by, and he waved at them as if they were his best friends.

For the next two hours they talked about everything: the city, movies, books, favourite travel places. He could tell from the things she said that she was a cut above him, but if she was aware of that, she didn't let on.

Whenever he could, he complimented her. He could tell she liked that. He also noticed that the compliments she liked best were about Sonny. She was obviously devoted to the boy and to raising him well. From what Dan could see, she was doing an excellent job.

"Would it be all right if Sonny helped steer the boat for a minute?" he asked.

When Megan nodded, Sonny leapt onto Dan's lap and put his small hands on the wheel.

The boy was light, and Dan guided his small fingers to the various toggle switches, explaining what each of them did. Sonny asked lots of questions, and Dan took his time to answer them.

"Smart kid," Dan said, smiling at Megan. He watched her face flush with pleasure. "Does Sonny get to see his father much?"

A soft vulnerability came into her eyes. "Not enough." She looked sad. "He needs a father, too. He's a handful sometimes."

"This little guy?" He tickled the boy, who laughed delightedly. Then Dan talked about his own kids and was surprised how easy it was to tell her things. She could be serious one moment and light-hearted the next.

By the time they got back to the resort, he was as elated as if he'd just won the lottery.

As he tied up the boat, he tried to think of a way to extend his time with her.

"Do you have time to give me a tour?"

"Sure, " she said. "And we'll see if Wayne is around."

They strolled around the grounds, Sonny swinging like a chimpanzee between the vines of their arms. Other guests looked at them, and Dan knew they thought he, Megan and Sonny were a family.

Unfortunately, when they found Wayne, he was just heading off to a meeting, but he suggested Dan come to dinner in a few days. Dan accepted and said his goodbyes.

"Yes!" Dan cheered aloud as he sped down the highway, his spirits flying up behind him like a cape. Finally, something good was happening.

Just don't fuck it up.

I won't, he swore to himself. He already had the boy rooting for him, didn't he? And Megan liked him. He could tell. When he went for dinner, he would take them both presents. A huge bouquet of flowers for Megan. And for Sonny? A good set of coloured pencils, that's what. The boy had talent. He wanted to help him develop it.

He was on his way to Bracebridge to get some things anyway, so he'd see if he could pick up a set. Whistling, he parked and walked through town. It was a pleasant little place with the usual array of tourist stuff. Nearly all the stores had items with "Muskoka" on them—mugs, T-shirts, bumper stickers, post cards. It reminded him a bit of Niagara Falls. He wandered into the other shops. Things were expensive. The prices were obviously set to go along with the real estate.

Seeing a store called Scott's that looked as if it might have art supplies, he went inside. There were mostly books at the front, but near the back he found what he was looking for and bought a pad of drawing paper and a set of bright coloured pencils. He was heading towards the door, his purchases in hand, when he glimpsed a pregnant woman looking in the window.

His heart slammed against his ribs. Wrenching his body around as quickly as he could, he hid behind a stand and grabbed the biggest book he could find to put in front of his face. A flood of sweat pulsed down his arms into his hands. Was that Christie? It couldn't be.

It took him several tortured minutes to get up the nerve to sneak another look. His knees felt weak and shaky. Not seeing anyone, he edged closer to the window. There was no one standing there now. Cautiously, he moved to the door, craning his head around to give him as long a view of the street as possible. There was no sign of any woman, and certainly not a pregnant woman.

Had he imagined her? There was no question in his mind that he'd seen a pregnant belly, but as he calmed down, he realized he really couldn't say that the belly had belonged to Christie. After all, he hadn't gotten a good look at the woman's face. The woman could have been any pregnant woman.

He did some counting on his fingers. Even if Christie had decided to keep the baby, she wouldn't be that big. Not yet, anyway. He was obviously going to have to get more sleep. His mind wasn't functioning right.

When he got back to Meat's, there were three other cars in the driveway. He parked beside a champagne coloured Lexus. Meat had told him a few days ago that he was having a gang of his buddies up. Meat was suffering from a gruesome groin injury, but that wasn't stopping him from partying. Nothing stopped Meat from partying.

Dan stood by his car for a few moments, wondering whether to go over to the main cottage and join them or head down to the bunkie. If he went to the party, there would be copious amounts of food and liquor. That had some appeal. But there wouldn't be a person there with an income under six figures. Except him. And what was he going to say when they asked him what he did? Admit he managed the water and sewer department? He didn't think so.

Grabbing his purchases, he headed down to the bunkie. The cabin was small, but it had its own kitchen and bathroom and was tucked far enough away from the main cottage to give him some privacy.

He sat down on the deck and stared out through the trees to the still, blue lake. The scene in front of him looked so peaceful. He wished he could suck some of its tranquillity into his body. He felt stirred up, first from meeting Megan and Sonny and then from his imagined run-in with Christie.

Cartoons began to race across the screen of his mind. He didn't like it. This is what used to happen to him in the old days. The cartoons would come to him unbidden, demanding his attention, twitching at his hands until he disgorged them from his mind onto paper.

He shook his head, and most of the cartoons dispersed. One image remained. It started as a bubble, then expanded, getting bigger and bigger, like a huge balloon. But then a strange thing happened. Just when he thought the balloon was going to explode, a hand burst through. A baby-sized hand. And it reached for him.

Chapter 11

The cool water slipped and slid around Jessie as she swam. She bumped into something floating in the water, something round and bone-coloured. It bobbed against her and, frightened by it somehow, she tried to push it away. It had eyes. They weren't alive eyes, only sockets or holes where the eyes should have been. And there was hair, long black hair streaming away from the skull. Hair like Harley's. Horrified, she woke up.

She fanned her arm out over the bed, scanning the landscape of the mattress for a shoulder, a leg, a pulse of Harley's heat. Her hand moved as if through air. Where was he? Probably with Hope-in-Hell, she thought. Harley was still getting up a few times a night to check on him. The beaver still needed constant attention, and Harley was unfailing in his willingness to give it.

Jessie pulled herself up and switched on the light, grateful for the way it filled the room with the present tense. Hearing her yellow Lab's tail thump against the side of the bed, she patted the place beside her.

"Come on, Charlie, it's okay…"

He eyed her uncertainly, then hopped up. She buried her head in the silky fur around his neck and fell asleep again.

When she woke, she thought about the dream. It was

no surprise she was having nightmares, she thought, given what she'd been doing lately: reading about the environment. She and the Grannies were about to do an environmental review of Muskoka, and each of them had taken a different area to research. She had chosen water. What she was finding disturbed her deeply.

Last night, for example, just before going to bed, she'd been reading a report on the status of rivers, a report that concluded, after surveying hundreds of rivers all over the world, that only two were fit for drinking in their "wild" state. Two! No wonder she was having bad dreams about water.

Besides, she still hadn't recovered from the explosion of the beaver dam. Being that close to such an evil act had put her on a strange sort of alert, and hard as she tried, she couldn't get her body to relax. There had been no time to relax anyway. Not with a sick beaver that needed twenty-four hour care. But she was grateful that he was alive and was only too glad to attend to him, as was Harley. Both of them knew his state of health was still precarious, but his burns were healing and he was eating, so, as scary as it was, they were allowing themselves some optimism.

Noticing the time, she pulled herself out of bed, had a shower and went in search of Harley.

"Thought I'd find you two down here."

Harley was sitting beside a large hay-covered platform that overlooked a pool he had fashioned out of an old hot tub he'd found at the dump. Hope-in-Hell was sitting on the platform, nibbling some fruit slices, and Harley was making a pair of leather moccasins. On the arm of his chair was a tray of beads.

"How's the patient?" Jessie asked, her attention

focussed on the beaver.

"In yam heaven," Harley said as he threaded a long, slender needle.

Jessie watched him with momentary fascination. The needle he was using had been made from the penis bone of a marten and had a small slit in just the right place for the thread. He loaded on some blood red beads and then a few butter-yellow ones as well.

Harley looked at her for a long moment, then put his leather making things aside.

Jessie eased into his lap and let herself relax into the reassuring substantiveness of his body.

"He's looking better, isn't he?"

Jessie yawned her agreement. "At least his skin has lost that black, burned look."

Harley nodded and yawned too.

"We need more sleep," Jessie said. It had been a long time since either of them had slept more than three hours at a time.

"Let's go to bed right now," Harley quipped, nuzzling his face in her neck.

"I've got a meeting with someone at the District to talk about water," she said, but her attention was on her neck, and how lovely it was to have his mouth there.

"You world saviour types." His voice was muffled.

Harley rested his head against hers, and for a few moments, they both were quiet.

"Sometimes I just feel so discouraged," she said, feeling her eyes beginning to droop. "All this reading I'm doing. It's hard to keep hopeful. Don't you ever wonder just how the earth is going to survive?"

"I'm not worried about the earth," Harley said. "The

earth is smart. Way smarter than people think. The question is whether people are going to survive. And the way we're acting, sometimes I wonder if we should." He paused. "But if we get too out of hand, the earth will just get rid of us. Blow us away with hurricanes. Or flood us out with rains. Maybe kill us off by refusing to grow food—"

"There have been a lot of floods and droughts lately," she said.

"I know," he said. "The earth is talking to us."

"It's been one extreme or the other."

"Extremes are like that," Harley said. "One calls to another."

"But if there are floods and hurricanes and famines, the animals, the birds, everything will die, not just people."

Harley nodded. "For a while, maybe. But the Creator will just make them again when the time is right."

It was an interesting thought. "Maybe all the New Age talk about Atlantis and those other civilizations is true," she said.

"Maybe it is."

"Maybe we knew each other in an earlier incarnation," she said.

"Yeah, I was your love slave, don't you remember?" He chuckled. "And we were supposed to switch roles this time."

Jessie grinned. "But you said you liked it so much, you were going to be my love slave for four more lifetimes. Or was it five?"

"Okay, but you can't just keep me tied to the bed all the time."

"Aw—"

Hope-in-Hell made a small, impatient sound.

"Okay, buddy, okay." Harley gave him another yam slice. "In the native tradition, there isn't just one world but four: the physical, the animal, the plant world and then the world of man. Of the four, man's is considered the most insignificant, because he depends entirely on the others for his survival. Whereas the three other worlds can get along well on their own. In fact, they might even exist better without man." He smiled. "At least without the white man."

"Wait a minute. You were the guys who sold beaver pelts by the millions to the fur traders. You're not as clean as you'd like to think."

He laughed and stretched. "I need to be outside today. I feel like I've been cooped up for days."

"That's because you *have* been cooped up for days." Normally, Harley spent most of his time outside. "For a guy who judges a good day by how many times he can pee outside, you've done well."

Harley grinned, and she planted a kiss on his forehead. Harley always made her feel better. The lightness of his being and the plumpness of his trust always made her feel as if everything would work out.

"I'll be back in a couple of hours," she said and pushed herself up. A few minutes later, she was heading for the door when she remembered she wanted to phone Warren. She felt guilty about the level of care she'd been giving to Lyn. First of all, she'd missed her appointment with Lyn the other day because of the beavers, and secondly she didn't know enough about E.I. to help Lyn decide whether she did indeed have it. From her last conversation with Warren, it sounded as if he were a library of information. Besides, he was level-headed and someone she could talk to freely.

Luckily, she found Warren at home. She began by telling him Lyn's complaints, all of which he said were the symptom list for E.I. Then he asked her if Lyn had been exposed to any sort of pesticides.

"I don't know," Jessie said.

"Check it out," he said. "My sister got sick after she'd had her house sprayed for carpenter ants."

"Did she go to the doctor?" Jessie asked.

"You know the medical profession, Jess. They're being pretty cautious about giving any legitimacy to E.I. Besides, the symptoms are so close to other psychological disorders, most docs tell patients it's all in their heads."

Jessie murmured her agreement.

"Besides," Warren said, "at this point in time, there's not much a doctor can do. With some illnesses, the body can fight back, create antibodies, but with E.I., the body becomes even more sensitive to chemicals. It's like they become allergic to the world. My sister's so sensitive now, she can't even be in a car without throwing up."

Warren was quiet for a moment. When he finally spoke, he said, "That's what makes it such hell—the person has to practically go into seclusion to survive."

They were both quiet for a moment.

"Be careful, Jess," Warren said finally. "E.I. has a really high suicide rate."

Chapter 12

Dan pulled up to Carlingview in his black Jeep, and Sonny ran towards his car as if it were an ice cream truck. Over the weeks he and Megan had been dating, the boy had become his biggest fan.

Dan got out of the car and picked Sonny up, swinging him in the air. He was as light as a pillow. Sonny laughed wildly, and Dan grinned as Megan, dressed in a snug-fitting cotton blouse and long flowery skirt, came towards him.

"You look gorgeous," he said, pulling her soft, womanly body towards him. She made him feel strong and virile, so much so that he lifted her up too, twirling them both in a big generous circle. Happiness swelled in his chest, and for a moment, he felt dizzy from the swirl of it.

"You two ready to go?"

They had planned on taking the pontoon boat out for a ride before dinner.

"There's a problem in the kitchen," Megan said. "Can you wait for a half-hour?"

Dan nodded. "Sure. Why don't I take the monster-eater here and we'll head up into the woods and see if we can snag some dinosaurs. What do you think, Sonny-son-son? Want to do that?"

In answer, Sonny shot off into the trees. Megan gave him a warm, appreciative kiss. He knew it pleased her when he took care of Sonny, and he liked pleasing her. Besides, it felt great that she was letting him play the role of part-time parent. If his wishes came true, maybe one day, he'd be more than that. Meanwhile, he enjoyed spending time with Sonny. Being with someone who adored you wasn't hard to take.

Dan followed Sonny up the hill, making a game of their adventure, chasing after the boy, then letting him run ahead. They went past the tennis courts and up into the woods. As they climbed, Dan could see most of the Carlingview property. He'd been wanting to take a good look at the place for a while, and this was the perfect opportunity. Although he hadn't said anything to Megan, he kept thinking about ways to become involved with the resort, and walking around it might give him some ideas.

"Faster, Danny, faster."

The way Sonny said "Danny", it sounded like "Daddy". It felt good to Dan to be thought of as a daddy again. He certainly wasn't getting to do much "daddying" with his daughters. Although he'd called Franny and Claire a few times since he'd arrived, he'd only caught them home once. He'd given them his new number, but they hadn't phoned him. As usual, it was up to him to make contact. In the past, that would have depressed him, but not now. Since arriving in Muskoka, it was as if a whole new life were being offered to him.

As willing as he was to leave his past behind, Megan wanted to know all about it. As they'd gotten closer and more intimate, she had become especially interested in knowing about his marriage and what had gone wrong.

One day, after he'd vented a long time about Barb, she'd wrinkled her face and said, "You're so bitter."

"Wouldn't you be, after someone like that?"

She sidestepped his question. "But how can you go forward in your life if you've got all that unfinished business?"

Dan didn't know what to say. As a child, he'd been taught to clean up after himself, but he couldn't see how it was possible to apply that to relationships. His marriage to Barb was like a nuclear waste area—far too toxic to venture anywhere near, let alone clean up.

A week later, she'd asked if they could have a talk. He'd winced but agreed. He could tell she was geared up to tell him something, and for a moment, he worried she was going to break up with him.

"Ever since Sonny's dad left," she began, "all I've wanted was to be a family again. For Sonny to have a father and…" She stopped herself. "I like you," she told him, "and Sonny adores you. And I've been thinking there might be a future for us, someday, but I can't see how we can go forward if you can't resolve things from the past."

"You don't know Barb—she's a viper!" He could feel Megan bristling.

"Sonny's father used to talk that way about his ex too," she said. "He kept telling me he was ready to get married again, but he wasn't. Not really. He was still on the run from her. We didn't have a chance."

After admitting that, she cried a little.

"After we broke up," Megan finally continued, "I went to see someone. A therapist. She helped me. To complete things."

Dan didn't know much about therapists, but if going to one had been helpful for her, he was glad. He kissed her hair.

"Would you see her for a session or two?"

Dan pushed his fingers back through his hair. The idea did not appeal to him, but wanting to appear open, he said he'd think about it.

He should probably think about it now, he told himself, but it was hard to think and walk at the same time. He trudged up the hill. They had climbed almost to the top of the ridge behind the resort. Dan looked down at the tennis courts, the swimming pools and various white wooden buildings. It was stunningly beautiful. He envied Megan and Sonny living here.

If he and Megan continued to get along as well as they were, they might get married. If that happened, he would invest what was left of his savings in Carlingview, and they would both be part owners. The idea filled him with pleasure. He would love nothing better than to leave the water treatment business and hang around this place all day.

His imagination tumbled forward, and he saw himself waking up with Megan, going for a swim first thing every morning before heading to his office in the resort. He saw himself discussing various decisions with Wayne and giving orders to the staff. Then he was out in the ski boat, taking the kids tubing. He could hear Franny laughing, Sonny shrieking as the boat bounced up and down. Claire would be sitting on Megan's lap.

The fantasy brought tears to his eyes. His kids would love it here. Maybe he'd get them up at the end of the summer when the resort wasn't so busy. He imagined the kids returning home and raving about Carlingview to Barb. They might even want to move up here and be with him and Megan. That would certainly wipe the smug smile off Barb's face once and for all.

Maybe he should consider this therapy idea after all.

He knew from Megan's tone that she really wanted him to give it a try. A few sessions wouldn't kill him, although he couldn't imagine talking to a stranger about things he couldn't even talk to Megan about. Nevertheless, if he could get the therapist's stamp of approval, it could be to his advantage.

Would he tell the therapist about Christie? No. Christie was in the past. He didn't even like thinking of her any more. It felt like bad luck somehow. He sighed, and hearing Sonny call, turned and made his way further along the ridge. When he reached the boy, Sonny was squeezing his nose with his little fingers.

"Pee-yuu," Sonny said. "Something stinks."

Dan made a visor of his hand and surveyed what he had hoped to find: the sewage lagoon. All the resorts that were too far from town services had such lagoons, but this one was particularly large, probably holding a thousand gallons when at full capacity, which this one certainly was near now.

Dan explained in as simple terms as he could, how when someone came to stay at the resort and used the toilet, what they flushed away was sent out here to this "lake".

"Why?"

Dan smiled. The favourite kid question. "Basically because there's no other place to put it. It's too far from town to take it there." He pointed to the sun. "So, they clean it here on the property. With the help of the sun. The sun kills the bacteria. That's the bad stuff. The stuff that might make you sick. And when the liquid is clean, they'll open up the outlet valve and let it run off." Dan remembered how one of the books had called this process "decanting the liquid".

"Ewww!" Sonny pulled at Dan's hand.

"Wait here." Dan walked closer to the lagoon. What was that growing in there? The sun was in his face, so he couldn't see as clearly as he wanted, but he thought he could see bullrushes. That wasn't a good sign. He'd have to tell Wayne. It would look good on him to be the one bringing this to Wayne's attention. This was a chance for him to start proving his value.

Sonny was wandering up closer to the lagoon, and Dan grabbed him.

"Hey there, big guy. Stay back." The idea of the boy being anywhere near the lagoon gave him the willies. He knelt down. "Climb on. I'll give you a piggyback."

Sonny scrambled up and put his small arms around Dan's neck, and the two of them took off down the hill.

When they reached the lodge, Dan went immediately to Wayne's office. Wayne was on the phone but waved them in, pushing a newspaper towards Dan. Then he pulled open a drawer and offered his nephew a cherry sucker.

"Thanks, Uncle Wayne," Sonny said, pulling at the wrapping.

Dan read the headline on the paper. TORONTO HEAT AT ALL TIME HIGH. He smiled. No wonder the resort was so busy. People were dying to get out of the city. He watched Wayne jot down some figures. Wayne had freckles, like Megan's, but they were smaller and darker.

Wayne put down the phone and rubbed his face. "This hot weather is great for the resort, but I'm bushed."

"You can sleep all February when this place is closed and you're in Bermuda," Dan said.

Wayne laughed, and Dan smiled.

"You should get yourself some more help, that's all."

Wayne smiled wearily. "Come on, I'll buy you a beer."

"Now you're talking."

Wayne picked up the phone. "Brian? Wayne. Send over two Budweisers, will ya? And a juice for Sonny." He leaned back in his chair. "There are a few perks to owning the place. The beer is free, and you can get some kid to deliver it."

When the beer came, Dan took a long sip and mentioned that he'd seen the sewage lagoon.

Wayne rolled his eyes.

Dan carried on. "There are some bullrushes that should get cleaned out."

"Bullrushes! What do I care about bullrushes?"

"It's not the bullrushes—it's the animals they attract. You might get a beaver in there or some other animal that could burrow into the 'berm', or side wall. That could weaken it. You don't want that. 'Specially with it being so full."

Wayne frowned. "I bet it's those fucking beavers. Tim told me there were a bunch of them up there. I told him to get rid of them a few weeks ago."

"There's no sign of any beavers right now," Dan said, but Wayne wasn't listening.

"A beaver took twenty trees down at my last cottage," Wayne said. "I finally shot it, but not before he'd shot the hell out of my property value."

Sonny was starting to draw on Dan's shoe with a pencil. Dan pulled his foot away. "All you have to do is clear away the bullrushes." He was about to offer to do that when the phone rang. Wayne picked it up and turned his chair so his back was to Dan.

Feeling dismissed, Dan chugged the rest of his beer, took Sonny's hand and went in search of Megan.

Chapter 13

J essie stood outside her house and breathed deeply. The pungent, primal smells of spring were streaming through the air like ribbons on the end of a kite. The woods around her house were all green now, that new pulsating green that she sometimes called "believer green". It always filled her with hope.

She was feeling good today. Harley hadn't talked about going away for a while now, and Hope-in-Hell was recovering nicely. For the moment, anyway, things were calm. Her only concern was Lyn. Lyn hadn't called back to make an appointment, but Jessie knew there was nothing she could do about that. She could hardly chase after the woman. She knew Lyn would call when she was ready.

She got in the car and made her way to the seniors' residence. Today was the day she and the Grannies were reporting back on the research they'd done, and she guessed the meeting was going to be both provocative and feisty.

She parked the car in front of the home and made her way along the sidewalk. Coming towards her was a stooped old woman, her hand clutching a cane that shook despite the ferocity of her grip. Jessie could feel the incredible energy the woman was exerting just to keep upright.

Getting old was daunting, Jessie thought, as she nodded and passed the woman. The only thing good about it was that it beat the alternative.

As Jessie entered the room, Joey threw her thick arms out to the sides in greeting.

"Yo! Jess!"

Jessie was pulled into the generous pillow of Joey's body.

"We wanted to meet down here so we could be away from all the old people," Elfy said, winking at Jessie.

"How's Hope-in-Hell?" Estelle asked, her eyes protruding like ping pong balls.

"He's still alive," Jessie said.

Grace sneezed and there was a chorus of bless yous from the other Grannies.

"I must be getting the cold that's going around," Grace said.

Jessie and Elfy exchanged glances. A year ago, Grace had undergone surgery for bowel cancer and had seemed to be continually sick ever since.

Jessie looked at the others. They were all old, but lately, they were beginning to look aged. Aggie still had her substantial, authoritative body, but it didn't make anyone step out of the way any more. Estelle, who had always been so bird-like in her features, was now as thin as an egret's leg. Even Joey, who had the energy of a bulldozer and the body build to be a decent replica, could hardly hear any more. Elfy still had some sparks left in her, but they didn't fly as fast or as far.

Grace, bless her, seemed to be fading away like a photograph left out in the sun. Would Grace be the next to go? Jessie wondered. She was the logical one, but really, death was just a heart squeeze away for any of them.

Aggie took a small dumbbell from her bag and began pumping it, making the gold bangles on her wrist clink.

"You should try weights, Grace. Build yourself up. My trainer, Roberto, swears by them."

Elfy rolled her eyes. "The only reason I'd take up exercise is to hear heavy breathing again."

Joey's belly jiggled. "Good one, Elf." She patted her stomach. "I joined a health club once. Cost me four hundred bucks. Didn't lose a pound!"

Estelle elongated her neck. "Maybe you didn't go often enough."

"You mean you had to go?" Joey gave her thigh an "I got'cha" smack. "HA!"

Aggie spoke over the laughter. "You know what they say—you're as young as you feel."

"That'd make me about two hundred!" Joey said. She was sitting on a plastic chair, and her rump spread over the sides like whipped cream over a cupcake.

"It's what keeps me out of an old folks' home," Aggie said smugly.

Jessie frowned. Although Elfy still stayed at her cottage in the summer, Aggie was the only Granny who was able to live on her own the entire year.

"Rub it in, Aggs, rub it in," Elfy said.

"Rub what where?" Joey asked.

"Oh, for crying out loud, Joey, move in closer if you can't hear," Elfy said.

Joey slapped her head. "Damn hearing aid."

"I didn't know you wore a hearing aid," Grace said.

"Yes, you did," Joey said. "You just forgot." She pulled in her chair. "When I was a kid, everyone thought I was retarded, until someone finally figured out I had ear trouble. And they called me slow!"

Elfy was still staring at Aggie. "Nothing so bad about

living here. You get your meals done, your laundry done—"

Aggie's mouth twisted wryly. "Your diapers changed—"

Jessie winced. "Okay, you two—enough." She pulled out a spiral notebook. "Time to get started." She looked up and began.

"My job was to research Muskoka's water, remember? What I did was start by calling the District. They're the ones who do the water testing. According to them, the water is fine."

Elfy frowned. "They're paid to say the water is fine."

Aggie lifted her chest indignantly. "Maybe what they're 'paid to say' happens to be the truth." She took a swig from her bottle of water.

"Why are you drinking that stuff then?" Elfy challenged. "Bottled water costs more than gas, for crying out loud."

"Come on, let's stay on track," Jessie said. She flipped through her notes. "The woman I spoke to sent me some charts, but what I'm wondering is whether we're testing for the right things. Do any of you remember those signs that used to warn everyone about the poison in the fish?" She nodded to Estelle, who held up a booklet. "That's a government pamphlet describing what's currently in our fish. Estelle's going to talk about that in a minute. But what I'm wondering is how we can talk about the water being fine if our fish aren't."

"Tell them that stuff about two-stroke engines," Elfy said.

Jessie nodded and handed out the paper she'd copied from the Internet.

"Yo!" Joey said loudly. "Two-stroke engines discharge twenty-five to forty per cent of their gas and oil unburned into the water?"

"What about snow machines?" Elfy asked. "They can't be much better."

"The problem with snow machines," Jessie said, "is they pack their emissions into the snow over the winter months, and it gets dumped into the water when the lake thaws. Which causes a kind of 'toxic shock'. During the spring, too, when fish and frogs are laying their eggs."

"When I was growing up," Grace said wistfully, "we used to swim in Lake Ontario."

Jessie checked her notes. "In the U.S., over forty-five per cent of the lakes are too polluted for fishing or swimming."

"Forty-five per cent!" Joey crossed her heavy arms. Her elbows jutted out like bazookas.

"That's disgraceful!" Aggie said. "Egregious! It's—"

"Nutso!" Elfy said.

There was a stunned silence.

Elfy broke it. "What else does that book say, Estelle?"

Estelle picked up the pamphlet. "According to this, in Lake Muskoka, you can't eat large lake trout or any small-mouthed bass. They're too contaminated. The other fish you can eat, but only a few times a month. If," she emphasized, "you're not a woman of child-bearing age."

"Oh, I get it," Joey said. "It's okay to poison the general population but not a potential mother. Right!"

Estelle nodded in a slow, funereal way.

Elfy scowled. "What you're telling us is that each and every fish in the lake is polluted, but the water is fine."

Jessie thought about Sushi and Gumption and all the other wildlife that ate fish for their survival.

"What kind of pollution are we talking about?" Joey asked.

"Mercury, PCBs, mirex, toxaphene and dioxin,"

Estelle read from the book.

"It's those damn businesses," Elfy said. "They don't care about anything but profit."

"It's not just businesses," Jessie said. "Ordinary people still do most of the polluting." She checked her notes. "Apparently individual Canadians dump millions of litres of used motor oil into the system every year. That's seven times the Exxon Valdez disaster."

Joey began to pace. "I've heard just about as much as I can stand."

"Let's get through all the reports, "Jessie said. "Aggie? You ready? You were going to research air pollution, right?"

Aggie nodded. "I chose that topic because I thought it would be good news. But it isn't. Last year Muskoka had more days in the red-zone than downtown Toronto!"

Joey stopped pacing. "What? Muskoka had more air pollution than Toronto?"

Aggie clamped her teeth together.

"Is most of that from the U.S.?" Jessie asked.

"Yes," Aggie said. "Which makes it darn hard to do anything about!"

Elfy shrugged. "Oh, I wouldn't say that. A few of us Grannies could threaten to take our clothes off in some automaker's board room."

Aggie's eyebrows shot up.

Elfy chuckled. "I bet those big time geezers would do almost anything to avoid seeing an old woman's wrinkled body." She turned to Aggie. "And if you threatened to peel too, we'd really have something to bargain with."

Jessie sighed. "Who haven't we heard from? Wasn't someone going to report on golf courses?"

"Me!" Elfy said. "Anyone want to guess how many

we've got in Muskoka?"

"Too many!" Joey answered.

"Thirty-one!" Elfy said. "And from what I'm reading, you might as well call them Pesticide Pits. Although I couldn't get Canadian figures, in the U.S. the average golf course dumps fifty-five pounds of pesticides per acre, per year."

Joey whistled.

"That adds up to over twelve million pounds of chemicals," Elfy said.

Estelle's eyes bulged. "I can't imagine some of that doesn't get into the lakes."

"The lakes and everywhere else," Elfy cried. "Know what one of the most toxic foods on the planet is? Mother's milk!"

Aggie looked distraught. "I don't believe it!"

"That's the most depressing thing I've ever heard!" Joey said.

Grace put her hands over her ears.

"Cover your ears, stick your head in the sand," Elfy said, "but that won't change anything."

Jessie felt numb. Maybe it was a mistake to look at the whole picture all at once. It was too much. Entirely too much.

Aggie dragged her eyes up to Jessie's. "It's disheartening. Very disheartening."

"Maybe we should stop the meeting now. Carry on another time," Grace said.

"Or take a pizza break," Joey suggested. "That'll make us feel better."

Elfy frowned. "We can't stop now! Not at a low point like this."

Jessie didn't want to stop either, but was at a loss as to

how to re-inspire the group. "I have an idea," she said suddenly. All eyes turned to her.

"Do any of you remember Green Schools?" she asked.

"Wasn't that when the schools went ecological?" Aggie resumed pumping her dumb bell. "My grandchildren made me buy them all plastic containers so they didn't have to take those cardboard juice cartons every day."

Mustering as much enthusiasm as she could, Jessie said. "What if we created the idea of a Green Cottage? We could draw up a check list, just like the schools did, and start to talk it up."

Seeing Aggie nod, she carried on. "The check list could have stuff on it like getting the septic tank pumped, not using pesticides, taking toxic material to the dump."

Elfy looked at Jessie meaningfully. "We know one garbage dumping bozo who'd flunk that all right."

Jessie stayed on topic. "Once we have the list," she said, "we could get it printed out, then talk about it at cottager's associations, maybe even give out certificates to people who comply. Call them Green Awards or something…"

"At least that would be doing something," Aggie said seriously. "We have to do something."

Elfy grinned. "And we could give out imaginary tickets for infractions." She pretended to be writing out a ticket for someone. "Sir, that will be ten enviro points for leaving your boat running."

"HA!" Joey hooted. "We'll get Elfy a sheriff's badge. And a cowboy hat."

Elfy stood up gingerly, spread her feet and held her hands out from her thighs like a gunslinger. "Turn off that engine, or else." She grabbed her imaginary guns and shot them into the air.

Chapter 14

As Dan and Megan's relationship deepened, he hoped her idea of him going to a therapist would float away, but it stayed anchored to her idea of what needed to happen. Finally, Dan gave in and made an appointment. Now, however, as he sat in his car on the road outside Jessie's house, fifteen minutes early, he fiddled with his keys and wondered what he was going to say.

When his marriage to Barb was breaking down, she had wanted to go into therapy, but he had refused. It was bad enough listening to Barb's endless list of complaints when it was just the two of them, but he wouldn't have been able to stand such an onslaught in front of someone else. Besides, by the time he and Barb had talked about marriage counselling, rigor mortis had already set in.

He looked up at the house at the end of the treed lane. On his way here, he'd pictured a severe woman with penetrating dark eyes, but this house didn't suit someone like that. Although he could only get a glimpse of what looked like a cottage, he could see bird feeders and flower boxes scattered around the property as it rolled down to the water.

A car drove by, and he resisted the impulse to duck down. He hoped no one he knew was going to see him here. Wishing he hadn't arrived so early, he stared down the driveway. There were two cars parked there. Did that mean someone was already in there? Was that person going to come out of the house at any moment and see him waiting to go in? He checked the time once more and rehearsed again what he was going to say. His plan was to admit that the appointment had been Megan's idea. That would put him in a good light right off the bat, establishing him as a responsive partner. Barb had always called him stubborn, and he was eager to show his willingness to do what it took to make a relationship work.

In a way, it was a good sign that Megan wanted him to resolve the past. It meant she was giving serious consideration to a future with him. The problem was, he couldn't imagine anything being able to heal the damage his marriage had caused. Even now, the wound of it felt embedded in his gut like a piece of shrapnel. How could a therapist dig out something like that?

He stuffed his keys into his pocket and reminded himself to stay on topic. He'd heard psychotherapists were famous for raking up the coals of the past. The last thing he wanted was to talk about his parents or his childhood. And he certainly was not going to mention Christie. He didn't want Jessie thinking he was just one big relationship fuck-up. That wouldn't do at all. He was here for one reason: to get a clean bill of psychological health, which he would take back to Megan and deposit into their future.

He checked his watch again. Restless now and wanting to get the appointment over with, he got out of the car and walked to the door. If there was already someone in there, too bad, it was his turn now. His legs felt shaky, but he told himself not to be a wimp and went to the door. An older but vibrant woman with long, light-coloured hair and bright green eyes opened it. Her hand felt warm and strong. Strong enough to pull a person out of the ditch.

"Would you like some water? Or a hot drink?" she asked on the way to her office.

Her offer took him off guard. He'd gathered himself up for this appointment, like a kid going into the principal's office, but her casual demeanour suggested no such gathering was necessary. That made him nervous. He didn't want to relax too much and say things he shouldn't say.

"No. No, thanks."

Jessie handed him a form and a slender black pen. The form was an exercise in itself, asking him everything from why he was there to the name of his favourite fairy tale. He answered the questions as best he could and was doodling on the page when she returned.

Suddenly aware of his scribbling, shame rose to his face. "I'm sorry, I—"

"No, carry on. I like it when people draw." She handed him a fresh piece of paper and took the form. "Keep going."

He looked up at her, surprised. He couldn't remember the last time someone over the age of ten had asked him to keep drawing. He lifted the pen but stopped himself. He didn't want to draw something embarrassing. Or revealing.

Seeing his hesitation, she said, "Why don't you draw a picture of your life?" She looked at him warmly. "Don't think about it. Just let your pen do whatever it wants."

Let his pen do whatever it wanted? He felt wary, but the pen leapt to the page like a skater to the rink. A figure appeared. Dan recognized it immediately. It was InkBoy. InkBoy! What was InkBoy doing here, now? Elation washed through him, but within it swam a snake of alarm.

InkBoy had always got him into trouble. He scrunched the paper up. Now Jessie was really going to think he was nuts.

He looked at her, expecting disapproval, but her eyes were soft and full of concern.

"You didn't like what you drew? Or you didn't want me to see it?"

Flustered, he said: "It's silly. It's just a cartoon I used to draw."

"You used to draw cartoons?"

He squeezed the ball of paper tighter. "Yeah. I had a regular spot in the school newspaper." He began to describe it to her. She seemed so interested, that he told her about the comic strip. He was doing just what he hadn't wanted to do—telling her everything.

Jessie leaned back in her chair. "Did your parents enjoy this talent of yours?"

Dan sighed. "My father thought it was a waste of time."

"How about you? What did you think?"

"I could see his point of view. Not many people can make a living out of cartooning."

"So what happened?" Jessie asked. "To InkBoy?"

"He disappeared. One day I went to draw him, and he wasn't there any more." She raised her eyebrows.

"I didn't have much time to cartoon anyway. My dad got sick, and I had to take care of him." He expected to see approval on her face for his willingness to be the dutiful son, but there was none.

"Sick? How so?"

The ball of paper began to soften from the moisture in his hand. It felt dangerous to be talking about his father here. "He had a heart attack."

"How old were you when that happened?"

"He almost died." Dan's mouth felt dry. "I was fifteen."

Jessie was watching him. "Was that when InkBoy disappeared?"

Dan swallowed. "Yes. I haven't seen him since until five minutes ago." He groaned silently. Why did he tell her that?

"How does it feel to connect with him again?"

"Dangerous." The word was out of his mouth before he could stop it.

"Dangerous?" she probed.

Dan didn't like where this was going. "My father thought I should be doing something more substantial with my life. He was just trying to save me from making a mistake." Jessie was staring at him dubiously, so he added, "I wouldn't have married Barb, my ex-wife, if I'd listened to him."

Jessie was pensive. "I get the sense that it's sometimes difficult for you to listen to your own counsel—trust your own sense of what is right."

Dan winced. Barb used to accuse of him of listening to his father too much as well. "You always do what he says," she used to shout. At times, standing between Barb and his father was like being caught between a megaphone and a road drill.

"Sometimes," he admitted. "But I know that Megan is right for me." He went on to tell her about how well he and Sonny got along and what his hopes were for the relationship, adding that his reason for being here was to clear up the past so his relationship with her could go ahead. He paused, hoping this last point would sink in.

Jessie began asking him some questions about his marriage, and Dan told her all she wanted to know.

"My father couldn't stand Barb," Dan said.

"You keep mentioning your father," Jessie said.

Dan frowned. It was true.

Jessie looked down at his form. "You wrote that 'The Ugly Duckling' was your favourite fairytale as a child. Do you remember what was so special for you about it?"

Dan's frown deepened. First they were talking about cartoons, now they were talking about fairytales. And he was paying for this? He shook his head.

"Let me see if I remember it," she said. "It was about a swan growing up in a family of ducks. If I remember rightly, the swan doesn't know he's a swan and spends his time trying to be a duckling. Do you relate to any of that?"

Dan said nothing. He felt a sinking sensation in his gut.

Jessie's eyes softened. "It can be like that in families too. Kids learn quickly what they need to do to get their parents' love and approval. If that means pretending to be a 'duck', so to speak, most kids will learn to quack as quickly as the swan in the story."

Ducks! Swans! Fairytales! This was ridiculous. "Look, I'm not here to talk about fairytales."

"It's not the fairytale itself we're interested in," Jessie said. "It's what it means. If, for example, you weren't able to be yourself as you grew up, you probably didn't know yourself well enough to pick a marriage partner who was right for you." She looked at him with warmth in her eyes. "And, given what a strong personality your father was, you probably chose someone equally strong. But at times, that probably felt like you were between a bull and a buffalo."

Dan nodded. She was dead on. But he brought the topic back to what he was here for. "Megan's worried I have too much bitterness from my marriage to go forward into a relationship with her. That's what I'm here to clear up."

Jessie nodded and asked more questions about his marriage and family life. Finally, she said: "The sense I'm getting, Dan, from all you've said, is that you're still trying to figure out who you are. You had a strong, almost domineering father and then, a strong, almost domineering wife. Even though you didn't always like their strength, in a way, it made things simpler because then you didn't have to figure things out for yourself."

"But the relationship with Megan is asking you to be your own person. It's asking you to grow up and come to terms with your past. Not just Barb, but your father too. That may be why InkBoy's reappeared."

"What do you mean?"

"InkBoy's the creative part of you. The part that can do anything. The part that doesn't have to play by the rules your family set out for you. When he came into your life, just as you moved into puberty, he expressed the part of you that needed to break away from the family and become your own person. Unfortunately, your father's heart attack, coming at the time it did, shut that process down. But it's a normal process. And one you need to carry on with now. Explore who you really are and stand up for that. Then you will be able to make decisions that are right for you."

She paused for a moment. "And as you stand up for yourself, you won't be so mad at Barb, or anyone else. Because they won't be able to push you around any more."

Her eyes found his. "And The Invader, whether that's your father or Barb or any other person who's trying to 'invade' you, will have no power."

Dan sat in the chair, stunned. Blood was pulsing into his hands, like ink.

Chapter 15

J essie sat looking out over the water. It was as still as a pond this early in the morning and a deep, blue grey. The sun had yet to rise completely over the horizon, but already the day was sullen with heat. Whatever happened to spring? When she'd been little, spring used to last for weeks, beginning with that lovely trickling sound of melted ice, followed by the softening of the ground as it became penetrable once again to her feet. And then everything thawed, and the world became lush and plush with greenery.

Spring was a time of year she loved, but nowadays, it seemed to last such a short time. This year, there had been snow on the ground one week and the hard heat of summer the next. And for almost a month now, the temperatures had been higher than ever before.

She went inside and looked at her appointment book. Today was "G-Day", the day she and the Grannies were going to take the Green Cottage concept on the road. G-Day! She shook her head at the military-sounding lingo. Next thing she knew the Grannies would be saluting each other.

But first, she had a 9 AM counselling session scheduled with Lyn. Jessie didn't like to see clients so early in the morning. Seeing clients meant she had to be extroverted, and she wasn't so good at that early in the day, but an appointment with Lyn was long overdue, so she'd made an exception.

Trying to get herself organized, she went over to a box by the door and pulled out a handful of informational pamphlets on the Green Cottage campaign, as well as a stack of Environmental Fitness Checklists, and put them in a bag. Thanks to Aggie, there had already been two articles in the paper about the campaign, so she hoped people would have heard about them.

"Remember, the checklist is optional," Jessie had reminded Elfy last week when the group had picked straws to determine who was going to pair up with whom. "Don't you try and bamboozle anyone into doing it."

"Me? Bamboozle?"

"I see that glint in your eyes," Jessie had said. "Listen, not everyone's going to appreciate someone coming in and telling them how to run their lives."

"Why? Aggie tells people what to do all the time."

Jessie ignored the comment. The whole idea of going to people's homes made her nervous. She was even more nervous having Elfy as her partner. She loved Elfy, loved her dearly, but the old woman could be feisty. Old people, really old people, seemed to go one way or the other, becoming compliant and childlike or ornery and self-determined. It was obvious which category Elfy fit into.

Pouring herself a cup of tea, Jessie went to her computer and checked her email. The first message offered her free photographs of hardcore teen sex. The second one told her about a scheme guaranteed to make her a millionaire in just a few weeks. The third described how the world's resources were going to run out by the year 2050. The statistics were daunting. She felt tense and irritated, partly because of the content, but also because the article had used the word "resources". The author talked about mineral resources, forestry resources, water resources. There was an egocentrism in the entire concept, she thought. As if trees, fish and other living things only existed for the consumption of the human race.

She leaned back in her chair, and Charlie, her dog, nuzzled her hand.

"Okay, my little animal resource. We'll get you out for your walk soon," she said, smoothing her palm along his velvet face. Charlie wagged his thick yellow tail.

She clicked on the last two emails. One was a health newsletter that she decided to read later and the other was an outline of the demographics of the world's wealth. She scanned it quickly.

"According to this, Charlie, if the earth's population were shrunk to a village of a hundred people, six of those people would have fifty-nine per cent of the entire world's wealth."

She stood up. The unfairness of it was colossal. Yet, if she could distribute the earth's wealth more evenly, she doubted if she'd do it. That would mean even more cars. And more pollution.

She set her laptop aside and wandered down to the enclosure Harley had built for Hope-in-Hell. The beaver was much better now. One day, they'd have to release him back to the wild, but not until he had completely recovered. Meanwhile, to make his stay more comfortable, Harley had built an enclosure that replicated his natural habitat as closely as possible.

Jessie attempted to make the sound Harley usually made to call Hope-in-Hell. To her surprise, the beaver lumbered towards her. She gave him an apple slice and watched as he delicately ate it. His elegant black hands intrigued her. She would have thought an animal that slogged such heavy logs around would have huge, meaty hands, but it was not so. How could such small hands move huge trees around like pickup sticks?

Thank God, his hands hadn't been damaged in the explosion. One of his back paws had been burned, but it didn't look so raw any more.

"Yup, you're definitely on the mend," she told him as she gave him another apple slice. He took it but looked to either side of her as if waiting for something. Or someone.

"I know who you're looking for," she said softly, massaging the soft fur on his chest. "Remember he came to say goodbye to you last night? And fed you that bowl of strawberries?"

Harley, unable to put off supplying his stores with his handcrafted leather goods, had left at first light that morning. Since he had to go north anyway, he thought he might take a few extra days and head into the bush.

"I know. It was a surprise to me too," she said. "He should be in Sudbury by now." Knowing Harley and his disinterest in cities, he'd get his business finished as quickly as he could and head west to the Sault, then north to Agawa Bay and the grandeur of Lake Superior. "Where it still feels wild," he'd said.

She knew he would be scouting around for other opportunities. For all she knew, he might come back and want to pack up right away. Harley was like that. He could move with the moment. But could she? Even if she could, did she want to? She had a life here in Muskoka. Not only a personal life, but a professional life. She wasn't just going to pick up and leave all that because of some man! Come on! Maybe it was time for the two of them to live apart for a while. They could visit each other and act like young lovers again. Not that they'd ever stopped acting like young lovers.

The phone rang and Jessie rushed back to the house, picking up on the third ring. It was Lyn.

"Jessie, I'm too sick to come. I can hardly get dressed. I think the drive will just be too much."

Jessie could hear the exhaustion in Lyn's voice. "Are you well enough to talk on the phone? Maybe we can have our appointment that way."

"Jess, I'm bad."

"Just keeping talking," Jessie said.

"It's taking every last bit of energy I have just to keep working," Lyn said. "God, Jessie, I can't lose my job on top of everything else!" She paused as if to gather more energy. "Some days I feel almost paralyzed, Jess, paralyzed. I have to make my body move. By the time I get home, I have to go straight to bed."

"When did all this start?"

"I'm not sure, but I think my first symptoms came after we did this spraying at the garden centre. I didn't think much about it. It wasn't like we did a lot of spraying. It wasn't more than someone might do at home."

Jessie tensed and waited for more.

"I wore gloves and everything, but I remember feeling really sick after. Now, if I even go near the shed where we did the spraying, I feel sick." She paused again. "There's something else. For a week after the spraying, I had this red rash on my arms above the line where my gloves ended."

Jessie debated whether to broach the topic of Environmental Illness. Lyn beat her to it. "I think I might have that environmental allergy thing. Bill got me some books on it. I've got nearly all the symptoms."

Jessie nodded. "I was wondering that too."

"But meanwhile, I have to survive. And now my boss wants me to do some painting."

"Painting!" This was not the time for Lyn to expose herself to the noxious chemicals of paint. "Can't you get out of it?"

"I tried! I even told my boss about the pesticide thing, but he just thinks I'm overreacting. Jess, he'll fire me if I don't. And we'll lose our place to live!"

Why would you lose your place to live, she was about to ask, when she remembered. Lyn's job had come with the offer of accommodation in a small cabin at the back of the garden centre property. Lyn and Bill lived in that cabin now.

"I couldn't face moving right now."

Jessie sighed and began asking questions. When confronted with a knot like this, sometimes questions had a way of loosening things up. She was hoping Lyn's answers would provide some new options.

Together they came up with a list of possibilities: Lyn could try talking to her boss again. Lyn could see if her doctor could give her a note excusing her from the work. Lyn could ask her boss if Bill could do the painting instead of her. And, if worst came to worst, and she did have to do the painting, she could minimize her exposure to it by wearing not only gloves, but a boiler suit, and a hat. She could even wear one of those filter masks the workers used in paint shops.

"You could even put a fan in the window to blow the fumes outside," Jessie suggested. "If you did all that, and took plenty of breaks, you might be all right."

There was silence on the other end of the phone. Finally, Lyn said, "I'm writing some of these ideas down," she said. "That's one of the other symptoms. Brain fog. Some days it's all I can do to remember my name."

They talked for a few more minutes. Finally, Lyn said, "My doctor wants to give me medication. He says it will help."

Jessie felt nervous. According to the reading she'd done, there weren't any drugs that were helpful with E.I. "Are these drugs for Environmental Illness, or are they tranquillizers?"

"Who knows? But it scares me to take them. I'm so sensitive to everything."

Jessie made a mental note to talk to Warren again. Meanwhile, all she could offer Lyn was support and encouragement. It seemed like so little.

"I need to go," Lyn said weakly. "I have to lie down."

"Take care," Jessie called through the phone. "Keep in touch."

But Lyn had gone. She'd hung up as if even one last word of goodbye was too much.

Jessie whistled for Charlie. She needed solace. And she needed it quickly. When Charlie came, she went outside, and the sun hit her like a club. She headed towards the woods. A drop of sweat oozed down from her armpit, and she pressed the cloth of her shirt against it to absorb it.

Sometimes she felt so helpless with clients.

Once she was in the trees, the temperature was cooler. The dappled light was dim and gentle, and she walked until she came to her favourite tree: Candelabra. It was one of her oldest friends. Resting her hand on its wide girth, she looked up its trunk several feet to where the tree had been hit by lightning many years ago. Because of the hit, the main trunk had been severed there, but now, instead of one trunk, the tree had split into five smaller trunks. These trunks grew like ordinary trees, and in the middle of them was a small sitting place. Jessie climbed there now.

This place was her little personal sanctuary, and she often came here when she needed rejuvenation. The tree's injury and subsequent growth pattern gave her heart. Yes, life could be devastating, but even devastating situations could be overcome. As this tree clearly demonstrated.

She leaned back and let her eyes drift through the forest. When she'd tried to save this tree and the others surrounding it a few years ago, some people had criticized her. Canada had so many trees, some argued. But as far as Jessie was concerned, given the amount of air pollution, every single tree was needed.

She closed her eyes and let herself feel the quiet, strong energy of the tree. How could anyone doubt that a tree was a living intelligence? A tree couldn't add or subtract figures, its intelligence was not of that ilk, but it knew a great deal about supporting life. In fact, one tree did more to support life than the average person she knew.

Sometimes, when she was invited into a school to talk about nature, she took the students outside and had them do this, press their backs up against a tree. Most of them were surprised how alive the tree felt. Which always shocked Jessie. What had they thought, that a tree would feel like a lamp post? But there were always a few who couldn't feel anything. These were boys usually—not because of any innate insensitivity in that gender, but because boys so often had their sensitivity socialized out of them.

She had no doubt that was what had happened to

Dan. It was sad. From what he'd told her, he'd been derided for every nuance of emotion, diminished for every aspect of his artistic nature. As a result, he had no emotional map. Guiding him home to his authentic self was not going to be easy. Especially if he didn't tell her the truth.

Whether he was telling her the truth or not, she wasn't sure, but she couldn't get rid of the disquieting feeling that, at the very least, he was holding something back. This wasn't unusual for a new client. All clients had secrets, secrets about things they had done in the past, or should have done, and it usually took them a while to trust her enough to tell all. But with Dan, she could almost feel a kind of deep refusal.

She shook her head. He must feel so unsafe. She reminded herself to go slowly. It took time for someone to know himself. Meanwhile, she would keep after him about being honest. Without that, there would be no firm ground for either of them to stand on.

She cleared her mind and took a few long breaths. Then she climbed down and made her way to Wildwood where she was to pick up Elfy.

About an hour later, as she arrived at Wildwood, Aggie drove in behind her. Elfy, wearing green shorts, green knee socks and a T-shirt that said "Grannies for a Green Muskoka", came out on the porch.

"You look like The Girl Guide From Mars," Aggie called out.

Elfy bristled, and Jessie shot Aggie a warning look. From the tangle of lines on Elfy's face, she was in no mood to be joked about.

Aggie suppressed her laughter, but a snuffling noise came from the back of her throat anyway.

"Elfy, you look fine," Jessie said.

Aggie took an armful of pamphlets to her car and handed Jessie a map. She gave Jessie a meaningful look, whispered "Good luck" and was off.

Jessie looked at Elfy worriedly. Irritation was radiating out of the old woman like heat. She and Elfy got into the car, Elfy slamming the door.

As they followed Aggie out, Jessie rolled down the window, determined to keep her own sense of wellbeing despite Elfy's mood. She took a few deep breaths. The strong, snappy scent of spring was over now, and the air smelled of summer. It was a ripe, almost steamy smell, filled with the sensuous aromas of berries and hot rocks.

"Hotter'n Hell's fire," Elfy said.

Jessie pressed her lips together. To her, complaining about the weather was a waste of time.

"We've had more scorchers so far this year than the whole of last summer," Elfy said fidgeting. She darted her head towards the side-view mirror. "Some bonehead's right on our tail."

Jessie pulled over, and the car raced past.

"Turkey!" Elfy said. "You should've just slowed down. That would've got his dander up."

"And have the driver cursing me upside down and sideways? No thanks!" She softened her tone. "What's eating you today?"

"What isn't? It's hot. I'm old. And my niece's got herself in a mess over some dickhead guy."

"Is this the niece you're so fond of?"

"Yup."

"Do you want to talk about it?"

"Only to tell you she's going to be staying with me for

a while." Elfy's attention turned to the map. "Turn here."

"If I can help, let me know," Jessie said.

They drove up a winding road. "Our first one's just up there, so you can pull over anywhere."

They parked and got out of the car. "I figured she could stay at the cottage with me for the summer anyways. I can handle that."

"That's kind of you," Jessie said and touched Elfy's arm. Despite Elfy's gruffness, she had a heart of gold. "But listen, are you sure you feel up to this today?"

"What do you think, I'm going to bite someone's head off?"

"You've got a lot on your mind right now."

"Okay, okay. I promise, I won't take a strip off anyone."

"Good."

"Unless they're a complete idiot—"

"Elfy!"

"This one looks easy, anyway."

"The road hasn't even been paved," Jessie said as they made their way along a gravelled driveway.

The cottage they were approaching was a one story, L-shaped structure with brown wooden siding and a deck along the front. Various bird feeders had been placed around the deck and nearby trees.

"They like birds—that's a good thing," Elfy said.

A short woman with a square face appeared around the side of the cottage as they approached. The woman pushed back her greying hair with the back of a hand covered in a flowered gardening glove. Jessie gave her the Green Cottage brochure and began explaining their visit.

The woman's hand jabbed the page. "We read about

this!" She called her husband over. "We were kind of hoping we'd get a visit."

A tall man with silky white hair came up behind his wife and after introductions, said, "Let's show these folks around and see how we measure up."

Jessie gave Elfy a relieved smile, and they began their tour of the Smythes' cottage. They started with the cleaning products under the sink and in the bathroom.

"As you can see, we just buy the biodegradable stuff," Mrs. Smythe said. Jessie put a check mark on the sheet and went on to the next point. "When did you last have your septic pumped?"

"At the beginning of the season," Mr. Smythe told her.

As Jessie walked around, she could see that for the most part, the property had been left in its natural state. The Smythes had even left a fallen log down by the shore. She put more checkmarks on the sheet. "So far, you people have a perfect score."

Together they all walked down to the boathouse.

"You'll lose a point for not having a floating dock," Elfy said, "but it's good that you've built most of it away from the shore."

Mr. Smythe lifted a metal latch to the boathouse. Jessie stepped inside, smelling the wet wood and life jackets. Waves from the lake splushed up under the dock.

Elfy whistled. "Holy cow!"

It was dim in the boathouse, and with the other three ahead of her, Jessie couldn't see what they were staring at. Some antique mahogany launch, she thought. A picture of the couple cruising the water in a long sleek wooden boat came into her mind. She poked her head around the group and saw it.

A huge fibreglass boat with two twin outboard motors filled the water slip.

"It's our grandson's," Mr. Smythe said. "We tried to talk him into buying an inboard, but we weren't successful." He frowned. "But next summer, if he wants to keep his boat here, he's going to have to buy a four-stroke." He turned to Elfy. "So, do we flunk the whole test now?"

Elfy shook her head. "As long as you or your family are committed to buying a four-stroke next time," she explained, "you still get points, just not as many." She took her pencil and tabulated their score. "You've still got enough to earn you a certificate. You don't get a five star rating, but four isn't bad."

Jessie nodded, pulled a certificate out of an envelope and handed it to them.

The couple smiled happily, and Elfy and Jessie said their goodbyes and made their way back down along the path. Jessie felt easier now. Maybe this wasn't going to be as difficult as she'd thought.

Chapter 16

Dan untangled himself from the damp, twisted sheets and fumbled his way into the kitchen. The bad dream followed him like a shadow. He'd been having bad dreams ever since he'd started psychotherapy. Wasn't therapy supposed to make you feel better? If so, it was failing miserably. Each time he went, he felt as if he were being dismantled.

Jessie had warned him the therapy might make him feel discombobulated. "It's just like when you're renovating a house," she'd told him in their last session. "Things can look messy for a while."

How long was a while?

He opened the fridge and blinked as the light hit his face. Leaving the door open, he sucked back some orange juice from a carton while the cool air radiated towards his belly. Last night he'd dreamt about shoes again. In the first dream about shoes, the one he'd had last week, he'd woken up in a sweat because he'd been forced to wear shoes that didn't belong to him. In last night's dream, he hadn't been wearing any shoes at all. He was at work, and everyone was staring at his naked feet, making him feel exposed and humiliated.

Cradling the carton of juice, Dan walked out on the deck of the bunkie and leaned his arms on the wooden railing. On the far side of the lake, he could see a blush of pink rising up over the dark trees. The hushed air felt gentle on his skin, and he eased down into a deck chair to watch the new day creep into the world. It had been a long time since he'd seen the dawn, and he had forgotten how lovely it was. And how sweet it could smell. He breathed in the lake, washed air deep into his lungs.

Maybe he should stop seeing Jessie. Wasn't it dangerous to have someone mucking around in your mind like that? How could he be sure she knew what she was doing? If she did, why wasn't he feeling better? Of course, Megan would be disappointed if he stopped going, but who said he had to tell her? Megan had told him after he'd made his first appointment that she wasn't going to ask him about it, so she wouldn't know the difference. That wasn't exactly lying, it was simply leaving something out. He would tell her later when their relationship was more stable.

He wandered down to the little dock. His presence startled a duck, and he watched it take off across the lake, its wingtips dimpling the surface of the water as it flew. Being a city kid, he hadn't spent much time in nature and hadn't realized how relaxing it could be. No wonder people paid such big bucks to be on water. He hoped Meat didn't mind if he stayed on for a while. At least until he got things more together with Megan. If things continued to go well with her, he was going to suggest they live together. At Carlingview. Then, all he'd have to do was move up the lake.

Thinking about Megan made him want to see her. Deciding to ask them out for breakfast, he called them, then dressed and made his way over to the resort. He stopped at the treatment plant on the way. As usual, everything was functioning well. There was no need to worry.

Sonny leapt into the air at the sight of him.

"Hey, big guy, look what I got for you." He pulled a tri-coloured pen from his pocket.

"Look, Mom! Look."

"Dan, you shouldn't have."

"It was only a few bucks," he said as he swung the boy up on to his shoulders. Megan slipped her arm through his and gave it a squeeze.

"Someone's got a major crush on you," Megan said as they got into the car. "All I hear these days is Dan, Dan, Dan."

Dan grinned. The boy's admiration was endearing. And emotionally rejuvenating. It had been a long time since the very fact of his existence had brought so much pleasure to someone. "He's a great kid. Smart, good-looking, fun to be with—just like his mother!"

Now it was Megan's turn to grin.

They went to Nibbs and he ordered three muffins, two coffees and a hot chocolate.

After they ate, Sonny insisted on sitting on Dan's lap, and Dan showed him how to use the pen.

Megan looked from her son to Dan. "Yup, it's definitely a case of hero worship."

Dan tousled Sonny's copper-coloured hair and stood up. The sidewalks were busy as they strolled through town, but Dan didn't mind. From the clothes and jewellery the people around them were wearing, he figured he was hobnobbing with the who's who of the country. He squeezed Megan's hands. He was proud to be with someone like her. She fit right in.

Just like the other tourists, he and Megan looked at the hand-made pottery, slid their palms along the smooth back of hand-carved birds and tried on expensive sunglasses. Everything was three times what it would cost in the city, Dan thought, but if he were a store owner and had a clientele with enough money to buy a two million dollar cottage just for a few weekend getaways each year, he'd inflate his prices too. Obviously, beautiful people expected to have beautiful things.

"Swings, Dan, swings."

They were past the stores now on the main street, so Dan steered them down Bailey Street to the park. There were two kids playing on the slide, and they waved Sonny over, so Dan slid the boy down and patted his bottom as encouragement to run off. He and Megan sat at a picnic table and watched him play.

Megan was wearing a short denim skirt, and Dan thought about slipping his hand up under it so he could feel the skin of her thigh. Megan had told him she wanted to go slowly, but he had gone to see Jessie, hadn't he? Thinking he was in a good position to advance his interests, he leaned forward and kissed Megan's neck.

"Dan! There's people!"

He looked up. All he could see was a fat woman and a couple of babysitters at the far side of the park. "Not close enough to notice," he said and returned his attention to Megan's neck, pressing his mouth to her delicate skin. It was like kissing a flower petal. He reached up under her hair and brought her face towards him so he could kiss her lips. He knew how she liked to be kissed and was pleased when she pressed herself into him, wanting more. A small hand pulled at his cell phone.

"Don't touch," Megan said. "That's for Dan's work."

"It's okay," Dan said. He really shouldn't let Sonny play with it, but he was grateful for something to distract the kid. He gave Sonny the phone.

"Oh, Dan, I don't think—"

"It's okay." He watched Sonny walk off, the phone pressed to his ear.

The fat woman on the other side of the park was staring at them. Dan slipped his arm around Megan and turned her so they were both facing the other way. What was that woman's problem, anyway?

He kissed Megan again, and this time she allowed him to thrust his tongue into her mouth. The thrusting excited him. He wished he could reach into his pants and straighten himself out. His jeans felt like a vice.

"Dan!"

Dan broke away from the kiss, yanking his eyes open. The fat woman was standing right in front of them. He peered into the swollen features of the woman's face and felt his penis shrivel.

"Christie!"

Because she was standing and he was sitting, her monstrously huge belly protruded into his face. He leapt to his feet, his palms spreading wide behind him as if feeling for a wall.

Christie looked from him to Megan and back again.

Dan felt his legs twitch and thought about sprinting across the park and leaping over the fence. "What are you doing here?"

Christie stared at him, her eyes pounding into his face like fists.

Megan reached her hand towards Christie. "Hi. I'm

Megan." Her voice rang out like a bell in a brawl, sounding strong and clear.

Stiffly, Christie took Megan's hand in the tips of her fingers.

"Go away," Sonny cried, pushing against Christie's side.

"Sonny! That's rude!" Megan pulled her son's hands away from Christie. She shrugged an apology and took her son over to the swings.

Dan watched her go, then forced himself to look at Christie. Her face looked bloated, and her long brown hair hung in strings to her shoulders. Her eyes bruised him with their fury, and it was all he could do to meet them.

"You fucking liar!"

"Shh!" Dan squeezed his buttocks hard. He felt like he was going to fill his pants.

"You said you wanted to think."

He turned his face as if she'd slapped him. He kept his voice low. "I didn't plan this, I—"

"You didn't call me, you didn't answer my phone calls, my letter…"

"I didn't mean for this to happen, I—"

Sonny ran back to them, just as Christie tossed her final words. "I hope you rot in hell."

Dan watched her stomp away, so relieved he thought he might cry.

"Who was that?"

Megan was at his side now, and he wanted to throw his arms around her and squeeze her tightly, but he knew he mustn't make any more of this situation than he was going to pretend it was.

"Who was that?" He repeated her words so he could

settle his voice down. "She's the girlfriend of someone I used to know." He looked into Megan's trusting face. He hadn't exactly told a lie. He didn't feel like the person Christie had been with. Not any more.

"What was she so upset about?"

Dan busied himself with bending over and putting Sonny back on his shoulders. "She and her boyfriend split up."

"That's too bad," Megan said. "With her pregnant and everything."

Dan made himself nod in agreement. He could feel Sonny's small fist tapping on the top of his head.

"What's 'hell'?" Sonny asked.

Turning in the opposite direction to where Christie had gone, Dan said, "You don't want to know, buddy, you don't want to know."

Chapter 17

The water was slipping and sloshing over itself as Jessie set out in her kayak. She knew she probably shouldn't be out here when it was rough like this, but she needed the open space of the lake. Besides, a kayak knew how to handle waves like this. With slender elegance, it didn't confront the waves, but simply nosed its way through them, the very grace of its bearing parting the waves like a dignitary parting a rambunctious crowd.

If Jessie had been in a canoe, she would have had to concentrate on paddling just to keep herself afloat, but the kayak's assuredness allowed her to enjoy the wildness of the waves. She was like a cork bobbing on the water, and she liked that. It made her feel more a part of things.

As she played in the waves, she thought about an article she'd read on the Internet the other day. The article had said that when water was free to move in its own rhythm, it took on a natural spiralling motion. Apparently, that spiralling was what allowed the water to recharge itself. Furthermore, freely moving water had snowflake-like geometric patterns that resembled the patterns of the healing waters in places like Lourdes. Water that was restricted in its movement, so the article said, became stripped of its magical geometry.

She paddled up the lake, staying near the shore, where

the waves weren't as large. Maybe Harley was paddling somewhere at this moment too. She imagined him in Water Spider, the aluminum canoe he'd taken along, paddling on some isolated lake. When he'd telephoned yesterday, he'd been in Wawa. She'd missed the call but had played back his message several times just so she could hear his voice.

If he were in Wawa, did that mean he was starting to head back? Of course, he hadn't said. For all she knew, he might be getting supplies so he could stay in the woods longer. She didn't want him gone longer. She wanted him back home.

She wished now that she'd gone with him. But, unlike Harley, who set up his life in an uncomplicated way, she had commitments. Today she would be doing more canvassing for the Green Cottage campaign, and she had some clients to see. She didn't have many clients now, but sometimes the energy it took to help even a few was more than she wanted to spend. Was it time to close up shop? She tried to imagine moving her clients on to other therapists, but she couldn't think of anyone who would see Lyn for the small fee she was able to pay. And she doubted if Dan's therapy would survive a transfer. As it was, he was hanging on by a thread.

Dan. She was surprised that he was continuing with his therapy. For a man who was totally unused to introspection, he was doing remarkably well. Her work with him was going slowly, but already she was beginning to see what shone in him. A psychological gold miner, that's how she thought of herself sometimes, bringing what was valuable to the surface, making it accessible so the person could use it for their own best interest. It was a noble endeavour, despite all the discouraging situations.

Although she was seeing the gold in Dan, she was also seeing the extent of his self-deception. He had a way of asserting something strongly, then imagining his assertion must be true because of the strength of his pronouncement. Then, rather conveniently, he ignored anything that was contrary to what he wanted to believe.

A psychological propensity like this usually arose in people who didn't have a strong sense of self. It was as if they were trying to erect a solid outer reality to compensate for the weak, inner reality. She hoped that, as Dan developed a deeper sense of who he was, he would be more able to open up and get whatever feedback the universe was giving him. At the moment, she suspected he missed a lot of things. That could be dangerous.

From what Dan had told her about his father, she imagined he'd picked this pattern up from him. What did his father do again? Oh yes, he ran the water treatment plant in Bracebridge. She found that a little scary.

A speedboat raced by, and she could smell its fumes. Jessie thought about Lyn and wished there were more she could do for the woman. As it was, the situation seemed to be going from bad to worse. Yesterday, she'd received a call from Bill, Lyn's partner, informing her that Lyn was in Penetang, a psychiatric hospital. Penetang! Jessie could hardly believe it. Apparently, Lyn had started to do the painting her boss had demanded she do, but had passed out halfway through the day. Bill wasn't sure whether she'd passed out because of the fumes or because of a reaction to the medication her doctor had given her. Nevertheless, an ambulance had taken her to the hospital, where, after some tests, they'd shipped her over to Penetang and committed her.

How was someone as sensitive as Lyn going to survive the heavy-duty drugs, the noise, the fluorescent light and antiseptic smells of an institution? It would be like pulling a little violet from the damp and dappled woods and throwing it into a pinball machine.

Jessie sighed. Right after her conversation with Bill, she'd called over to Penetang and set up an appointment to talk with Lyn's psychiatrist. Jessie was going to talk to him when she drove over later. If all went well, she might even be able to get Lyn released.

The question was, could Lyn cope on her own? As challenging as the hospital was, at least she was safe there. Warren's words came back to her.

"It's not that people with E.I. don't want to live," he'd said. "It's that living becomes impossible."

Hearing distant shouting, Jessie focussed her eyes and saw Elfy waving. Jessie paddled in.

"Sorry," Jessie said, "I guess I lost track of the time out there."

"You looked so happy, I hated to wave you in," Elfy said. She helped Jessie tie up the boat, and they headed up to the car.

Once they were on their way, Jessie asked, "How's it going with your niece?"

"It's going." Elfy crossed her bony arms in front of her small chest.

"That all you're going to tell me?"

Elfy rolled her lips inside her mouth as if afraid to speak. She shook her head. "She was fine for the first few days, but something sure got her dander up yesterday. She was fit to be tied. I can't see how that's good for the baby."

"Baby! What baby?"

"Didn't I tell you?"

"No!"

"That's why she's coming here. To have the baby!" She blew air out her mouth. "She's asked me to be her birth coach."

Jessie whistled. "Did you accept?"

"No one else is volunteering."

"The father not around?"

"Nope." Elfy clenched her hands.

"That's gutsy that she's going ahead without him," Jessie said. "But then, no one in the Pepper family ever suffered from a lack of guts!"

If Elfy heard the compliment, she didn't acknowledge it.

Jessie tried to sound cheerful. "It will be special to be at the birth, I'm sure." Elfy nodded and pointed to their first cottage. Jessie pulled the car over and they gathered their pamphlets and checklists.

The cottage they were approaching was made of wood and had a huge verandah around its exterior. As they knocked on the door, Jessie could see that the owners had done some extensive tree cutting at the front of the cottage. She saw the lawn and frowned. Why would anyone want a lawn at a cottage? She felt nervous. How were they going to handle a situation like this? First of all, nothing they could say was going to bring the trees back. But they could perhaps educate the owners about the importance of keeping the shorelines and hopefully lessen the risk of further destruction.

When no one answered, she felt relieved. They left a pamphlet in the door and walked on down the road. To get to the next cottage, they had to pass through a white wooden gate that was partly open.

"Must be some big shot," Elfy said as they went through it. "Or someone who thinks he is."

They walked up a long, paved road. Along the side, the trees had been cut and a lawn planted. There were signs on the bright green grass. "Pesticides. Keep Off!" Every few hundred feet, there was an ornate wrought-iron streetlight.

"Looks like we've got a real doozy here," Elfy said.

Jessie winced. So far, the place was showing itself to be an environmental disaster.

"I'll do this one," Jessie said. They'd gotten in the habit of having one or the other of them take the lead. It was Elfy's turn, but Jessie felt nervous about Elfy taking on this one.

Elfy pushed up her cotton sleeves. "I can handle it."

They continued along the hard, black tarmac of the driveway until they saw the cottage. Elfy stopped.

"For crying out loud! That's not a cottage, that's a hotel!"

The cottage was a three-story affair with turrets and balconies and windows two stories high.

"Can you imagine trying to heat it?" Jessie whispered.

"Give me a match, and I'll show you how to heat it."

As well as not liking the look of the house, Jessie didn't like the way it sat on the land. When a house and a property were happy with each other, they showed each other off like lovers, each eager to make the other look good. But this house flagrantly denied any relationship with the land that surrounded it. It was too busy shouting, "Me. Me. Me. I'm what's important here. Everything else can go to hell."

Jessie had to push herself forward. If the house said "Screw you" to the environment, what was the owner going to say to them?

In the garage, they could see the back end of a red Miata.

"Hope he's not the turkey who tailgated us the other day," Elfy said. "Be just our luck." They stepped up to the doorbell. "Here goes nothing."

The sound of a stereo thumped from somewhere deep in the house, but no one came to the door.

"Come on," Jessie said, eager to get away. "Let's go."

The door sprang open. A muscular man, naked except for a towel he was holding around his waist, stood in the doorway.

"Oh, ladies, sorry, I was expecting—a woman!"

Elfy rolled her eyes and said out of the corner of her mouth, "Guess my birth certificate was wrong."

Feeling something wobble in her stomach, Jessie looked up at the man. He had a fixed grin on his face, as if he were smiling for a camera. He had very white teeth. "Step inside." He disappeared down a hall. "I'll be right with you."

Elfy and Jessie looked at each other.

Jessie hesitated. Her body was telling her to turn around, but the rope of social convention kept her where she was.

Elfy stepped into the foyer. "Get a load of this place!"

Jessie took a look. The inside of the cottage was like a huge glass cavern filled with chrome, white carpets and black leather furniture.

"Nothing like the rustic charm of an old-fashioned Muskoka cottage," Elfy said.

Jessie's eyes moved from the high open ceiling down to a cliff of windows that gave a spectacular view of the lake. Beside her, the walls of the foyer were covered with card table-sized photographs of hockey players.

"Hey, maybe this guy is some big time hockey hero," Elfy said. "That would explain the big bucks." She moved closer to the photograph. "If we play our cards right, we might get some tickets."

"You'd like that," Jessie said, knowing what a hockey fan Elfy was.

"Darn tootin' I would."

Jessie read some of the signatures underneath the pictures. She didn't know a lot about hockey but recognized some of the more famous names.

"Hey, there's our host!" Elfy pointed to one of the photographs.

Jessie looked. Sure enough, there was the man who'd answered the door. In the photograph, he was wearing a shirt with a big Indian face on the front. The Indian was frowning and seemed to be trying to warn her somehow.

"Elfy, I really think we should leave, I—"

Footsteps pounded on the thick carpet and the man reappeared, dressed in tight jeans and a snug-fitting black T-shirt. On the front of it were the words, "Bite me."

"Sorry ladies. Now, what can I do for you?"

Jessie looked at Elfy, expecting her to launch into their spiel, but the old woman was engrossed in the photograph of their host. Not sure what to do, Jessie handed the man a brochure and started explaining the Green Cottage concept.

Suddenly Elfy shot around and jabbed her index finger into the hockey player's chest. He stepped back, but she went after him, jabbing away with her bony forefinger.

"You're that bonehead that dumped the garbage!"

The man looked at Elfy as if she had foam coming out of her mouth.

"Pardon?"

"You heard me, fella."

Alarmed, Jessie tried to pull Elfy back, but it was like tying to hold back a bull at full charge.

"He's the idiot who keeps dropping his garbage at Wildwood," Elfy cried, incensed that Jessie was trying to hold her off.

Jessie looked from the man to Elfy. Beside the hockey player's tall, muscular body, Elfy looked as small as a child.

The man's face bunched up like a fist. "What? You're crazy, lady!"

Elfy whipped the Visa slip she'd been saving from her little change purse. "Explain this then, Smarty Pants." She slapped the Visa slip beside the signature on the photo. "Looks like the same John Henry to me!"

The hockey player lunged forward. "Gimme that!"

Small and impish, Elfy snatched the paper out of his reach and jumped clear. "No way, mister!"

Jessie pulled Elfy's arm. She had to get Elfy out of there before something worse happened. Sparks were practically shooting out of Elfy's eyes, and the hockey player's face was as red as a stick of dynamite.

"Elfy, let's go. Let Mike deal with this." Mike was the local bylaw officer. "It's his job."

Elfy jerked her arm out of Jessie's grip. "I'm not leaving until this idiot says he's sorry."

The hockey player exploded. "Get off my property!"

Elfy shook her fists at him. "You're the one who trespassed first. And you're the one who did the illegal dumping! What would your fans have to say about that, Andy Malowski?"

Jessie sucked her breath in. Andy Malowski? She didn't follow hockey, but even she had heard of Andy Malowski.

He was always on the front page of the sports section with a black eye or bloody nose. If he wasn't fighting another player, he was fighting with the owner of the club over the paltry millions he made.

"Mr. Malowski," Jessie said, determined now to intervene. "Maybe you don't realize just how close the town dump is—"

"I don't give a rat's ass how close the dump is. Get out of here!"

Grabbing the womens' arms, he marshalled them towards the door.

Elfy yanked herself away. "Stop that! You're hurting me!"

To stop her from getting away, Malowski grabbed Elfy with both of his meat hook hands. Elfy cried out from the pain of his iron grip and clawed at Malowski's face. Jessie watched as three long red scratches appeared between his ear and jaw.

The hockey player touched his skin. He yanked his hand away and stared at his bloody fingers. "You cunt!"

If there was ever a word that could cause a knee-jerk reaction in Elfy, it was that one. Unfortunately, when her knee went up, it found a particularly tender part of the hockey player's anatomy. Malowski reacted as all men do when kneed in the groin—he jack-knifed back and put his hands over himself, pressing his knees together as if trying to squeeze out the pain.

Jessie and Elfy rushed to the door, but Malowski lunged at them, barring the door. Pulling a cell phone from his back pocket, he jabbed three numbers.

"Get me the police."

Chapter 18

When Dan stepped out of his air-conditioned truck, the heat came at him. When he'd first arrived from the city, the warm and sunny weather had felt like a validation for moving here, but the temperature had gone from hot to hotter than hell. Being from the city, he was used to the weather being hot, but there was a sting to this heat he didn't like. It was as if the good times were over.

Maybe the good times were over. Now that Christie was on the scene, he wasn't going to be able to relax. He still couldn't believe the odds of her moving to the same town as him. And in a town as small as Port Carling, they were bound to run into each other. But part of him still suspected that she had tracked him down and followed him. For all he knew, she might have used a private investigator. What a nightmare!

Now he lived in fear of running into her again. What if she found out where he worked? Or where he lived? Maybe this idea Meat had of putting an electric fence around the cottage wasn't so bad. Meat had been investigating it ever since those two demented old ladies had assaulted him. Imagine an assault like that happening right here in Muskoka! And for no reason. Dan wished he'd been around. He might have been able to stop it. Although why a big strapping guy like Meat should have needed help with a couple of old biddies was a bit confusing. But Dan had taken a hit or two in his groin during his lifetime. That kind of pain could disable Hercules.

For a day or two after it had happened, Meat'd had trouble walking. But that certainly never stopped him from talking. He was telling everyone who would listen what "those crazies" had done. He was talking to the police, to his lawyers, even some judges he knew. He was obviously well connected. Which meant those women were going to pay and pay big time. A man like Meat had the money to make people pay, too. As they should. What was the world coming to?

Dan had meant to get a paper and see if there were more details about the incident, but the local paper only came out once a week, and he could never remember which day that was. Having a paper only once a week was something he was having a hard time getting used to. It was one of the aspects of small town life he didn't like. At first, everything about Muskoka had seemed so perfect, but now he was starting to see things he wasn't so happy with.

Dan sat at his desk and took the messages off his machine. There were two from his father. One from today and one from yesterday. Why did his father have to call every goddamned day? It didn't exactly exude confidence in his abilities.

He set the messages aside. He didn't want to talk to his father now. He forced his attention to the paperwork on his desk. He had a session scheduled with Jessie at lunch today, so he only had the morning to answer calls and read the report on his desk. At the end of an hour, however, the pages of the report were covered in doodles.

Jessie had told him to pay attention to what he drew.

"Your drawings are like dreams," she'd said. "They may give us information about your unconscious."

He wasn't sure he liked the idea of having an unconscious. If there were parts of him beneath his awareness, he was content to leave them there. Looking at what he'd just drawn simply confirmed this. There were spears and guns and other instruments of torture. Many were projected out of the opening in a huge letter "C". A person didn't have to be Sigmund Freud to figure out that symbolism.

He buried his face in his hands. What was he going to do about Christie? Everything he wanted was so close, so very close, and now he might lose it all.

He picked up the phone. There was no way he could go ahead with his appointment with Jessie today. She always made him feel so safe and relaxed that he found himself blithering on about himself with dangerous abandon. Things he'd never told anyone seemed to crawl out of him.

If he went there today, she would know something was wrong. She would extract the truth out of him. Even though part of him would have been relieved to talk to her about Christie, a bigger part of him couldn't stand the idea of Christie gaining a foothold in his world. No, he would not even utter her name!

As the phone rang, Dan hoped Jessie was with a patient and that he'd get her machine. That would allow him to simply leave a message saying he couldn't make the appointment and be done with it. After that, he would keep forgetting to make another one.

"Hello?"

"Jessie?"

"Yes. Is that you, Dan?"

Her voice was so warm, and he was so surprised to hear it, he blurted, "Yes, I—"

His voice stopped, and a space loomed between them. The space was black and cold, and he rushed to fill it. "I just wondered what time our appointment was. Twelve or one?"

"It's for twelve, Dan."

"That's what I thought," he said. "See you soon." He put down the phone quickly, feeling like an idiot.

Half an hour later, he was sitting unhappily in her office.

"So, how are you feeling today?" Jessie asked.

Dan sighed. Feelings. Feelings. Feelings. "Fine. I feel fine."

She looked into his eyes for a moment, quizzically, and seemed about to comment, but didn't. They sat in silence for several moments. Jessie's round, caring face was facing him, as warm and full as the sun. He felt hot suddenly. Why was she looking at him so expectantly? Did she know he had something to tell her?

Finally, Jessie spoke. "Sometimes people grow up in families where there are a lot of rules about how they have to behave in order to be accepted. When they come here, they think it's going to be the same. But my job is not to judge you, Dan, it's to understand you. And to help you understand yourself."

Dan was careful to keep his gaze on the wall behind her. There was no way he was going to look into her eyes. If he did that, he wouldn't have a chance. But he could feel her face, feel its compassion and warmth. And his resolve became like so much gelatin in the heat.

"There's this situation," he finally said, unable to stop himself.

Jessie nodded, encouraging him to go on.

"There's a woman I used to go out with." He wasn't going to say her name. That far he wouldn't go.

Jessie gave him a small, encouraging smile and waited for more. God, did he have to spell it all out?

"This woman, she thinks she's pregnant..."

"Thinks?"

Dan frowned. As usual, she was asking for details. "Actually, she is pregnant. And..."

"And..."

She continued to look at him in her sunny, supportive way.

"This woman—she thinks I'm—the father."

Jessie nodded, her eyes neutral. "Are you?"

Encouraged by her non-judgmental tone, he said, "I don't know."

"Don't know or don't want to know?"

Dan shrugged. He wasn't going to go there. "Megan doesn't know about her." He stole a look at her. Was it his imagination, or did she get tense when Megan's well-being was involved?

If Jessie were protective of Megan, there was no evidence in her tone. "What stops you from telling her?"

Dan's throat felt dry. "I will tell her. One day. I just don't want to tell her yet."

"So, you're lying to her?"

How did she do this? Accuse him of something so terrible and keep her tone so light?

"Maybe tinkering with the truth..." That's as far as he was going to go.

"Is there a difference?"

Dan winced. "Look, lots of people tinker with the

truth. Politicians do it all the time. And not just scummy ones either. The President of the United States, the Prime Minister of Canada. Sometimes it's a political necessity."

Jessie just looked at him, her green eyes large. "I don't care what other people do. I care about what you do. How does it feel to you to lie?"

Dan looked down at his hands. "Look, I'm going to tell her, I just didn't want to toss all my dirty laundry into her face right at the start, that's all."

"But if she finds out about this other woman, and I can tell you from experience that these things have an uncanny ability to find their way into the world, aren't you risking the future of the entire relationship?"

Dan swallowed hard. Probably. Jessie made it sound so obvious. "I just can't imagine telling her. Besides, I don't even know what to tell her. I could be the father, but I could also not be. I just don't know."

"What's your gut telling you?"

Dan felt a twinge in his belly, but said nothing.

"Tell her what you've told me," Jessie finally said. "That a past girlfriend is pregnant. And you're not sure the baby is yours."

"You make it sound so easy."

Jessie smiled. "What's the worst that can happen?"

Dan cringed. "She'll dump me."

"Maybe. But maybe not. It will certainly give the two of you an opportunity to see what your relationship is made of. Because, as you know, mistakes are going to happen. You're human, and so is Megan. How you handle them, both your own and one another's, is what's going to count."

He looked at Jessie fully now, and the warmth of her face buoyed him. Optimism flooded through him. Of course, Megan would understand. He would make her understand.

"I'll tell her," he said.

They talked on for a few more moments, and when the appointment was over and they were at the door, she said: "Speak from the heart. If you speak from the heart, she'll listen from the heart."

He nodded. Yes. What Jessie was saying was wise and true. He gave her a warm handshake and felt her approving eyes. She was right. It was time for him to stand up and tell the truth about himself. As Jessie had said, if the relationship was going to last, it had to be on solid ground. The truth would provide that solid ground.

He repeated the important phrases of their conversation as he walked to the car. When he drove away, however, he left all memory of them behind.

Chapter 19

Jessie walked hurriedly through the rain to the variety store. Usually, when it rained, the temperature cooled, but not today. Today, the rain was like water on the hot rocks of a sauna.

Inside the store, she left the hood of her poncho up. She didn't want to be recognized by anyone. Striding past shelves lined with everything from fishing lures to Swiss chocolate, she made her way to the cooler at the back of the store. She pulled open the heavy glass door and took out a carton of skim milk.

For days she'd kept a low profile, hoping that no one would find out about what had happened with the hockey player. She hated the idea of her name being skewered by the long tongue of gossip. Besides, she knew that any gossip involving her would also involve the Green Cottage campaign, and she didn't want that project jeopardized.

Despite the fact that she'd told no one, rumours seemed to be sparking up everywhere. Yesterday, her paper girl had congratulated her for "creaming the guy". Jessie had tried to explain that she hadn't "creamed anyone", but the girl had only yawned. Jessie knew it might be just her imagination, but neighbours seemed to be either snubbing her or regarding her with amused smiles. For all she knew, the whole town might be talking behind her back.

Jessie was going to have to muzzle Elfy. According to Aggie, Elfy had gleefully regaled the entire Guerrilla Granny group with a blow-by-blow account of what had happened with Malowski. This had to stop. Jessie resolved to talk to her when she took the old woman to the dentist later that morning.

Jessie walked quickly towards the counter.

"Well, well, well, if it isn't the famous Jessie Dearborn."

Jessie cringed. "Hello, Mr. Burton." Mr. Burton was an insurance agent and liked to know everything about everyone.

Although he'd arrived at the cash register at the same time as Jessie, he waved her ahead with exaggerated gallantry.

"Be my guest," he said emphatically, smirking at the girl behind the counter. "You wouldn't want to get in this woman's way. No siree! Not if you care about certain parts of your—anatomy. If you know what I mean. Heh, heh, heh."

Jessie focussed on the change that was being pressed into her hand. She slipped the milk into a bag and headed towards the door.

"Maybe you should get that knee insured," Burton called after her.

Jessie rushed through the rain to her car, stepping in a puddle just before getting in. She turned on the windshield wipers and watched as Burton came out of the store. He looked pleased with himself, the self-satisfied old bugger! It was all she could do not to roll down her window and shout: "IT WAS ELFY!"

Jessie drove away slowly. It stung her that people were so willing to believe her capable of such an act. It wasn't her style to hurt anyone, let alone attack a man's private parts. Was she going to have as much trouble making the police believe her too? Officer Tamlin had been over twice asking questions. Apparently, he'd been over talking to Elfy too. There was no doubt in her mind that if Andy Malowski had not been involved, the investigation would be over and done with by now. But with the reputation of a veritable Canadian icon at stake, a man who could afford the most famous lawyers, the police were going to be cautious. Which was fine by her. She'd done nothing wrong.

When she returned home, she went outside and cut some twigs for Hope-in-Hell. The woods were wet, and by the time she was finished, her clothes were soaked. She changed quickly and drank some iced tea. As she sipped it, she tried to call Lyn again. She felt discouraged and embarrassed. First, she'd cancelled an appointment because of the beaver incident, then she'd missed talking with the psychiatrist at Penetang because of what had happened with Malowski. Of course, as soon as she'd left the police station, she'd called to apologize and make another appointment, but the hospital told her that Lyn had already left. Left? Had they released her or had she run?

Jessie had called Lyn's home number but had not been able to get her. It took another day to finally reach the psychiatrist, who said that although he didn't know what was wrong with Lyn, he had released her because he didn't think her condition warranted committing her. Which meant Lyn should be back at home. But if she were back home, why wasn't she answering the phone? Jessie had been trying for days now. She hadn't been able to leave a message either, because the answering machine wasn't on. Jessie found that particularly disturbing.

But now as the phone rang, Jessie heard a click on the other end of the phone. Someone was answering. Her heart leapt.

"I'm sorry, this number is no longer in service," an automated voice said.

On an impulse, she grabbed the phone book and quickly looked up the garden centre where Lyn worked. Why hadn't she thought of this before? Maybe Lyn was putting in some extra hours there. To make up for being away. She knew this was unlikely, but she called anyway.

"Lyn Bryden no longer works here," the person who answered the phone said.

"No longer works there?" Jessie felt a deep sense of alarm. Things were tough enough in Lyn's world. Being unemployed was going to knock her stress up one more notch. "Do you know what happened? Or where she is?"

"I'm sorry, I don't have that information."

"Can I speak to the owner?" She had to get more information. There was another clicking sound and more ringing as the call was put through to someone else. Another automated voice greeted her. "Have a great day," the voice told her. She banged the phone down.

The noise startled the dog, who came to her side.

"It's okay, Charlie. But I think she's been fired. Fired and kicked out of her accommodation." That was the only possible explanation. The owners of the garden centre probably thought they had a nut case on their hands. A crazy. "If she's not crazy yet, she's being pushed damn hard into it," Jessie said quietly.

Although the rain hadn't started up again, the clouds were dark and looked as though they were carrying a great weight. The air felt so saturated with wetness, it was difficult to breathe.

Lyn could be out of a job and a place to live. A double whammy of stress like that would be difficult, even for a healthy person. Given Lyn's weakened condition, it was nothing short of scary.

Jessie felt a limp helplessness move through her body. There was nothing she could do now but wait, wait for Lyn to contact her. She watched a raindrop drool down the window and disappear.

Charlie barked, and the screen door slammed. Only Elfy slammed a screen door like that, Jessie thought and pulled herself up. She found Elfy in the kitchen.

"Thought I was picking you up," Jessie said.

Elfy nodded towards the outside. "I brought Christie. Thought it would do her good to get out. She's been stewing in her own juices these last few days."

Through the window Jessie could see a short, very pregnant young woman lumbering along in front of the cottage. Her head was down, hidden behind the curtains of her long brown hair.

Elfy slumped into a kitchen chair. "I finally found out what was bugging her. Apparently, she ran into the father the other day. Making out with this other lady."

Jessie winced. "Ouch!"

"He'd be saying more than 'ouch' if I'd caught them."

So, Christie was not only dealing with the mood swings of pregnancy and the daunting prospect of raising a child alone, but the humiliation of seeing her ex-lover with another. There was something truly degrading about that. Like having someone's dirty underwear shoved in your face. Jessie felt a swell of sympathy for the young woman.

"Is the father anyone we know?" Jessie asked.

"She won't tell me." Elfy's face tightened into a knot. "Which is just as well, 'cause if I knew him I'd, well, I don't know what I'd do."

Jessie put her hand on Elfy's shoulder, and Elfy reached up and squeezed it gratefully.

"It's hard watching someone you love get hurt," Jessie said.

"I'll say." Elfy wiped her eyes, and Jessie handed her a tissue. "You know what's weird?" Elfy asked, looking up into Jessie's eyes.

"What?"

"She told me that even after all he's done, she still thinks they're going to be together."

Jessie was quiet. She'd learned a long time ago that in the territory of love, none of the usual rules applied. "What makes sense to the heart makes no sense to the head. You've lived long enough to know that, Elf."

Pushing her hands against the table for support, Elfy stood up. "Geez, I feel old!"

Jessie gave her a hug. "Want some strawberries?"

Elfy shook her head, but Jessie took a bowl of them outside anyway and walked down to where Christie was standing by the beaver enclosure.

Jessie introduced herself, but Christie's eyes were on Hope-in-Hell, who was lumbering towards them.

Jessie placed a strawberry in Christie's hand. "You can feed him if you like. Hold it out like this, and he'll take it from you."

Christie pushed her hair off her plump face and looked at Jessie uncertainly.

"He won't bite," Elfy said.

Hesitantly, Christie held out the berry, and Hope-in-Hell reached out his thin black fingers as if he had all the time in the world.

"That'a girl," Elfy said.

Pleasure blossomed on Christie's face as she watched Hope-in-Hell eat.

Jessie smiled. Animals had a way of disarming people. A few minutes ago, Christie was locked into an emotional box of pain. Now she was outside that box.

"His fingers are so tiny," Christie said. "They're just like a child's." She looked at Elfy and smiled.

In search of more berries, Hope-in-Hell went up on his haunches, exposing the burns on his underbelly.

Christie's hand flew to her mouth. "Oh, my God! What happened to him?"

"Someone blew up his lodge," Jessie said. "He was the only one we could save."

Christie gently caressed the beaver's head with infinite tenderness. "You poor little guy."

"Poor little guy nothing," Elfy said. "He's living in a five star hotel, gets his bed changed every day, has room service—next thing he's going to want a TV so he can watch his favourite nature shows."

Christie laughed, and Jessie and Elfy exchanged a smile. Jessie checked her watch.

"You can stay here if you like," Elfy said. "I'm sure Hope-in-Hell would love the company. We won't be long."

Christie nodded, not taking her eyes off the beaver.

A few minutes later, in the car, Elfy said, "That's the first time I've heard her laugh since she arrived."

"Hopefully she'll feel better once the baby arrives," Jessie said.

"Which reminds me, I'd better start practicing my breathing!" Elfy crossed her arms. "I just hope court's over by then."

"Court? What do you mean court?"

"You think Malowski's going to let us get away with what happened? I bet you dollars to donuts he's going to have us charged."

"Us? If anyone's charged, it will be you. Not me. I didn't do anything but try and calm you both down." Jessie put her arm out the window. She suddenly needed air. "And I'd still like you to calm down. Aggie told me you've been gabbing about what happened to everyone who will listen. You've got to stop fanning the flames."

Elfy smiled thinly. "Who, me?"

They were in town now, and Jessie stopped the car in front of the dentist's office to let Elfy out. When she came back an hour later to pick her up, the old woman was waiting by the curb, the newspaper opened like an oversized book in front of her. At the sight of Jessie, she stuffed the paper quickly into her bag and got into the car.

"Is that today's paper?" Jessie asked.

"Yup," Elfy said, looking out the window.

Jessie's stomach tightened. "Was there anything in the paper?"

"Look, there's Doris McKinnon coming out of the variety store. I heard she's sold the—"

"Elfy. Answer me."

Elfy crossed her arms and stared out the window.

Jessie's unease increased. "You talked to the press, did you?"

Elfy turned, her voice full of fervour. "Andrew called me himself, he—"

Andrew was the editor of the paper. "Elfy! We agreed!"

Elfy's face bunched up. "People should know what that bully did."

"Elfy, this is Hockey Night In Canada country! Hockey

players are heroes up here." Jessie let her head fall back against the headrest and closed her eyes. When she opened them again, she reached for the paper.

"You're not going to like it," Elfy warned.

Jessie unfolded the paper Elfy handed her. On the front page it said, "GRANNIES ON THE ATTACK."

Jessie groaned loudly.

"At least the Green Cottage thing got mentioned," Elfy said.

"Oh, God." The last thing Jessie wanted was for the Green Cottage campaign to be mentioned at the same time as this incident with Malowski. "We wanted good press, Elfy, not bad press." She imagined herself trying to offer someone a Green Cottage brochure only to have the door slammed in her face. Furious, she threw the paper aside and started the car.

Elfy picked it up and poked at the article with her forefinger. "Says here Malowski already had a groin injury." She looked at Jessie triumphantly. "See? He was injured already. I just made it worse." She began to bob up and down with laughter. "At least now everyone knows where I got the guy."

Jessie could hold herself back no more. "Elfy, this isn't funny!" Elfy wheezed as she laughed harder. "Elfy!"

"Jessie, he manhandled me."

"You don't have to tell me what he did. I was there, remember?" She reined in her anger. "He had no right to do what he did, but you shouldn't have done what you did either."

"I was defending myself. You saw the bruise on my arm—"

"Defending is different from attacking. What you did

was attack."

"He deserved to be attacked."

"Elfy! An eye for an eye makes everyone blind."

"Wow. That sounds like something out of a book. Is that something you thought up?"

"No. Martin Luther King."

"Thought it sounded eloquent, even for you."

Elfy crossed her arms and looked out the window. For the next few minutes, they drove in silence.

"You get any fan mail yet?"

"Fan mail?" Jessie repeated. She hadn't been to the mail box in a few days.

"Yeah. I got three letters so far. Two in favour and one against. And some seniors' magazine wants to do an interview."

Jessie rubbed her temple with her free hand as she drove. She was letting herself get far too stressed about this whole situation.

At the lights on Pine Street, she turned left and saw the seniors' home up ahead on the right. They had planned to stop there for a few minutes so Elfy could pick up some things.

A police car was parked in front of the home.

Elfy straightened in her seat. "Dum-da-dum-dum."

With a feeling of trepidation, Jessie pulled over to the curb and watched Officer Tamlin extract himself from the car. His mouth was scrunched up tight as a fist as he walked grimly towards them. Jessie and Elfy got out of their car.

Tamlin handed Elfy some papers.

"Sorry about this, Elfy, but the chief has decided to lay charges."

Elfy read through the forms.

"Assault! And what's Mr. Hockey Night in Canada being charged with?"

Tamlin took his hat off, smoothed his thin hair and put his hat on again. "He isn't."

"How come?"

"The bylaw officer spoke with Mr. Malowski's lawyer, and Mr. Malowski has promised to use the dump from now on."

"So, just because he's a big shot hockey player with a big shot lawyer, he gets a warning? And I get charged?"

Tamlin pulled his thin lips back into his mouth nervously. "A bylaw violation isn't as serious as a criminal code offence."

Elfy wasn't listening. "He can dump garbage, hit old ladies, call them dirty names—"

"Elfy, calm down," Jessie said. She didn't think it was fair, but there was no point in arguing with Tamlin about it. He didn't make the decision, he was just the bearer of it.

Tamlin nodded at Jessie approvingly and handed her the same papers.

She looked down at them incredulously. "Trespassing? You're charging me with trespassing?"

Elfy mimicked Jessie's words of a few moments ago. "Jessie, calm down!"

Chapter 20

Outside, the weather was still sour and oppressive. Dan looked up at the sky, wondering if it were going to rain again. A gang of purple clouds was gathering ominously in the east. A storm was definitely brewing, and from the looks of the clouds, it was going to be a real ripsnorter. It was the time of year for hurricanes too.

When he left his Medora Road office, he could already see the big white water tower rising high above the tops of the trees to the right. Written on the white tank, in sky-blue lettering, were the words PORT CARLING.

He turned right and drove past the new golf course, then swung left into the laneway leading to the tower. He parked by the high chain-link fence and sat looking up at it. From way down here, it looked colossal. It was at least 130 feet to the top and probably two truck widths wide. Constructed out of rings of pre-poured concrete, it looked like a pile of corrugated tuna cans piled one on top of the other. He was going to have to be careful draining the sucker. A quarter of a million gallons was a lot of water. And one hell of a lot of pressure. He'd heard stories about water towers collapsing like giant pop cans if you released the water too fast.

Even if he drained it slowly, it was still going to take over a day to get the water out of it. When it was empty, he was going to have to climb up and look inside the tank. Every few years the tank needed repainting, and it was just his luck that the painting job was falling to him. Dan looked up dubiously. The thought of climbing up that high made him feel nauseous. He'd never been good with heights. That's why he'd never made it as a hydro guy. The height of the poles had terrified him. Yet, terrified or not, he was going to have to make the climb into the water tower.

He sighed. It seemed that much of his life required him to do things he didn't want to do. Like have this talk with Megan. For days now he'd been wavering back and forth about it. Part of him, a big part, wanted to tell her. It would be a relief to come clean. But another part of him, a stronger part, thought doing so would be relationship suicide.

If only he hadn't told Jessie he would do it. He didn't like the idea of having to tell her he hadn't followed through. He considered lying to her, but wasn't sure he would get away with it. Jessie seemed to know him in ways no one else had before, and this unsettled him. As did her belief in him.

He hadn't asked Jessie to like him. He hadn't asked her to believe in him. But now that she did, he didn't want to give that up. It felt good when someone believed in your potential.

In no hurry to get out of the truck, he sipped the last drops from a can of pop and spread open the *Toronto Star*. He read the entire paper, even the ads. One caught his eye. It was a large promotional advertisement for a musical he knew Megan wanted to see. LAST WEEK, a banner across the ad said.

An idea formed in his mind. He would buy tickets and treat Megan to a big night in Toronto. After the musical, they would go out to some posh place for dinner then maybe get a room for the night. He pictured the two of them snuggled up in a king-size bed in a hotel. He imagined her naked beside him, no, naked underneath him, moving and moaning. For weeks now, every time they had been together, he'd pressed on into new sexual territory. It was time to make the final plunge. Yes, he thought, imagining himself making long and lovely love to her. Afterwards, when he was holding her in his arms in their post-coital bliss, he would tell her about Christie. In his experience, in that afterglow of sex, a man could tell a woman almost anything.

He pulled out his cell phone and called the number in the ad. The tickets were expensive, but when he phoned Megan to tell her what he'd done, her pleasure made it totally worthwhile. Particularly when she agreed to farm Sonny out for the night so they could get back whenever they wanted.

He pulled out his daytimer to write in the event. "Damn." He was on call that night. Being on call meant he was supposed to stay within reach. Not that anyone had told him what "within reach" meant. And Toronto was just two hours away. What could go wrong in two hours?

Not wanting to think about that, Dan got out of the truck and unlocked the big blue doors at the base of the tower. As usual, the closed-in feeling of the place gave him the creeps. He shuffled his feet nervously and heard them echo. Stretching his head back, he looked up. Above him was a huge column of air. About eighty feet up sat the water tank itself, the tank he was going to have to climb up to. Feeling dizzy, he reached out and held onto the metal ladder that went up the side of the circular wall.

Jessie was always telling him he was more capable of facing things than he thought. She better be right, he muttered as he turned and went into the small operations room.

As always, his eyes leapt to the gauges that were fixed on the big pipes that took the water in and out of the reservoir. One of the gauges said 8.7, which told him that the reservoir was 87 per cent full. The other gauge said 4.3, so he knew the water pressure was good as well.

He looked at the large grey wheel. The moment he turned it, the reservoir would begin to drain. And once it drained, all the water people needed would have to be supplied by the little pump over at the pump house. Which was another reason why he should fix it. It was going to be under a lot of extra strain. He made a mental note to do that. Maybe tomorrow. He hefted his weight against the grey wheel, and immediately there was a thunderous flushing sound as hundreds and hundreds of gallons of water swooshed down from the tank.

It sounded as if some huge monster had just flushed a giant toilet. Which, if he thought about it, meant that one colossal load of crap was on its way.

Chapter 21

Jessie rolled over to Harley's side of the bed. The emptiness of it seemed to go on for miles. It was odd: when she woke up, she was convinced it was the morning when she missed him most, but when evening came, she thought it was night time that her yearning for him was the greatest.

She stroked the dog's back. "I guess I just miss him, eh, Charlie?" Harley had been gone three weeks now. Long enough, she thought.

She lay on her back and stared up at the ceiling. Nothing in her life was working right now. She still hadn't been able to find Lyn, the Green Cottage campaign was on hold since the incident with Malowski, and she'd been charged with trespassing. Trespassing! Every time she thought about it, her indignation grew. To think that she was going to have to go to court, stand up in front of all those people and defend herself against something she hadn't done. It was humiliating to say the least.

She wondered where Harley was now. Having breakfast in some diner in Wawa? Drinking tea as he rambled along some tree-lined road? If she'd gone with him, she would be sitting beside him, her body snuggled up to his as he drove, the two of them sipping the early morning silence.

She closed her eyes. A claw of yearning moved down her chest. Sometimes she could hardly stand how much she missed him.

Harley never admitted to missing her. "You're with me all the time," he always told her. "Right here," he'd say and touch the centre of his chest.

She carried him around with her all day too, even had conversations with him in her mind, but when he was away, her body always felt bereft. When he'd last called, he'd wanted to know all about Hope-in-Hell. When Jessie went on to tell him about the incident with Malowski, he had chuckled long and low.

"Laugh all you want," she'd said, "but I've been charged with trespassing."

She expected that would stop his laughter, but his chuckling only deepened. The sound of it was so loose and lovely, rumbling through the air with such abandon that even though she wanted to resist it, she couldn't and began laughing too.

After the laughter, they both became quiet. Jessie could almost feel Harley pulling his forearm across his eyes to wipe away the wetness.

"When's your court date?" he asked.

She told him, and by the careful way he repeated it, she knew he was writing it down on his hand. Or jeans.

"That's next week," he said. "Guess I'd better get back before they lock you up and throw away the key." He chuckled more.

"It's not the actual trial," she said. "Just a date to set a trial." She sighed.

When the call was over, Jessie leaned over and gave the dog a hug.

"He's coming soon, Charlie. That's what he said, 'soon'." Charlie nuzzled her face with his.

Sometimes she felt as if she had a special kind of radar when it came to Harley's whereabouts. It was as if she could feel how near or far away he was by the texture of the space between them. A hollow feeling meant he was far away, a less hollow feeling meant he was closer. This morning, the space between them felt dense and electric.

Hoping this wasn't just wishful thinking, she got out of bed and was dressing when she heard the flutey sound of a bird singing. She stilled her hand and listened. The sound was like a series of golden balls trilling down an airy set of stairs. A hermit thrush? The hermit thrush was one of Harley's favourite birds.

Charlie fetched his breakfast tin and dropped it loudly at her feet. She scooped two cups of kibble into it and made some tea. Today she was going to drive over to the garden centre to see if she could talk to the manager himself. She'd already waited two days for him to call her back and he hadn't, so she was going to track him down. If she went early, it wouldn't be busy, and she might be able to talk to some of the other staff. Surely, Lyn would have had some friends there. Even if just one person knew her whereabouts, it would be worth the trip. When the tea was ready, she took it with her in the car.

As she suspected, there weren't many customers in the garden centre this early. She found the manager, but he would tell her nothing. She hung around and finally managed to talk to one of the other female staff, who told Jessie that Lyn had been fired. Unfortunately, the woman didn't know much else. She certainly didn't know where Lyn had gone. Jessie wandered back on the property until she found the cabin she thought Lyn and Bill must have stayed in, but it was empty.

On the way home, Jessie stopped at Huckleberry Rock. Sometimes she needed the solace of the woods, but today she needed the feeling of wide-open space. Although earlier a storm had seemed imminent, there was no sign of it now, so she let Charlie out of the back and they made the short walk through the woods. Suddenly, the forest ended and she came out on a huge expanse of flat rock. Other than a few scrubby pines that had managed to find some nutrients in the odd handful of soil, the landscape was entirely barren. It looked like a huge beach.

Charlie bounded ahead, his nose yanked in various directions by different scents. When they reached the highest point, there was a house-sized rock, which Jessie climbed. Miles of lake spread out before her. The water was bright and strongly blue. In places where the clouds were thin and the sun could penetrate, the surface of the lake flashed with silver.

Water always did like light, she thought. Whereas the forest seemed intent on keeping the light out, or at least filtering it, water opened right up, as if wanting to fill itself to the brim. Right now the lake looked absolutely luminous.

The first time she'd ever gone swimming, she'd known water was a living thing. She felt in awe of the way it moved and how it felt. She'd always had an abiding reverence for it. She knew there were others who felt as she did. Lyn had been one such person. But now Lyn was nowhere to be found. And Jessie felt she had failed her. She hadn't been there for Lyn when Lyn had needed her. All she could hope was that Lyn was all right and not in some garage trying to kill herself with gas fumes.

After a long, quiet sit, Jessie made her way home.

Harley's mud-splattered truck sat in the driveway. Elation leapt through her. Eagerly, she got out of the car. Streaming her fingers through her hair a few times, she went quickly into the house. An earth-brown duffle bag was in the hallway. Further down the hall, she could see a pair of running shoes, laces askew.

Wanting to savour the idea that he was there, in the bathroom, only yards away, she walked slowly. The door was partly open, and she could smell the soapy steam coming from his bath and hear the sloshing sounds of water. Then there was silence. He was listening for her. Sensing her.

"Hey—"

She took a step forward. She could see him now, see the way his wet hair hung against the rounded muscles of his shoulders as he moved the washcloth over the glistening skin of his thigh. In the warm moistness, she could smell the woods, the lakes, the long days of their being apart.

He reached for her, and she knelt by the side of the tub. He pressed his lips into her open palm and brought the end of each of her fingers to his lips. She could feel the warm wetness of his mouth on her skin.

They looked at each other and were silent. Silence had always been kind to her and Harley, but today, the question of their future sat like a large egg in the nest of that quietness.

Harley looked at her, his face solemn, and moved the soapy cloth in a circle over his chest as if assessing how to say what he wanted to say. "There are some wonderful places out there. Wild places. Places we'd feel at home."

Jessie felt the air she was holding press against the sides

of her lungs.

"Do you want to leave? Is that what you're saying?"

His dark eyes rested fully on hers. "It still feels so wild up there, Jess."

She nodded. "So, you've decided."

"I've asked for a sign."

She frowned. "You're going to let your life, our life, be determined by a sign?"

Harley paused. "You always make it sound like a billboard advertising hamburgers."

She laughed and felt a loosening in her chest. "Sorry." She knew that to Harley, the Great Spirit was always talking, talking through coincidences, symptoms, dreams.

"It's just that, when you get a sign, how do you know who's talking? I mean it could be God, or it could be some lunatic subpersonality." They'd had this conversation before, but somehow she never felt she really understood what Harley was trying to say.

Harley laughed. "Even some lunatic subpersonality can have something smart to say sometimes," he mused.

"True. But there are millions of signs happening at any given time out there."

"I know. But certain ones get your attention. It's the ones that get your attention that are important."

Jessie nodded but felt far from agreement. "I guess I just don't like the idea of a sign determining our future."

Harley sat up. "It's not the sign itself that's important. It's your reaction to it. That tells you what's going on inside you—your own truth." He rubbed his face with the facecloth. "You'll understand it more when it happens." He smiled gently. "I've asked for a sign big enough for the both of us."

Jessie laughed. "I'm that dense, am I?" She pushed her hand through her hair. "I'm just scared, that's all."

Harley extended his hand to her. "Know what I want right now?"

"What?"

"You. Closer."

She moved her arms on to the side of the bathtub and put her head on them. Harley touched her face, sliding his wet thumb across the fullness of her lips. She closed her eyes and leaned into him. The warmth of the bath water flooded up the front of her shirt, but she didn't care. All she wanted was his mouth on hers.

Kissing him was like coming home to all that was good in the world. That goodness swelled through her body, washing her worries aside.

Maybe it was the steam from the bath, but she felt sweaty now, as if she'd been running in the sun, and there was a tingling on the tops of her thighs as if the grasses and flower heads had been slapping against her skin.

Harley pulled her close. All of her clothes were getting wet, but she didn't care. As Harley touched her, she felt as if bouquets of dark red pleasure were being pulled from hidden places in her body. Sensations erupted all over her skin.

They were both breathing hard now, and, eager to have her skin against his, they worked at freeing her of her clothes. When she was naked, she lay upon him completely still. She was eager to touch and kiss him, but for a moment, she lay without moving, grateful only for the beat of his heart.

Chapter 22

D an ran to his car, the rain pelting against him as if he were its personal target. Lately, everyone had been talking about the need for rain. Many of the lawns around town were straw-coloured and dry. Even the farmers' fields looked parched.

But goddamn it, the fields could be parched for another few hours, couldn't they? Why did it have to rain on the one day he was going to the city? When he'd bought the tickets for the musical, he'd imagined strolling leisurely through sun-dappled city streets, his arm around Megan's bare summer shoulders. With this downpour, they'd have to wear coats and take umbrellas. Rain! There was nothing sexy about rain.

He turned the radio up loud so that he could hear the forecast over the sound of the rain beating on the roof.

"Damn," he said. The forecast was for hard and heavy rain, maybe even a thunderstorm.

For weeks, the warm, sunny weather had been like an affirmation 3for moving here. Muskoka had seemed to open up its arms to him, offering him a fresh start. In the city, stepping into his life had been like putting on the same old clothes day after day, clothes stained from all his mistakes. Back in Toronto, people were always asking him, "How's Barb?" And he'd have to say, "We're divorced." As always, the person he was talking to would say, "Divorced? You're divorced?" Then he would get that look. It wasn't exactly pity, but it reminded him of the look his teachers used to give him when he'd failed something at school.

Here in Muskoka, however, not only did no one know Barb, no one even knew he'd been married before. He felt clean and new, as if he'd just jumped out of the shower. Meeting Megan and becoming involved in her life at the resort was like acquiring a whole new wardrobe. And a classy wardrobe at that.

He just had to make sure this situation with Christie didn't explode all over everything. As it would if Christie and Megan ever met. Given how furious Christie looked that day in the park, he knew she would roast him alive if she got the chance. For all he knew, Christie might even seek out Megan and try to tell her what a bastard he'd been. No, he had to tell Megan first, and tell her in such a way that she understood.

When he got to Carlingview, Megan was waiting for him in the lobby. She wore a cotton dress, as white as a new sheaf of drawing paper. And she had her hair down. The thick amber tresses spilled over the golden skin of her sun-browned shoulders. She smelled of wildflowers.

"You look gorgeous," he said, kissing her.

She pressed against him as they hugged, and he felt his chest expand. He picked up her coat and with an exaggerated flourish, opened the umbrella and escorted her to the car. Her breast was against his arm as they walked, and his mind leapt forward to what they might do later at the hotel.

"I hope Sonny will be okay," she said as he helped her into the car.

Dan squeezed her hand. "He'll be fine."

"How come you're wearing your pager?"

The question came at him like a wasp out of a daisy. He pretended to be busy getting on to the highway so he could have a moment to think. He didn't want to tell her he was on call. She might know what that meant: that he was supposed to be accessible. On the other hand, he wasn't going to lie. The whole point of this adventure was to give him an opportunity to speak the truth to her. He just wished lying wasn't so damn easy.

"I want to be reachable," he said. "Just in case."

His father's disapproving eyes appeared before him. Dan cringed. What he'd said wasn't exactly lying, but it was close.

Megan seemed to accept this, but the question unnerved him, made him wonder what else she might ask. Ever since their encounter with Christie in the park, he'd been waiting for more questions, but they hadn't come. What if she, too, had been waiting for this opportunity to talk? He braced himself.

"An interesting man came to see my brother yesterday," Megan said.

Dan felt an immediate irritation. "Who?"

"A Mr. King," Megan said. "Apparently he's got money to invest and might be interested in Carlingview."

"What?"

"Isn't that great? You know how Wayne wants to expand."

Dan gritted his teeth. He didn't want Wayne to partner with someone else. He wanted Wayne to partner with him.

"He drove a Jaguar," Megan said.

Dan bristled. A Jaguar! If ever there was an overpriced, excessive vehicle, it was a Jaguar.

"I love Jaguars," Megan said.

Dan imagined a tanned, good-looking man, a man closer to Megan's age, pulling up to Carlingview, stepping out of his shiny car. He could see the appreciative look in the man's eyes as he surreptitiously surveyed Megan's body. How could he tell Megan about Christie when there was this threat around?

Dan drove on. It was raining hard, and it took a lot of concentration to see the road. Megan chatted happily beside him until someone blasted a horn at him. As the car sped past, the driver's arm appeared out the window, middle finger extended.

"The prick! What's his problem?"

"You did cut him off," Megan said quietly.

Her tone was matter-of-fact, but he didn't like that she'd said anything. Barb used to do that too, criticize his driving.

"They're maniacs down here!" They were in the city now, and he drove past the hospital where Franny had been born. A few blocks later he saw the restaurant he'd gone to the night he and Barb had become engaged. His chest muscles tightened. Maybe this trip to the city hadn't been such a great idea after all.

When they arrived downtown, it was still raining, so Dan dropped Megan off at the Eaton Centre and went to find a parking lot.

"That's robbery!" he said when the dark-skinned man in the booth told him the fee for the day. He hadn't paid for parking since he'd left the city. As he fingered through his change, he noticed the beaver on the nickel and thought of the lagoon at Carlingview. All this rain would be filling it to the brim. He hoped Wayne had cleared out those bullrushes.

The musical was a romantic comedy, and although he had trouble concentrating on it, he liked the sound of Megan's laughter beside him. He also liked that she kissed him in appreciation when it was over and they were strolling through the lobby.

"Thank you," she said.

Dan put his arm around her. Like a warrior who'd brought home a pleasing bit of meat, he had made his woman happy.

"I'm going to check on Sonny," Megan said when they passed some phones in the theatre's lobby.

Dan watched her go. He had a nervous feeling in his stomach. He should call the treatment plant. After all, he'd had the pager turned off for a few hours now. Yet he loathed the idea of calling. What if the automatic responder at the plant said something was wrong? In a storm, it was easy for the computer to get things mixed up.

He forced himself to reach for the small box on his belt and fumbled nervously for the plastic switch. Jesus, he was acting as if the damn thing were going to explode. He flicked the button to "on". There was no beep.

When Megan came back, he threw his arm around her and led her outside. It was no longer raining, and the night was bright with city lights. The sound of a saxophone wailed through the air, and kids on skateboards whizzed past. Dan was used to this mélange of city life, but Megan clutched his arm excitedly. Feeling suave and worldly, Dan led them through the maze of streets.

They passed a small Chinese variety store, and Dan

spotted a poster of a large dragon in the window. He pointed it out to Megan.

"Sonny would love that," he said, then went inside and bought it.

"You treat him so well," Megan said, kissing him again.

"He's a wonderful kid."

They walked on until they came to a hotel.

"Let's go in," Dan said, seeing what looked like a posh dining room inside.

Choosing an intimate table near the back, he ordered an expensive bottle of champagne. He was in the mood for bubbles. By the time the main course came, Megan was giggling.

He administered the champagne, then the wine, with care. He wanted to anaesthetize any caution she might have, but not compromise his sexual abilities.

When the waiter came for their dessert order, Dan suggested sorbet. Megan nodded. He loved that she let him make decisions. She didn't fight for control over every little thing the way Barb used to do.

The desserts arrived. Dan dipped his spoon into the sorbet and lifted it to her mouth. Her lips parted, and he fed her a spoonful, then licked a small bit from the corner of her mouth.

The sound of her laughter filled him with strength.

"It tastes yummy, doesn't it?"

He nodded. "You taste better."

After dessert, Dan suggested a postprandial brandy. Postprandial. He liked that word. It had class.

"Oh, I shouldn't," Megan said. "I've already had too much to drink. Are you going to be okay to drive home?"

"I'll be okay if I sleep for an hour or two," he said.

Concern flew into her eyes.

He stroked the side of her face with the back of his hand. "Why don't I get a room? We can snuggle up and I'll sleep for a while. In an hour or so, I should be fine." He leaned forward and placed a chaste kiss on her mouth, a kiss that told her he would not pounce.

He stood up, waiting for her to argue, but she didn't, so he went to the front desk. A few minutes later, they were sitting on a large chesterfield in a lovely room overlooking the city. He made a show of setting his watch, then turned down the lights.

"Look, there's the CN Tower," he said, putting his arm around her. He liked being up this high and looking down at everything.

He yawned and lay down on his side. Megan lay so her back was curled into his front. The fleshy curve of her rump was against his loins, and her nipples were inches from his hands. His fingers itched to touch her, but he kept them still. In the distance, he could hear sirens wending their way through the city.

He buried his face in her fragrant neck. Her skin was moist and smelled of summer fruit. "A goodnight kiss," he said, nuzzling his mouth into her skin. Although she was tense, he could feel her back arch with pleasure. He liked bringing her pleasure. It made him feel masterful. And he needed to feel masterful, for any minute now he was going to tell her about Christie.

As he kissed the side of her face, she turned a little, so their mouths could meet. She was almost on her back now, her voluptuous body spread before him like a banquet. Looking at her made him feel like the luckiest man in the world. His resolved softened. How could he jeopardize all he had with her? Chances are, she would never find out about him and Christie. It was a risk, but so was telling her. And at the moment, telling her felt like a far greater risk.

Jessie's face appeared before him. He had promised her. Promised himself.

"You're the best thing that's ever happened to me," he whispered. He meant it. Sometimes he could hardly believe his good fortune. His words seemed to soften her, open her to him. It was funny how words could do that to a woman. What turned a guy on was a naked body, what turned a woman on was naked emotion.

They kissed deeply. She wanted him now, he could feel it. He took off his tie.

"You know when I first met you," she said, "I really wasn't sure." Her voice was round and plump with relaxation and warmth. "I wasn't sure you were the type of man who would stick at things. That was the problem in my marriage. Sonny's dad just wasn't willing to work things out. But when you went to Jessie, I realized I was wrong."

He let his teeth bite ever so gently into her neck. "God, you taste good."

"And you've really stuck with it too, even after all that controversy about Jessie—"

"What 'controversy about Jessie'?"

"You know, that incident with the hockey player."

"What incident?" His brain felt fuzzy, as if there was something right in front of his face that he should be seeing but wasn't. He sat up. "Jessie was the woman who assaulted Malowski? The guy I stay with?"

"I thought the guy you stayed with was named Meat," Megan said.

"That's what I call him, yeah, but it's Malowski. Andy Malowski."

Dan tried to put what Meat had told him together with what Megan was telling him now.

"I think the whole thing's ridiculous," Megan said. "Jessie's not the kind of person to assault anybody. Frankly, I'm not even sure she was charged with assault or whether it was the woman she was with."

Dan rubbed his forehead between his thumb and fingers. He couldn't believe what he was hearing. His therapist had assaulted his best friend? He was going to have to rethink everything now.

Megan snuggled into him. "Sorry. I didn't realize you didn't know."

"It's a shock, that's all." And it was. But it was also an out if he wanted it. As far as he was concerned, the deal he'd made with Jessie was off.

Megan began to massage his shoulders. "Having your friend fight with your therapist. That would be weird."

"Ex-therapist," Dan said to himself. How could he carry on with her after all this?

They began to kiss again, but Dan felt distracted. His mind was in overdrive. Even if he didn't have to keep his agreement with Jessie, what about his agreement with himself? If he didn't talk to Megan tonight, how could he trust himself again?

Megan pressed her whole body into his. He slid his hand under the fabric of her dress and stroked her skin. It felt so delicate, and there was a slight moistness to it like a flower petal. He began easing the dress off her shoulder.

There was a high-pitched beep from somewhere in the room.

Damn! Damn! DAMN!

He groped around the floor to find his beeper. When he found the small plastic box, it was all he could do not to throw it against the wall and smash it.

Furiously, he stood up, grabbed his cell phone and strode into the bathroom. "I'll be right back."

Closing the bathroom door, he flicked on the harsh light and punched in the phone number of the treatment plant. The plant was equipped with a chatterbox and as soon as the line answered, the automated system would feed him information about the nature of the problem. It'll be the water tower, he thought. The water tower wasn't functioning, because it wasn't supposed to be functioning. The computer should know that, but the storm might have confused it. He tensed as the automated voice began its computerized report.

"Channel 1: Normal."

"Channel 2: Normal."

Each of the channels represented a different part of the water treatment process. Channel 1 and 2 had to do with turbidity. At least everything was fine in that department.

Come on, come on. He'd never realized how slow the damn thing was. Feeling a sudden urgency to pee, he held the phone with one hand and unzipped his pants.

The chatterbox reported on the various channels. He was waiting for it to get to Channel 7. Channel 7 was the water tower. If the chatterbox said Channel 7 was not right, he'd know it was just a glitch in the computer. Nothing to worry about.

"Channel 7: Normal."

Channel 7 was normal? What the hell was going on?

"Channel 8: low chlorine alarm."

His pee hit the wall. Low chlorine? The pump must have busted. Fuck!

Quickly he rearranged himself and checked his watch. It said 1:13. At this hour, there wouldn't be many people using the water. And even if there were, using unchlorinated water from the lake for a few hours wasn't going to kill anybody. Some cottagers drank lake water all the time!

He washed his hands, flicked off the light and went back to Megan. There was no reason to rush home. As long as he was back before dawn, everything should be okay.

As he walked along the hall, he could smell her. The hotel room was dark, and he almost staggered across it, following the path of her aroma. When he reached the couch, he sprawled down beside her. He had planned to resume kissing her the moment he had her in his arms again, but worry pressed down on him.

"Is everything all right?" she asked. The richness in her voice told him she was totally open to him now. Ready and waiting.

He lay beside her, limp with exhaustion. "Everything's fine."

Chapter 23

Jessie lay in bed nervously, listening to the storm. She felt like a child listening to her parents having a bad argument. At times the wind blasted so forcefully, she could almost feel the wooden framing of the house grip the concrete foundation.

When a storm happened during the day, she and Harley often pulled up chairs and watched it from the porch. But storms at night were more frightening, at least to her. At night the wind sounded more ferocious, the rain more severe. Thank goodness Harley was home.

As she pressed her back into his warmth, the sky thundered, and a flash of lightning lit up the room. Despite the ferocious gusts, beside her, Harley slept peacefully. Storms never bothered him. Besides, he'd been up most of the previous night driving, so he was tired.

She was tired too, but whenever she began to drift off, the noise from the storm pulled her back from the brink of sleep. Finally, she got up and was in the kitchen making some hot milk when the phone rang. Startled, she picked it up.

"Yes?"

"She's started."

Started? Who had started what?

"Elfy? Is that you?"

"You've got to get over here. Christie's started her labour. I'm too scared to take her in to the hospital by myself. Not in this storm."

"Labour? But it's too soon!"

"Tell that to the baby!"

"I'm on my way."

Jessie put the phone down and raked her fingers through her hair. What a night for a baby to come into the world. She looked outside and debated whether to wake Harley. She wanted to ask him to come with her, but it didn't seem fair. He was exhausted.

It shouldn't take her long to get to Elfy's. It was just down the road. And it wasn't far to the hospital either. Another twenty minutes. That wasn't too much for her to do. Resolved now, she crept back into the bedroom, pulled some clothes out of a drawer and changed in the bathroom. Nearer to the door, she donned a rain poncho. It looked awfully wet out there. The dog stood close by her.

"You don't want to come, Charlie. Hear that wind? You'd get soaked just running to the car." She pulled on some rubber boots.

She wrote a quick note to Harley, took an old Hudson's Bay blanket and tucked it underneath her poncho. When she opened the door, rain slapped at her face. Tucking her head down, she trudged out into the storm. At the car, she saw that Charlie had slipped out and was standing beside her. She let him sit in the front seat. He whined as he stared into the darkness.

"Warned you, didn't I?"

She sneezed and started the car, putting the windshield wipers on full. Even so, she had to strain forward to see the road. The storm made the night so incredibly black, diminishing the power of her headlights so she could see only a small bit of road at a time. The dense forest seemed to press in on her, and the curves came upon her quickly, so quickly she had to pull the steering wheel one way and then the other, which was altogether too dangerous, given how slippery it was.

Although it usually only took her a little over ten minutes to get to Elfy's, it was well over twenty before she saw the diffused glow of Elfy's front door light. She proceeded towards it. When she was closer, she saw the old woman standing in the doorway, her arms crossed over her chest. Elfy turned away and reappeared a few moments later with Christie.

Jessie ran to the house, and she and Elfy began to help Christie out to the car.

Elfy looked haggard with worry. "I was starting to think about boiling some water."

Jessie was about to ask how far apart the pains were coming when Christie moaned and clamped her arm. Despite the intensity of the labour pain, they managed to get Christie into the backseat. Still standing out in the rain, Jessie leaned in and put her arm around Christie. Seeing how frightened Christie was, she pushed back the hood of Christie's raincoat and stroked her forehead. "It's okay," she said. "Breathe with me, and it'll pass."

The rain was running in under her collar, and her back was aching from being crouched over, but Jessie coached Christie through the contraction until it passed. When Christie unclenched her hand from Jessie's arm, she slowly pulled herself up to standing. It was difficult to get her back to straighten.

Elfy had scurried back to the cottage and returned with

her purse and a bottle of juice. "Here, drink some of this," she said to Christie as she unscrewed the top. "I just made it."

Christie shook her head, and Jessie got into the front seat. She started up the car and drove slowly down the gravel road, steering around branches as she went. It alarmed her how soft the road was. The gravel felt supersaturated with rain, and she worried about it simply giving way. When they got to the main road, she was relieved. It was paved, and she thought she would be able to drive faster, but the rain was so heavy, it was bouncing off the pavement. She found it difficult to get her tires to grip the road.

"Pardon?" Jessie shouted over her shoulder. Elfy had said something, but between the rain pounding on the roof and the whacking of the windshield wipers, Jessie hadn't been able to make out the words.

Elfy cranked up her voice. "This is taking longer than the second coming. Can you pick up the pace a bit?"

Jessie could hear the fear in the old woman's voice but didn't feel it was safe to go any faster. She was about to shout that back at Elfy when a loud cracking sound broke the air. Charlie made a frightened, high-pitched yelp. Jessie jammed her foot on the brake just as a tree limb crashed onto the road ahead. She yanked the steering wheel sideways to avoid the tree, and the car spun sideways. There was the snapping sound of wood breaking and a nasty bashing sound as the front left side of the car hit the tree limb.

Charlie barked again as the car continued to move forward, crunching into the limb so forcefully that Jessie thought the windshield was going to shatter. She fell over Charlie and pushed her face into the seat until the car stopped moving.

For a moment, no one spoke.

"Another few feet, and we'd'a been under that thing," Elfy whispered.

Jessie let her breath out. The old timers called branches like this "widow makers". The weight of one of those limbs would crush whatever was underneath as easily as a Mack truck would crush an ant. Nervously, she looked up to see whether the rest of the tree was going to come crashing down, but all was black.

Christie moaned. Jessie turned and held the young woman's hand. When the labour pain was over, Jessie pushed against her door. She wanted to assess the damage, but the tree limb was squashed against the car, pinning her in. She slid over and was able to get out the door on the passenger side. One headlight was still working, so she could see the road and the huge limb that was sprawled across it, blocking both lanes.

Jessie pushed back the wet hair from her face. Thinking that she and Elfy might be able to move the limb if they lightened it up by removing some of the branches, she began to break off the smaller ones. The wood was dead and dry and broke under her pressure. She tried to push the limb itself, but it wouldn't budge.

Elfy came to help. "Come on, put some muscle into it, Jess. I don't fancy becoming a midwife at this stage of my life."

Jessie spread her feet and wrapped her hands around the tree limb. They pulled together and pulled hard, but the branch didn't move.

"Let's try breaking off more of the branches," Jessie said.

They worked together, sometimes heaving both of

their bodies against a branch to make it break.

"Sure is hot in this raincoat," Elfy said, ruffling the green plastic of her poncho up and down. "I'm sweating."

Jessie looked at Elfy worriedly. This was heavy work for someone Elfy's age. "Why don't you go back and sit in the car? Rest for a bit."

"And let you take the credit for getting us out of this? No way!" Elfy retrieved her bottle of juice from the car, took a long swig and offered it to Jessie.

"Want some?"

But Jessie had already reached into the glove compartment for a small bottle of water she kept there. She took a sip and said, "Come on, let's give it one last try."

They got into position. "One, two, THREE!"

The limb moved. Not much, but it moved.

"A few more pulls," Elfy said, "and we'll have this sucker out of the way!"

It took a lot more than a few more pulls. Each time Christie had a labour pain, they had to stop to soothe her through it. But each push moved the limb a little farther off the road and after about an hour, they had made a narrow pathway.

"That wide enough?" Elfy asked.

"Let's try it," Jessie said. She looked at Elfy. The old woman had pushed the hood of her raincoat back, and her hair was plastered down so her head looked just like a skull. Jessie looked away. "You drive, I'll guide." She wanted to get Elfy out of the rain, even if it was just for a few minutes.

"Let's hope the damn thing starts," Elfy said, getting in.

There was a chugging sound of the ignition, but the engine did not turn over.

"Oh, no!" Jessie cried. Part of the limb must have

rammed itself under the car and damaged something.

What were they going to do? Jessie slumped against the car. Between the rain and her own sweat, she was soaked through. And she was exhausted.

Christie moaned in the back seat.

Light flashed and Jessie groaned, thinking it was more lightning, lightning that might sever more of the tree above and send it crashing down upon them. But the light moved, and she realized what she was seeing was headlights.

Chapter 24

Dan listened to the frantic fwap, fwap, fwap of the wipers as they tried to create a small fan of visibility in the storm. He wanted to turn on the radio, find some music to distract him, but he didn't want to wake Megan. He looked over at the childlike peacefulness on her face and felt grateful she was sleeping. Hopefully, any policemen in the vicinity would also be sleeping. He was driving like a maniac. If he got caught driving at this speed, the fine would cost more than the car.

Given the intensity of the rain, it was crazy to be going this fast, but he was still south of Barrie, so he had another hour to go. Another hour in which he would tell himself a thousand times not to think about the stupid pump.

He squeezed his buttocks tight. His bowels were loose. He knew he should stop and go to the bathroom, but he didn't want to waste one minute in getting back. And the moment he got into Port, he was going to hightail it to the pump house and put in the new chlorine pump. Once he did that, all would be well.

He was glad he hadn't told Megan anything. When they'd first got into the car, she'd asked if he wanted her to help with the driving so he could get some sleep, but he'd said no. There was no way he'd be able to sleep. Adrenaline was surging through his body, and he felt jumpy and agitated. Gripping the steering wheel tightly, he leaned forward so he could see into the darkness. It was black, black, black out there.

At the moment, Megan didn't even know there was a problem. All she was aware of was that his beeper had gone off. And he had downplayed that, telling her that things were a bit wonky because of the storm. When he told her he should be getting back, just to make sure everything was "A-okay", as he'd put it, she'd accepted that too. She'd kissed him and said, "You're so conscientious."

Megan didn't even know he wasn't supposed to be in the city. He hoped that she wouldn't find out either—that no one would. Especially not his father.

It was after 3:30 AM by the time they reached Carlingview. Without trying to look as if he were rushing, he dropped Megan off, then raced through the dark streets to the pump house. As soon as he unlocked the door, his eyes flew to the chlorine analyzer. It said: 0.00. That confirmed it. The pump was busted.

He reached for his tools and began to take the pump apart. His hands were shaking, and he had to concentrate hard to get his fingers to work right, but soon he had the old diaphragm off and was installing the new one. As soon as he had this sucker working, the chlorine would be injected into the water again, the reading would go back to normal, and everything would be fine. No one, not even his father, would know there had been a problem.

He dropped the screwdriver.

"Damn!"

He could almost feel his father's eyes drilling into him. Frank always seemed to expect him to make mistakes, but then he'd be mad at Dan for making them. But everyone made mistakes. Even Jessie said so. Sure, he should have changed this pump earlier, but how was he supposed to know it was that far gone? It hadn't looked that way to him.

Spurred on by thoughts of his father, he worked even faster. In less than an hour, he had the new pump in place. Nervously, he switched it on and felt a rush of relief when he heard it begin to chug smoothly. Now all he had to do was wait for a few minutes and watch the numbers on the analyzer start to rise. He leaned against the concrete block wall and wiped his brow. His shirtsleeve came away soaking.

He closed his eyes and counted to a hundred, then looked at the meter. It still said 0.00. Why was it taking so long? He checked the chlorine supply. It was three-quarters full. That was enough for weeks of chlorination. And the pump was obviously working. He could hear it, for Chrissakes. His eyes went back to the analyzer. It still said: 0.00.

"Move, you bastard! Move!"

He waited for a few more minutes, then thumped the analyzer with his fist. Maybe the analyzer itself was busted. He pounded it again.

"Work! For Chrissakes! Work!"

Turning on his heels, he grabbed a chlorine test kit from a shelf. He would do another reading with a different piece of technology. His hands shook as he turned on the tap and filled the little glass bottle to the line indicated. Quickly, he ripped open the small foil package. He'd done this a thousand times in his career, emptied the contents of the little packet into a test bottle and watched as the water turned bright pink. That was always the first sign that the water had chlorine: the bright pink colour. Then the dial at the top of the meter would give him a more precise reading of the actual amount of the chlorine residual, but it was the colour that would be his first clue.

Although he was positive the water would turn pink, as it had hundreds and hundreds of times before, he paused before dumping in the powder. It took him a moment to steady his hands enough to pour the powder into the opening. He closed his eyes and shook the bottle vigorously. Then he shook it again. If he could have shaken pink into it, he would have.

"Holy Jesus!"

He ran outside and emptied his bowels in the blackness of the shrubbery. When he was back inside, he took another sample of water and repeated the process. After adding the packet of powder, he shook the bottle in his fist as hard as he could. The water in the bottle was empty of colour. Just like the first one.

This time he continued through the test and pressed the various buttons to give him the actual chlorine reading. The dial said 0.00.

He backed against the wall. If he was pumping chlorine into the water, yet none was showing, that meant something was consuming the chlorine. What consumed chlorine was bacteria!

He shook his head violently, as if to wake up from some horrible dream. It was impossible. How could that much bacteria get into the water supply?

When the idea came into his mind, he had to clench his jaw so he wouldn't throw up. He bolted out the door, jumped into his car and drove to Carlingview once again. This time, however, he turned off his headlights and drove past where Megan lived. He careened past the tennis courts, and when there was no more road, forced the car along the grass. He grabbed a flashlight from under his seat and got out. He didn't need the flashlight. The smell told him all he needed to know.

He climbed the hill anyway and flashed the light on the sewage lagoon. The last time he had seen it, this lagoon had been almost full. Now it was one giant empty pit.

Some animal must have burrowed into the berm and weakened it, so much so that with the pressure of the huge dump of rain they'd had, the side of it had collapsed. He could see where it had caved in. The rim protruded out like a spout. And out of that spout hundreds of gallons of sewage had sluiced down the hill and into the lake. The current must have carried it towards town, and some of it must have passed over the intake pipe of the treatment plant. Now it was in the town's water system.

Dan gagged and spewed his dinner. He wiped his mouth on his sleeve and staggered back to his Jeep.

The wind whacked against the car as if it were trying to get at him. He needed to think about what he was going to do, but he couldn't. He felt crazy. His father's hard, accusing eyes appeared in the blackness. Dan shut his eyes and shoved his fists into them, but the image wouldn't go away.

He started the car and drove down the hill. He was going to have to phone his father and report this mess. The car bounced over the uneven ground, and he pulled it to a stop in front of Wayne's door. Wayne should be informed about this. Besides, Dan could use the phone there.

Dan banged and banged. Finally, a light came on inside the house and Wayne came to the door.

"What the—"

Dan could barely get his mouth to work. "The lagoon. It broke, it spilled..."

Wayne's eyes became huge. "No!"

Dan yanked Wayne outside and pushed him into the car, then drove back up the hill. They got out and made their way against the lashing rain until they were close enough to see the lagoon.

Wayne stood staring at the empty lagoon, his fists shoved into his soaking wet slacks. "I'll get Barney to shore it up with some cement blocks tomorrow."

Dan grabbed his shirt and spun him around.

"You don't get it! All that SHIT has gone into the lake. It's in the fucking water system!"

Wayne jerked his head back. He stared at Dan now, rain streaming down his stunned face.

"We need to notify people. My father. Public health," Dan said.

Wayne was alarmed. "Public health? They'll shut me down. I've got three hundred guests booked this week. And the next. I'll be ruined."

Dan's head felt heavy and thick, swollen from multiple blows. "We'll both be ruined."

The rain pelted them, but neither man noticed. They faced the lagoon dumbly as if a monster had just walked out of it.

Wayne looked at Dan hard. "Can't we flush the contaminated water out somehow?"

The agonized imperative in Wayne's voice forced Dan to think. "We could open up the hydrants, that would flush the system, but if the water coming in was still polluted—"

"But it wouldn't be," Wayne said as he shoved the sopping wet hair off his face. "The contaminated water should be past the intake pipe by now. It should be way out in the middle of the lake."

Dan's brain felt slow, and he had to work hard to get it to grasp what Wayne was saying. He made his mind follow the path of the water and saw it sluice down the hill from the broken lagoon and enter the lake, passing over the intake pipe for the treatment plant. Some would have entered the pipe, but most would have been washed out to the middle of the lake. No matter how lethal it was with E. coli, cryptosporidium or giardia, it couldn't do much damage out there. Meanwhile, if they cleaned out the contaminated water from the town's pipes now and refilled the system, all should be well.

"Do you know how much bad water got into the system?" Wayne asked.

Enough to give people diarrhea? Enough to make them vomit? Enough to kill them? Dan shook his head. He really didn't know. "Enough to throw the chlorine reading all to hell."

"Come on. What have we got to lose?" Wayne shouted as he ran down the hill to the car.

Dan took off down the hill. Feeling as if he were five again with his father chasing after him, Dan ran as fast as his legs would carry him. He had never felt so terrified in his life.

They worked fast, starting at the hydrant beside the pump house. Dan loosened the cap, and the water shot out. He was grateful now for both the darkness and the storm. The darkness gave them cover and with all the rain, no one was going to notice the gallons of water they were releasing. The rain would also wash away the smell.

Once again, he felt as if nature were on his side. He took that as a good omen. Validation that he was doing the right thing, even though it felt so wrong.

After about fifteen minutes, Wayne held the flashlight, and Dan took out his portable testing kit and checked for chlorine. He almost cried when he saw the slight hue of pink in the test bottle. It wasn't the strong pink he was looking for, but the fact that there was any pink at all filled him with hope. He held the meter in the light so he could get the actual reading. The chlorine level was at .2. They continued pulling more water out. Every few minutes, he tested again. When the meter said .5, he jumped in the air.

They raced to the next hydrant, the one on Bailey Street. Methodically, they moved from hydrant to hydrant, flushing out the polluted water. They were releasing water from the hydrant by the bridge in the centre of town when they saw lights.

"A car!" Dan shouted.

Wayne flicked off the flashlight, and they both ducked behind Dan's Jeep as a pickup truck went by. Dan held his breath until it had passed. He didn't think he'd been seen, but his skin had the feeling eyes had been over him.

The grey face of dawn was peeking into the black night when they finished the last hydrant.

"We did it," Wayne said, raising his hand for a high-five.

Dan looked at Wayne's hand. His palm looked as white as a corpse in the grey light. Dan felt no celebration as he hit his own hand against it.

Wayne looked him hard in the eyes. "I owe you, buddy. Big time!"

Dan nodded and slumped back against the truck.

Chapter 25

Jessie woke up feeling sluggish and tired. She knew she'd slept, but her body didn't feel as if it had. It had been two days since she'd been up all night getting Christie to the hospital, but she still hadn't recovered.

Seeing the time, she dragged herself up and threw herself into the shower. She couldn't afford to be sleepy. Not today, the day of her trial.

She showered quickly and went downstairs to find a cup of tea waiting for her in the kitchen. She sipped it and wandered outside. From the deck she could see Harley feeding some young saplings to Hope-in-Hell. She was going to walk down to him, but it seemed like too much effort, so she sat on a wooden Muskoka chair.

Already the sun was hot, so she got up and moved the chair into the shade. Once upon a time, she'd loved the sun, would have begun her day in its gentle warmth. But nowadays she avoided it, partly because of its scorching heat, but also because of its dangerous rays. She frowned. She hated that the sun had become something dangerous. But it *was* dangerous. As was the air. And the water.

She put her hand on her belly. Her stomach felt queasy. Pre-court jitters? She wished she knew whether Malowski was going to be there. She doubted it. Guys like him hired lawyers, hotshot lawyers from the city.

She yawned again and checked her watch. In a few minutes, she was going to have to go in and wake Elfy. The two of them had to be in court in just over an hour, but she wanted to give the old woman every last minute of rest that she could. The long, stressful night with Christie had taken its toll on Elfy too. For the last few days, she'd been looking haggard and depleted. So much so that Jessie had suggested she stay with her for a few nights to recuperate. Since Christie and the baby were still in the hospital, Elfy had agreed.

Both of them had gone to bed early, but Jessie had awakened to the sound of the toilet flushing a few times in the night, so Jessie knew Elfy had not slept well. She'd better get used to it, Jessie thought. When Christie and the baby came back, she'd be wakened in the night many times.

Of course, the whole ordeal with Christie on the night of the storm could have been much worse. If Harley hadn't come to their rescue, who knows, they might have had to deliver the baby themselves. But Harley had come, and he'd taken them all to the hospital where Christie, with both Jessie and Elfy acting as birth coaches, had delivered a beautiful six-pound baby boy.

A small smile climbed on Jessie's tired face. The birth itself had been incredible. To see a woman's body squeeze a new human being out of its fleshy folds was indeed a miracle. Afterwards, both she and Elfy had been so elated that they'd ended up sitting with the baby and holding it for the rest of the night. Newborns were so magical. They still had the glow of God on them.

It hadn't been until the morning that Jessie had found out who the father of the baby was. That had been a shock in itself. Now that she knew, she thought the baby looked just like Dan, but she might not have guessed if she hadn't seen his name written on the registration form. Christie had left the form by the side of the bed for only a few minutes, but Jessie had felt her eyes drawn towards it. She hadn't meant to look, had felt embarrassed that she had, but in a second, she'd seen his name: Dan Gorman, printed clearly in Christie's large handwriting under the heading that said, "Father."

Of course, she'd said nothing to either Elfy or Christie, but since then, she hadn't been able to stop thinking about it. First of all, she tried to remember what Dan had said about this woman he thought he'd impregnated. As far as Jessie could recall, he hadn't even said her name. No doubt he'd made a point of keeping that information to himself. As Jessie had learned, Dan was good at selecting the details he wanted people to know. And if she'd probed, he'd acted like he was on the witness stand, releasing every bit of personal information as if it might be used against him.

But now what was she going to do? Tell him she knew about the baby? How could she do that if she wasn't supposed to know? But how could she not? She could hardly withhold the truth after urging him to tell it! Of course, all this would be a moot point if Dan did not return to therapy. He hadn't shown up for his appointment yesterday, and if her intuition was right, he wouldn't be back. No doubt Dan, like everyone else, now knew about the Malowski incident. She shook her head, wondering how long she would be dealing with the fall-out.

Harley left Hope-in-Hell's enclosure and came towards her. His eyes roamed over her face. "You all right?" He put his palm on her forehead.

"I'm just tired," she said, leaning into him.

"Are you sure you don't want me to come with you?"

She shook her head. "All we're doing is setting a court date. That's when I'm really going to need you there."

"Where's Elfy? In the shower?"

"I haven't wakened her."

"Since when did Elfy need waking?"

"I was wondering that myself," Jessie said. Normally, Elfy was up before the birds. "I think she's still recovering."

Harley shrugged. "Good luck," he said, leaning over to kiss her.

She pulled him to her with a fierceness that surprised her.

Chapter 26

Tight. Dan's muscles were tight. His stomach was tight, his throat was tight, his whole body was tight. As tight as a turned-off tap. The tension made him feel in control, and since the night of sewage spill three days ago, keeping control had become his prime preoccupation. He didn't want a drop of sweat appearing on his forehead. People might start wondering. Or they might start asking questions. Questions could be dangerous. He wanted everything to appear normal. No one must know the terror that was gnawing at him.

He knew Wayne was doing just as he was, going to work, trying to make everything look normal. Even the lagoon looked normal now. They'd fixed it the following night, shoring up the broken wall so it looked just like it had before the spill. Luckily for them, the rain had washed any residual evidence away. They had flushed the system, so there was no contamination in the water now, and even if there were, the copious amounts of chlorine Dan was injecting into it were taking care of it.

During the first day after they'd flushed the system, Dan had agonized about whether to tell Peter, the Chief Medical Officer, about the problem. He'd finally decided not to. First of all, telling Peter would do nothing to change what had happened. And secondly, if a person, or a few people had been up that night drinking the water between two and five in the morning, there was nothing that could be done now. Once E. coli got into someone's system, it had to run its course.

So, what was the point of implicating Carlingview? Wayne was adamant about keeping their mouths shut. If Dan talked, he knew he'd lose Wayne's friendship. Which would not bode well for his ongoing relationship with Megan. Besides that, if he talked, he would also lose something else: the opportunity Wayne's indebtedness would one day offer.

As convincing as these arguments were, there was something far more visceral that kept him from telling. His father. The idea of his father finding out made him feel as if he had his own personal sewage lagoon inside his body. He would rather die than have his father find out.

All he could do was hope and pray that no one got sick.

Dan rubbed his neck as he drove to the post office. For the last four days, he had forced himself to go there—not because he had postal business, but because it gave him the opportunity to put the stethoscope of his ears to the collective body of the town. If that body were sick, it would begin to show symptoms soon. And he needed to know.

Because it was summer and the town was busy, he couldn't find a parking spot right in front of the post office, but he was able to squeeze into a place a few blocks down. He scanned both sides of the street. There were two people he must avoid at all costs. Jessie was one, his father was the other. Since his father was usually in Bracebridge, he didn't think there was much chance of seeing him here in Port Carling, but still, he wanted to make sure. His father had been calling repeatedly. Finally, Dan had called back at a time he knew Frank wouldn't be there. Like a dutiful son, he'd left a message, pretending he was sorry to have missed the call. Pretending, pretending, pretending. That was all he was doing lately. But what choice did he have?

Jessie, however, could easily be in the vicinity. Of all the people in his life, she was the most dangerous. She knew how to read him. And he didn't want anyone reading him just now.

He let his body slump back against the seat. For a moment, he thought he might doze off, he was so tired, but he was afraid to sleep. Sleep brought dreams, terrible dreams. Last night he'd heard a thousand people groaning in pain.

Opening the truck door, he pushed himself out and walked to the post office.

"Hey, Dan—"

A rotund man who worked as a chef at Carlingview stopped as Dan came towards him.

"Gorgeous day, eh?" Dan said, filling his voice with cheerful bravado.

"Coming over for dinner tonight? Arctic char is on special."

Dan said he couldn't, he was busy at work. It was the same story he'd been giving Megan the last few days. He wanted to see her, yearned to see her and hug her and hold her, but he was too agitated, too scared that she'd sense something was wrong. Besides, he wasn't sure he could lie to her either. Not up close. Lying was becoming more and more difficult. He felt as if he could taste all the lies he'd ever told, and they tasted foul.

Dan carried on inside. Inserting his key into the small

metal mailbox, he pulled out several envelopes, listening for conversation around him as he sorted through them. Two men were talking quietly in the corner. Dan strained to hear what they were saying.

"You're looking a little poorly, Jack," one said.

Dan froze, straining to hear more.

If there was going to be an outbreak, it would start any day now. This was the place he'd first hear about it. The first symptoms would be diarrhea. Others might have stomach cramps.

"It's my knees," the second man said. "Got a touch of the arthritis in the right one and…"

Dan tuned out the rest of the conversation and yawned again. God, he was tired. He'd spent most of the night at his computer reading about water contaminants: E. coli, cryptosporidium and giardia. Of them all, E. coli was the most frightening. There were many strains of E. coli, but one in particular that worried him: E. coli O157.H7.

Identified by a man named Theodor von Escherich, this E. coli O157.H7 was resistant to the stomach acid that usually killed off its relatives, so it was able to make its way to the intestinal tract, where, within three to five days, it began its destruction. The first sign of that destruction was diarrhea. According to Dan's research, at this point most people ignored the symptom—diarrhea was something people expected to happen from time to time, so they usually just put up with it.

As the bacterium carried on its systematic destruction of the inner lining of the bowel, however, it killed off the cells lining the small blood vessels, and the diarrhea could turn bloody.

Although there was seldom any fever, the lack of

which usually helped doctors differentiate it from flu, there was often agonizing abdominal pain. What made E. coli O157.H7 particularly frightening was that once it penetrated the intestinal wall, it could enter the bloodstream and get a free ride to other organs in the body, like the kidneys. Complete kidney failure was not an uncommon result. Or if the bacterium made it to the brain first, the person infected could die from a thousand tiny blood clots. Children and the elderly were the most susceptible.

All of this horrified Dan. But there was something even more appalling. Once the destructive process had begun, it couldn't be stopped. Drugs of any kind were almost useless. For the most part, people simply had to ride the illness out. Healthy people had a better chance of doing that than others, but still, even healthy people could get seriously ill if the contamination were severe enough. Dan pictured someone lying in a hospital bed in a coma, and sweat broke out over his skin.

According to what he'd read, there'd been incidences where entire towns had been infected by bacteria. Milwaukee, for example, had over 403,000 people as sick as dogs in 1993. As he read about these outbreaks, his hands shook so hard he had to sit on them.

Dan dumped the junk mail in the big, black bin and walked back to his car. On his way out of town, he drove past the doctor's office. He counted the number of cars in the parking lot. There were no more than yesterday. Although he wished he could be relieved by this, he knew that even if people were starting to get symptoms, they wouldn't be driven to the doctor by them for another few days.

Meanwhile, every water sample he'd taken since he'd flushed the system had tested normal. The water was as clean as a whistle. Unfortunately, all the testing in the world couldn't change the fact that for a few hours anyway, during that time he was in the city, the water might have contained some contaminants. Someone could have been up in the night and sipped some of that water.

The very thought made him want to throw up again. Not that there was anything left in his stomach. He hadn't eaten much in three days and even though he was still throwing up, it was mostly dry heaves now.

Wiping his sweating palms on the sides of his trousers, he headed back through town along Highway 118. As he approached the turn-off to his office, he thought for a moment about passing it by. If he kept on driving, he'd be at Highway 169 in half an hour. He could buy some camping supplies in Sudbury and just keep heading north. Disappear into the bush for a few months. Or years.

He parked the truck and went into his office. There were two messages from his father. Dan erased them.

Chapter 27

"Come on, lazy bones, you've got a date with a judge." Jessie walked into the bedroom where Elfy was sleeping. She spread the curtains wide, and the day leapt into the room, but the body in the bed did not move.

"Elfy?" Was the old woman sleeping so soundly that she hadn't heard? "Elfy!"

Jessie sat down on the side of the bed and put her hand on Elfy's shoulder. It felt as small as a child's. "Elfy! Wake up!"

Elfy was facing the wall, but Jessie could see her eyes open and float around the room as if she didn't know where she was. She seemed as disoriented as a swimmer surfacing in a strange lake. "Elfy—it's me, Jess!" She squeezed the old woman's hand with concern.

Elfy jerked her head around, and Jessie could see the old woman's grey and pallid skin.

"Were you up in the night?" Jessie wanted to get Elfy talking, then moving as soon as possible. They had a courthouse to get to. "I thought I heard the water running a couple of times."

Elfy tried to push herself up to sitting, but the effort was too much for her, and she collapsed back into the pillows. "Your toilet and I had quite a date last night."

"Were you sick? Throwing up?"

"Sort of. But out the other end."

"Oh, my. Are you well enough to go to court?"

Deep lines dug into Elfy's white face. "Not unless there's a Johnny on the Spot beside the witness stand."

Jessie leaned towards her and put her hand on Elfy's forehead. She expected the old woman to feel feverish, but, if anything, Elfy's skin was cold. She pulled the covers up to Elfy's chin.

Elfy pushed them back again. "Be right back. That darn toilet's calling again."

Despite her concern about the time, Jessie helped Elfy up and walked with her to the bathroom. She was weak, and they had to move slowly.

"The way things were running out of me last night, I'm surprised there's anything left to get rid of," Elfy said. When she was near the toilet, she steadied herself by holding on to the sink. She shooed Jessie away. "I can take it from here."

Worried about the time, Jessie took the opportunity to run back to her room and dress. She was quickly brushing the long silver strands of her hair when she heard the toilet flush and went back to help Elfy.

"I feel like I left my bowels in the bowl that time," Elfy said, flopping down against the pillows.

Jessie winced and sat on the side of the bed. She didn't like the sound of this.

Elfy looked at Jessie with solemn eyes. "What do they do when someone doesn't show up?"

"I guess I'll just have to explain to the judge," Jessie said. "I'll tell him you were out partying all night and couldn't get out of bed."

"Ha!" Elfy grinned.

Jessie felt relieved. If Elfy could laugh, she couldn't be that sick.

"It must have been something I ate," Elfy said.

Jessie reviewed what they had eaten for dinner last night. Leftover chicken soup and coleslaw, neither of which Elfy had eaten much of. Could the soup have been off? Or the mayonnaise in the coleslaw? If so, wouldn't she be sick too? And Harley? Realizing she didn't have time to think about this now, she stood up. "I'd better get going. Can I get you anything?"

"Yeah, a coffin."

"Elfy! Don't say that."

"I was just kidding."

"I know, but—" She took Elfy's hand. It felt dry and lifeless. "Want some water? Or tea? If you have diarrhea, you're probably dehydrated. You should be drinking lots of liquids."

The old woman reached down and picked up a bottle of grape juice. "I still have this to finish."

Jessie recognized the bottle from the night of the storm. "Wouldn't you like some fresh juice?"

"When you get home," Elfy said. "This'll be fine for now." She unscrewed the top and took a small sip.

Jessie felt uneasy. She didn't like the idea of leaving Elfy unattended. Especially when she didn't know what was wrong. Should she call the doctor? She would talk to Elfy about a doctor when she got back.

"Hey, I like your shoes," Elfy said.

Jessie looked down at her beat-up running shoes, splotched with paint. She liked wearing them around the house in the mornings.

Elfy put the bottle back on the floor and slipped back down in the bed. "Say hi to the judge."

Jessie kissed Elfy's temple and stood up to gather her

things. She reached for her shoes, then suddenly had an idea. She turned and picked up the phone.

"Oh, Aggs, I'm so glad you're home."

"Jess! Aren't you supposed to be in court?"

"I'm just going there now, but Elfy's got some sort of flu or something. And Harley's gone off somewhere…"

"Flu? At this time of year?"

"I know it's odd, but listen, she's here at my house, and I'm kind of worried about leaving—"

"I'm on my way."

"Thanks." Seeing the time, Jessie bolted out the door and drove quickly to Bracebridge. Usually the drive took her at least twenty minutes. She was going to have to do it in half that time, and she was still going to be late. She hated being late.

When she reached the courthouse, she rushed through the halls, looking for the room she was supposed to be in. The place smelled of wood and furniture polish. When she found the right courtroom, she went in and slid along one of the benches. Her heart was still racing. This was the first time she'd ever been in a courtroom, and she took a moment to look around. The judge wasn't there yet, but various clerks, lawyers and people were gathering, all talking in hushed tones. The room reminded her of a church, with its rows of wooden benches and elevated area at the front. And just like in church, a man wearing robes would soon appear to make decrees about behaviour.

Jessie scanned the small crowd for Malowski but didn't see him. She was fairly certain she could spot his lawyer, though. Even though she could only see him from the side, there was one man who had a scissor-sharp line of hair above a crisp white collar, with skin shaved as clean as a skyscraper window.

Suddenly, everyone was standing, and the judge came in, looking as brusque as a stern father. As he attended to some papers on his desk, the clerk called out the name of the first case. Other cases were called, and, as Jessie waited, she was glad she'd had the foresight to ask Aggie to look after Elfy. She smiled. For all the supposed animosity between those two, they cared about each other deeply.

"Malowski versus Dearborn-James and Pepper," the clerk called out.

The lawyer with the skyscraper skin stood up and watched as Jessie made her way up to the front. When she stood beside him, he squinted as he surveyed her, as if looking through the sights of a high-powered rifle. She watched as his eyes moved down her body, then stopped at her feet. One corner of his mouth lifted, and an eyebrow arched. Jessie looked down. Her paint-splattered sneakers were still on her feet!

Jessie groaned inwardly. The judge cleared his throat, and Jessie turned her attention to him.

"Good morning, your honour," Malowski's lawyer said.

"Good morning, Mr. Patten," the judge replied with easy warmth, looking up over the rim of his steel-framed glasses.

Jessie looked from one man to the other. Did these two know each other? They certainly sounded familiar. For all she knew, they might be old law school buddies.

"And you are?" The judge looked down at her unhappily.

Jessie introduced herself, but the judge continued to look around.

"And your lawyer is…"

"I'll be representing myself," she said. "As will Elfy Pepper."

The judge frowned. "And would you be so kind as to elucidate for me the whereabouts of—" he checked his papers, "Ms. Pepper?"

Jessie explained and watched as the corners of the judge's mouth dug further down towards his chin. The clerk, however, began suggesting various dates for trial. Malowski's lawyer was unable to make the first two suggested times, but a third was finally agreed upon.

Feeling like a fool, Jessie had to borrow a piece of paper from the clerk to write down the court date. Feeling mortified, she turned and hotfooted it out of the building. At this task, the running shoes totally redeemed themselves.

Chapter 28

*D*ay 5. Dan wrote the words in big black letters on his blotter. Then he wrote them again. The blotter was so full of his scribbling, it was getting harder and harder to find places to write in. The empty spaces were running out.

The phone rang, and his body jerked violently. He looked at the call display as if it were the timing device for a bomb. It was the health unit. Weird nerve-like impulses began firing off in his body.

On the fourth ring, Dan cleared his throat and grabbed the receiver. Throwing as much casual authority into his voice as he could muster, he said, "Dan Gorman."

"Dan, this is Dr. Wright, Chief Medical Officer."

Something exploded in Dan's gut. The last time he'd talked to "Dr. Wright", they'd been on a first name basis. The fact that Peter was now using "Dr." and reiterating his title made it clear that this call was official. And serious. Dan's hand wrote the word "Danger" at the top of the blotter.

"What's up, Pete?" If the man was going to call him by his first name, Dan was going to do the same.

"The doctor in Port Carling is reporting a high incidence of people with stomach and intestinal distress."

Dan's throat constricted, and he had to pull hard to get his breath. It was all he could do to push a question out his mouth. "Does he know what kind of intestinal distress?"

His pen retraced the word "Danger", making the letters bold and black.

"It's a she, not a he and no, there's no diagnosis yet."

Dan fought to get air into his lungs. People were sick. SICK! He imagined putting the phone down and taking off, running as far as his legs would carry him.

"It could be anything," Dr. Wright said. "Even some sort of flu. I just don't want to take any chances."

"Of course not." Dan's words sounded loud and forced. He pulled himself into a rigid sitting position. Strange twinges and twitches erupted all over his body. He had to stay calm, stay in control. Stomach upsets could be caused by anything. There was nothing implicating the water yet!

"The lab reports showing everything okay?" Pete asked.

Dan stood up and paced in front of his desk. He forced his mouth to eject more words, the words he knew Pete would want to hear. "I took samples again this morning. Everything is fine."

"And there's been no breach in chlorination?"

He held his breath, then said, "No, the chlorinator is working fine."

There was silence on the phone now, and Dan imagined Pete's brain going around and around, like a mouse in a cage, trying to figure out what was going on. These medical guys didn't like not knowing the answer.

Dan picked up a file folder. "I can send the lab reports over. But there's nothing suspicious." Suspicious. Why had he used that word?

"Send the reports for the last week too, will you?"

"Sure." Dan had worked with enough bureaucrats to know they always wanted to cover their backsides. He'd already faked the numbers for the day after the storm.

"Give me your fax number," Dan said. Dutifully, he wrote it down. His hand, like some malfunctioning machine, wrote the number again. And again.

"I've got people checking all the fast food outlets and restaurants," Pete said.

"Good," Dan said emphatically. A few years ago, a fast food place in town had served some egg salad that had made people sick. He knew it was a long shot, but that could have happened again.

"We've taken stool samples from some of the people who are sick," Pete said. "That should tell us something."

Dan felt a stab of pain in his chest. Was this what a heart attack felt like? He imagined someone finding him, his nose flattened by the desk, ink smeared on his forehead, his brain dead to any concern about stool samples and what they might reveal.

Dan stopped pacing. Even if the stool samples showed the presence of E. coli, that still didn't implicate the water. People could get E. coli from a variety of sources. In the summer, when it was hot, food was a far more likely source than water. Pete would know that.

Until there was definite proof that the water was a problem, he was going to keep his mouth shut. For all he knew, this whole thing could blow right over. Sure, a few people had diarrhea, but so had half the people on the plane the last time he'd come back from Mexico. Diarrhea wasn't the end of the world. He'd had it himself. There had been a few days of discomfort, but, like everyone else, he'd recovered. The same situation could happen here in Port Carling. By next week, everybody could be chowing down hamburgers like there was no tomorrow. Then all this worry about the water would end. And he would fall on his knees and give thanks to the God he would never doubt again.

He looked down at the paper on his desk, and the breath caught in his throat. The words, "Tell the truth," were written over top of all the other scribbling. Beside them stood InkBoy, his hands firmly on his hips, his broad shoulders squared. Dan turned the page over.

"Well," said Pete, "keep me informed."

"Will do," Dan said and hung up.

He collapsed into his chair and put his head in his hands. He should have told Peter. He should have confessed.

But what if all this turned out to be nothing? He had to hold on. Just a few more days. There was so much at stake.

Dan pushed his hands through his hair.

Outside, there was the sound of a vehicle crunching on the gravel. Dan lifted his head sharply. Who the hell could that be? Dan tensed as the sound of the vehicle's engine was turned off. He waited for the slam of a car door. It seemed to take forever. Finally, he heard footsteps on the loose stone outside. The footfalls sounded laborious and slow.

Wayne appeared in the doorway. He was swaying a little, and at first Dan thought he was drunk, or had been in a fight, for his face looked swollen. It took Dan a minute to realize what was causing the contortion—it was anguish.

Wayne's glance swung up to the rafters, and Dan's hand went up to his own neck. Wayne's eyes found his, and the two men stared at each other.

When Wayne spoke, he said only two words, but they were enough to yank Dan up and out of his life as he'd known it.

The words were: "Sonny's sick."

Chapter 29

Jessie lay in a hammock down near the water, wrestled into submission by the heat. She knew she should go and check on Elfy, but it was difficult to find the energy to move. She pushed herself up.

Inside, the house was as hot as a sauna. She went over to the windows and pulled the curtains to shield the room from the sun, then went into the room where Elfy was sleeping. She sat down on a chair by the bed. The clock on the night table was softly ticking, and Jessie found its sound soothing.

Elfy looked no bigger than a child lying in the bed. It had been the better part of a week now, and she still looked withered and pale. Whatever this virus was, it was hanging on. Elfy was adamant she would be "right as rain" any day now, but her diarrhea and cramps weren't going away. It was time to see a doctor.

Jessie closed her eyes. A tight ball of dread was huddled just under her rib cage. It had been there all morning. Or at least since she'd heard the rumour that other people in town were also sick. Last night, Harley had been up—was he catching it too?

The old woman flung an arm out to the side of the bed as if reaching for someone or something to pull her from her sickness. Jessie shifted forward, and the skin on the back of her thighs stuck to the seat of the chair like adhesive. She took Elfy's hand and said her name softly. Elfy opened her eyes.

"How are you feeling?"

"Like dog vomit."

"That good, eh?" She squeezed Elfy's hand. "I want you to go to the doctor."

Elfy tried to wet her lips. "My mouth's so dry."

Jessie stood up. "I'll get you something to drink." She went into the kitchen and found Harley finishing off a glass of juice.

"Want some?"

Harley poured a glass for her. She looked at it with unease. Wasn't this the same jar that Elfy's juice had been in? Had Harley washed it out before making up the new juice? Knowing him, she doubted it. She sniffed the juice. It smelled fine. Telling herself not to be so paranoid, she lifted the glass. It was almost touching her lips when she stopped and poured the juice down the sink.

"I think we should drink bottled juice for a while," Jessie said, opening the fridge in search of some. Noticing a bag of oranges, she decided to squeeze them and make fresh juice.

"You worried about the water?"

Jessie shrugged. "I seem to be worried about something."

"I checked the ozonator a few weeks ago, but I can check it again."

A few years ago, Harley had installed an ozonator that purified all their incoming water. They both liked to drink a lot of water and wanted to make sure that what they were drinking was safe.

"How's the Elf?"

"Pale as a corpse. I'm going to take her to the doctor."

"Is it that serious?"

Harley didn't like doctors, not Western white ones. "I don't want to take any chances." Jessie put her hand gently on his back. "I heard you up last night too. Are you all right?"

He shrugged. He had never been one to give energy to ailments of his body.

Jessie eyed him with concern. She couldn't stand the possibility of him being sick.

Harley put his arms around her, and for a moment, they just held each other.

When he let her go, she cut the rest of the oranges and squeezed them. She liked oranges. They seemed so bright and optimistic.

When she'd made the juice, she took a glass to Harley who was sitting out by Hope-in-Hell's enclosure. In his lap were the various pieces of some doeskin moccasins he was sewing together.

Harley nodded towards Hope-in-Hell. "Soon we're going to have to think about finding him another lake."

Jessie leaned forward and stroked Hope-in-Hell's head. He had become such a part of her life, she couldn't imagine him not in it. Wearily, she turned back to the house.

She found Elfy's bed empty. Setting the glass down on the night table, Jessie walked down the hall to the bathroom and tapped on the door. "You all right?"

There was silence.

"Elfy?"

She heard the toilet flush. "Everything okay?"

The door opened, and Elfy hobbled out. Jessie took her arm and helped her back to the bedroom.

"Damn hemorrhoids!"

"You have hemorrhoids?"

"Now instead of squirting water every time I go, I'm squirting blood."

"Blood?" The ball of dread Jessie had been feeling burst and spread through her body. Blood!

"Do you have any pain?"

"Nope."

That didn't sound like hemorrhoids to her.

"Elfy, I want you to go to the doctor."

"I'll go tomorrow, if I'm not better."

"I want you to go today," Jessie said. "Particularly now that there's," she hesitated, "blood." She passed Elfy her cotton housecoat. "Just wrap yourself up in this, and I'll help you out to the car."

A few minutes later, they were driving to the medical clinic in Port Carling. The clinic was small and only operated in the summer. It was seldom busy. This morning, however, the parking lot was full. Jessie drove past it and tried to find another parking place nearby. There wasn't one.

"Damn!"

What was going on? She drove back to the clinic. Elfy wasn't well enough to walk any distance, so Jessie thought she would settle the old woman into a chair in the waiting room, then go and park.

Leaving the car running, Jessie helped Elfy out.

"I must look a sight," Elfy said, pulling on her Toronto Blue Jays cap.

Inside the clinic, people were everywhere, sitting in the chairs, leaning against the walls. Somewhere in the mass of people, a baby wailed.

Jessie took Elfy's hand and pulled her through the

crowd to the reception area. "Excuse me," she said. "Excuse me." When she reached the harried-looking receptionist, she said, "I have a very sick woman here. We don't mind waiting, but she's going to need a place to sit while—"

The phone rang. Jessie wanted to reach out and stop the receptionist from picking it up, but didn't. She could feel Elfy's weight against her.

When the receptionist put the phone down, it rang again immediately. "Wait," Jessie said. She was worried that Elfy was going to collapse. "Is there anywhere she can sit down?"

The receptionist sighed. "I have people sitting on examination tables as it is." Her eyes roamed over Elfy's face then returned to Jessie. "Take her to Emergency at the hospital. She'll get seen sooner there."

"I'll be fine," Elfy said to Jessie. "Just take me home."

Now it was Jessie's turn to sigh. There was no way she was going to take Elfy home. She turned, rallying her energy for an argument, but Elfy saved her the trouble. She fainted.

Chapter 30

Dan ducked into the stairwell of the South Muskoka Hospital, his heart thudding in his chest. His legs threatened to buckle under him, but he trudged up the steps, keeping his eyes down. The suitcase he was carrying was white and belonged to Megan. It contained some of the things she'd asked him to pick up for her. Sonny's condition was so serious now that later today, he was being transferred to The Hospital for Sick Children in Toronto. Megan, who hadn't left her son's side since he had taken ill, was going as well. Dan was supposed to be following her down later.

It had felt odd to go through her clothes, pick out underwear and socks and blouses. He felt as if his hands were somehow dirty and might soil her clothing, so he had made himself work quickly. This was the last act he was going to be able to do for her, and he wanted to do it well.

At the top of the stairs, he gripped the white suitcase more firmly and hurried along the hall to Sonny's room, praying he wouldn't run into anyone. When he got to Room 320, he eased open the door and entered. The curtains were still drawn, and there was a hushed, funereal stillness in the room. Megan was in a chair, her head resting on the bed beside Sonny's inert body. She had been there all night. He had been with her most of that time, listening as she whispered to him, holding her while she cried. His self-hatred had beaten him senseless, and now he was so exhausted, he could barely move.

Moving with extreme quiet, he put the suitcase down in the corner. Megan looked as if she were sleeping, and if she were, he did not want to wake her. She had a brutal day ahead of her.

Standing in the corner, Dan made his eyes go over to the boy. Sonny looked so terribly small and fragile in the large metal-framed bed. Dan wanted to go over and touch him, even if that was just to place the end of his finger on the soft skin of Sonny's arm. But he would not let himself. He had damaged the boy enough. His eyes filled with tears. He was the one, not Sonny, who should be forfeiting his life.

Megan made a small moaning sound, and a lock of her hair tumbled from her shoulder to her bare arm. He could still remember the silky feel of it in his fingers and the way it smelled of ripe strawberries when he'd lain with her in the hotel. Holding her in his arms that night had been like hugging summer. He would take that memory with him to his death.

What a fool he'd been to think things might be different. For a while, he'd let himself believe his luck was changing. And it had. Life had given him some new opportunities, but he'd ruined it all, dumped the mess of his life over Megan and Sonny like garbage over a garden.

Worried that Megan might wake up, he stepped towards the door, taking a last look at her face. Even in sleep, her face was contorted with worry.

He wiped the wetness from his face and turned away. Keeping his head down, he made his way quickly along the hall. He passed a patient reading a newspaper. His own smiling face greeted him from the front page.

Yesterday, a reporter had caught him on his way out of the hospital and snapped his picture. Dan had said a few quick comments about the safety of the water and had almost run to the car. He felt hounded all the time now, by reporters, health officials, his father—everyone was after him with questions.

He ducked into the stairwell and began making his way to the main floor. A strange, guttural sound echoed up through the dead air of the stairwell. Shit. Someone was down there. He quickened his pace, hoping that if he moved faster, he would be able to hurry past the person and get out the door to his truck.

He was almost at the bottom when a baby shrieked. It was a loud, shrill sound that seemed to explode in the enclosed space. Sneaking the quickest of glances, he saw someone by the door holding a baby. The baby was being held up near the woman's face, so he couldn't see either the woman or the baby, but he didn't care. All he wanted was to get past them and out of there.

Keeping his eyes down, he moved quickly, planning how he would duck around them and reach for the door. He was about to lift his arm for the door handle when the person holding the baby stepped in front of him, blocking his way.

"Don't you want to see your son?"

Dan lifted his eyes.

Christie. Her long, glossy hair fell around her radiant face as she smiled proudly at her son. Dan followed her gaze to the baby she was holding and met eyes that could have been his own.

"He looks like you, doesn't he?"

The baby jerked his small chubby arm out into the air. Dan thought about letting his hand touch the tiny fingers, but he did not let himself.

Christie nuzzled her head down into the baby's neck happily. Then she turned and looked at Dan with tentative shyness. "I saw you."

"Saw me?" Saw him in the hospital and came here to wait for him? Saw him somewhere else?

Christie leaned closer and whispered. She might as well have shouted the words for the effect they had on him. "Flushing the hydrants."

Dan's eyes widened.

"We passed you as we were going to the hospital."

Dan tried to swallow the hard stone that seemed to have found its way into his throat as he remembered the truck that had passed them just as he and Wayne were letting the water out of the last hydrant.

Seeing his alarm, she said, "I won't tell. Honest."

The baby shrieked, and Christie took her eyes from Dan, found the child's nipple-brown soother and put it in his mouth. She moved her hand tenderly over the baby's soft fuzzy head.

"He's gorgeous, isn't he?"

Dan stood immobile, unable to move or speak.

"Want to hold him?" Christie asked. She extended the baby towards him like a contract.

Chapter 31

Jessie squeezed Elfy's hand. Her flesh was warm, and Jessie waited for some small pulse in response, but there was none. She's sleeping, Jessie told herself. No one squeezed your hand back while asleep.

Despite the fact that Elfy was in the hospital now, and the doctors were doing their best to help her get better, she wasn't getting better at all. As yet, no one knew for sure what was making the old woman ill. Although Jessie had heard that the stool samples of some of the other sick people were showing E. coli, Elfy's had shown nothing. The doctors suspected this was because Elfy's stool sample had been taken after she'd eliminated the toxic organisms from her body. Jessie blamed herself for not getting Elfy to the doctor earlier.

But even if no toxic organisms still remained in Elfy's body, the damage would continue. A nurse had told Jessie yesterday that they were worried about Elfy's kidneys. If her kidneys were attacked, she could go into a coma. Listlessness was one of the first symptoms, and Elfy was as limp as wet rope.

However, even if E. coli had shown up in Elfy's stool, the doctors still wouldn't have been able to do anything. There was no medicine that could cure E. coli. People just had to endure the symptoms until they passed. For people with strong immune systems, that meant about a week of illness, but for the elderly and the young, it could take longer, and they were at far greater risk of having other, more serious complications.

Jessie rubbed her eyes. She felt as if the salt of a thousand tears had dried just under her eyelids. Her hair felt gritty too. She thought about going home and taking a long bath, but even though the thought was good, the idea of actually doing it felt too tiring. Maybe she'd just go home and sleep. Last night Harley had been up again. He kept telling her he was fine, but she was so worried, she'd hardly slept. And she would need her sleep if she were going to think straight.

Please don't get sick, Harley. Please.

She leaned forward and whispered into Elfy's ear that she would be back later. She smoothed the old woman's ginger hair back off her face and made her way to the door. Pulling it open felt like trying to pull a slab of concrete away from a wall.

Compared to the dim quiet of Elfy's room, the hall was bright and busy. As she stepped into it, she almost bumped into someone.

"Peter!"

Dr. Wright looked at her, bleary-eyed.

"You look as exhausted as I feel," Jessie said.

"I was just about to say that about you."

They shared a small smile. Peter and his wife, Marjorie, had been supporters of the bird refuge for years.

"Thank God for Marjorie," Jessie said. "With Elfy sick, she's practically been running the bird refuge with Alex—"

"Is Elfy any better?"

Jessie shook her head. It was all she could manage.

Peter ran his fingers through his thinning brown hair. "This thing has got us all running around in circles. We've interviewed every person who's showed up at the clinic, every person who's reported symptoms to their doctors, and we still don't know what's going on. We can't find a water source or a food source. We've checked the restaurants, grocery stores. It's confusing as hell. And the people who are sick are from all over the map, like that boy from Carlingview."

Jessie had heard that a small child was ill, but she hadn't known where the boy was from. Didn't the woman that Dan Gorman was seeing live at Carlingview? And didn't she have a son, a son that Dan was fond of?

"The boy that's sick, is he about five?" Jessie asked.

Peter nodded.

She remembered now. "Sonny." She leaned against the corridor wall. Somewhere, behind one of the doors, someone was moaning. It was a muffled, agonized sound, and Jessie tried to block it from her awareness.

"They're flying the boy down to Sick Kid's Hospital today," Peter said. "To put him on dialysis. Which he may be on for the rest of his life—if he's lucky enough to live." He leaned against the wall too. "It's just so strange," he said, grinding the fist of one hand into the palm of the other. "From what's showing up in people's bodies, you'd think it was the water. But apparently the water's okay."

"Apparently?" Jessie thought it an odd choice of words.

"According to Gorman's reports—"

Jessie gripped the corridor railing.

"Do you know him?" Peter's eyes scanned Jessie's face.

"Yes, but not in a capacity that I can talk about."

Peter nodded, getting the message. "According to his lab reports, the water is fine. But I'm starting to wonder if he's telling me the whole truth." He shook his head and blew air out his mouth. "Things just aren't adding up."

There was a beeping sound, and Peter pulled a pager from his pocket. Shrugging his shoulders, he gave her a small wave and turned into the lounge to take the call. Jessie staggered out of the building and stood leaning against her car. It was a long time before she got in and drove away.

Chapter 32

Dan drove from the hospital to his parents'. He knew as long as he was moving, no one could get to him and ask him questions, so he took his time. So many of the houses on his parents' street were shaped like small brick boxes. The one next to his parents' had a large, stained glass angel hanging in the window. He'd never noticed that before.

He swung into the driveway, left the car running and went inside. The radio was on, so his mother didn't hear him come in. He could see her long, thin back as she stood at the sink washing dishes. She looked so frail and alone standing there, he was overwhelmed at the sight of her. He wished he were little again and could bury his face in her apron.

He understood now why people who killed themselves took their loved ones with them. That way, the pain would be over for all of them at the same time.

She turned, the palm of her hand leaping to her chest.

"Dan! Why didn't you tell me you were here, I—"

Not wanting her to see his eyes, he ducked away and went downstairs, calling behind him, "I just stopped by to get something."

She followed him to the top of the stairs, but came no further. The basement was his father's territory, and he knew she would not enter it.

"How's Sonny? Is he any better?"

Although Dan couldn't see all of her, he could see her hands. They were wringing the flowers of her apron and leaving damp spots on the cloth.

"About the same."

"Your father says he's called and called you…"

"I'll be up in a minute," he shouted, pretending not to hear. He walked past his father's fishing gear and hunting stuff, making his way to the far wall where two shot guns were displayed. Although the law required guns to be locked up, Frank ignored this regulation.

Beside the guns was a cupboard. Dan opened it and pulled a beaded metal chain. A light flashed, there was a "plink", then darkness. Not wanting to take the time to go upstairs and find another bulb, he knelt down and felt for a box on the bottom shelf. Yes, there it was. He pushed back the lid and groped around inside. The metal grip of the gun greeted him like a handshake.

He brought the gun out, wrapped it in some newspaper and put it in an old aquarium.

"Is that for Sonny?" his mom asked when he carried the aquarium upstairs. "Are they going to let him come home?"

He couldn't allow the heartache in her voice to enter him, so he moved quickly through the kitchen, ignoring the newspaper with his picture on the front.

All his attempts at covering up seemed silly to him now. Jessie was right, the truth had a way of floating to the surface, despite a person's attempts to keep it under. His only hope now was to be out of the way when the facts about what had happened were dragged to the shore.

At the door, Dan turned to call out goodbye, but his mother had followed and stood before him. There were tears in her eyes as she searched his face. She moved towards him and gave him a strong, fierce hug. For a brief moment, he was ten again, holding on to her for dear life.

"I pray for Sonny every day," she whispered. "And I pray for you."

Dan felt a wash of grief fill his chest and move up into his throat. Afraid he might cry, he kissed her cheek quickly and left. As he pulled out of the driveway, he caught a glimpse of her standing on the stoop, waving goodbye. Hoping she wouldn't be able to see the tears that were streaming from his eyes, he raised his hand in a salute and drove away.

On his way home, he stopped at the liquor store in Port Carling and picked up a twenty-sixer of rum. When he handed the woman at the cash register his money, he stared at her. Unless Meat showed up unexpectedly, this was the last contact he was going to have with another human being.

"I'm going to kill myself," he told her with his eyes.

She gave him a dime and two pennies and moved on to the next customer.

Dan put the change in the head slot of a plaster seeing-eye dog that stood by the door and drove to the cottage. He pulled his car into the empty parking area and carried the aquarium and bottle down to the cabin. As he walked along the stone path, he remembered the day he'd carried his things here from the city. He'd been so optimistic then. As if he'd had a new clean sheet of drawing paper in front of him. But now there were no new pages to be had.

Placing the gun under his arm, he took the bottle of rum, a deck chair, and a pad of paper down to the lake.

"You first," he said to the rum and cracked the bottle

open. He took a long swig. The liquid burned as it went down, but he could feel the anaesthetic effect of the alcohol almost immediately. He drank more.

There was a strange relief in him now. Knowing he was going to die meant there would be no more screw-ups to face, no more worries about hurting people. The game was over. He was calling it quits. But first he had a letter to write.

"It's confession time," he said aloud.

He expected the letter to be difficult to write. He wasn't used to telling the truth, and he thought it would be hard to do so now. Particularly since he knew others, his parents, the police, perhaps Megan, maybe even Jessie, might be reading what he wrote. But his pen flew across the paper, filling one inky page after another. He wrote about Megan and what meeting her had been like for him. He wrote about Sonny and how terrible he felt that the boy was sick. He wrote about Christie and acknowledged his son. He said he was sorry to all of them, but particularly to his parents. It seemed like such a feeble thing to say.

Hating himself utterly and completely, he took a large gulp of the liquor in the bottle. What a horrible, horrible man he was. He didn't deserve to live. He doubted that even his death would be an adequate apology for all the pain he'd caused, but he would offer it anyway. At the very least, it might alleviate some of his parents' public humiliation. And, if there were such a thing as a beneficent God, maybe the act of terminating his own life would allow Sonny's to be spared.

He pulled out a fresh piece of paper and wrote out a will, leaving everything to his four children—the three of his loins and the one of his heart. It made him feel better to be able to give them his savings. And confirmed that it was right for him to be taking his life. He had more to offer dead than alive.

Finally, he wrote about the sewage spill and the night of the storm. This part was harder, but instead of choosing his words carefully, he simply blurted everything out. His pen moved quickly, in the same way it did when he was cartooning. And the writing was dark and bold just as it was when he was drawing InkBoy. A sudden realization made him lift his pen from the page. It wasn't him doing this writing, it was InkBoy. Only InkBoy could drop ink on a page this quickly. Only InkBoy had the clarity of thought to leap over obstacles in his mind like this.

A smile came to his lips. Jessie would be happy to know that in the end, InkBoy had been free to fly again. She, more than anyone, would celebrate this. But her celebration wouldn't last long. Not when she heard how he'd screwed up with the sewage and contaminated the water. The thought of her finding out what he'd done was so sharp that he swilled another inch of rum. He had drunk over half of it now and was feeling its effect.

Good riddance to bad rubbish. That's what she and everyone would be saying. And all the alcohol in the world wasn't going to take away the pain of that. There was only one thing that could.

"This baby here," he said aloud and lifted the gun. It felt heavy in his hand, so heavy he could hardly hoist it up. He pressed the muzzle to his forehead and curled his finger around the trigger. A trigger was such a fragile thing.

The woods around him began to spin, and for a moment he thought he might pass out. Was he that drunk?

Jessie's face appeared before him. Of all the people in his life, Jessie had been the one who had believed in him the most. She was the one who thought he had value. Well, she was wrong. He had no value.

He pulled the trigger.

At least, he made the move to pull the trigger. But something held his finger back. InkBoy? He yanked the gun away from his head and looked at it. Everything was blurry now and swaying slightly. Dan closed his eyes. Something was gripping his index finger and holding it back. Only InkBoy had that kind of superhuman strength.

"Listen, pal," he said, "if you want to rescue someone, get down to Sick Kids and save Sonny."

The thought of Sonny lying in a hospital bed rallied his determination. He lifted the gun again and pressed the metal into his scalp.

Chapter 33

Jessie heard the warning hoot of the train, and by the time she began racing down Taylor Road on her way from the Pines in Bracebridge, she could see the huge blunt nose of the locomotive coming down the track. There were no cars in front of her, and for a mad moment, she thought about gunning the car and trying to get across before the train barricaded her way, but it was throttling towards her quickly, and at the last minute, she pressed hard on the brakes.

She sighed and let her head fall back against the seat as the big clay-coloured railway cars clacked by. She checked her rear view mirror and saw the man behind her drumming his fingers on the steering wheel, staring fixedly at the train as if it were his personal enemy. Here life was, offering both her and this man a small gift of unstructured time, but it was hard to take advantage of it. She was worried about Harley and wanted to get back to him. Harley. Now there was a man who never waited. To him, waiting meant you were out of tune with things. Life took its own time, and he was willing to flow with that. Unless he was standing in some sort of government line— then it was foot tapping, capital W, Waiting!

Her conversation with Peter had unsettled her deeply. Why did she keep having the feeling that Dan was involved in this somehow? She closed her eyes. There was only one way to find out—go to him and demand the truth. Of course, there was no certainty he would tell her the truth, but she had good intuition about when someone was trying to cover something up.

She made herself breathe. It was hard to get her chest to move. It was always like this when she was feeling stressed: she moved into a shallow breathing pattern that wouldn't meet the oxygen needs of a mouse. She elongated her inhalation and exhalation until she felt herself starting to relax. She knew that in order to listen to her intuition, she had to be in a place of relative calm.

She envied Harley's neutral mind. He didn't have to breathe deeply to find that neutrality, it was just there. His neutrality allowed him to be quiet and to listen at a micro-level for what was right for him to do. Not right in a religious moral sense, but right in terms of what was most congruent with him and his relationship to life itself.

Jessie stared at the train. Most of the brick-red cars were covered with spray painted names and designs. "Paul was here" was printed in white paint and a few cars later, "Martin rules" was written in blue.

She shut her eyes and concentrated on her breathing again. If she did decide to track down Dan, she would have to go to his workplace. After all, it was the middle of the day. And if she went to where he worked, she probably wouldn't be able to talk to him anyway, so what was the point? She sighed. No, she would go home and check on Harley. That's what she wanted to do.

Since the idea wouldn't leave her, she came up with another plan. She would go home, check on Harley and, if all was well, go and see Dan at his cabin that night.

Then she would have a better chance of catching him alone. A riffle of fear went down her body. If she went to Dan's home, she might run into Malowski. The thought of that was off-putting in itself. The last thing she needed was another trespassing charge. No, it would be foolhardy to go anywhere near Dan's place. It was a stupid idea, and she would abandon it.

Jessie peered down the track and saw the last railway car. As soon as it passed, she would head home. She watched the last car coming towards her. It seemed to be pulling a curtain of landscape along with it. She was so focussed on the backdrop of trees and greenery that was being revealed, moment-by-moment, that she almost missed the word that was spray-painted on the side of the railway car.

The word was Dan.

Chapter 34

Jessie's Toyota lurched forward, leaping across the track where the train had just been. In that split second, she decided she would go to Dan's and felt immediately afraid. The idea of just dropping in on him was frightening. It wasn't her practice to do that with clients—especially clients who hadn't completed their therapy. Dan might be angry that she'd sought him out. And even angrier at her questions.

It was crazy to go, but the rightness of it pushed her on. As she drove, she focussed on making her belly rise and fall with each breath. All too soon, Malowski's road appeared, and she turned in.

All of her senses jumped to the alert as she drove the car slowly up the laneway. Thank God. There was only one car in the driveway: Dan's black Jeep. She parked and stared down the flagstone path leading to the main house. She'd been along that path once before and didn't want to go down it again. Then she saw a path leading off into the woods. The woods were dense, but now that she was looking for it, she could just see the small bunkie nestled in the trees.

She closed her eyes and reminded herself to be extremely careful. Dan might be feeling desperate. Desperate people did desperate things.

Forcing herself out of the car, she closed the door quietly and walked along the path. She kept her eye on the bunkie, watching for the smallest movement, listening for the smallest sounds.

She was so focussed on the bunkie that she was fairly close before she saw him sitting in the woods down by the water. There was a compacted darkness to him that alarmed her. His hands were resting on the paddle-shaped arms of the chair, and there was something black in his right hand. She strained forward to see what it was, but couldn't. Yet there was something so ominous about it, she kept her eyes riveted to it as she edged cautiously forward.

When she realized it was a gun, she jerked back the step she was about to take and stood perfectly still. Blood thudded in her ears. Then, as if he could feel the stunned pressure of her frightened glare, he turned.

His eyes were like black pits excavated into his face, and Jessie felt as if she might fall into them, but she kept her focus back so she could keep the periphery of her awareness on the gun. The gun. She felt herself shift into a state of heightened vigilance about it and any movement that might involve it. For it was clear to her, bone chillingly clear, that in no more than a second, he could raise the gun and shoot her. She was too far away from any cover to protect herself.

She stared at him, waiting. Seconds passed. Neither of them moved.

Finally, her lips parted, and she was aware that words were trying to come out, but her mouth was dry, and her tongue seemed to be stuck.

"If you're going to try and talk me out of this, don't," he said.

She tried to speak again, but all that came out was his name. "Dan—"

He pulled his eyes from hers.

Alarmed that she had lost contact with him, she said, "Can I come closer?"

He shrugged.

"Could you..." She swallowed and tried again. "Would you put the gun on the ground?"

He picked up the gun. For a few terrified moments, she held her breath, waiting for him to point it at her, but he didn't. He laid it on the ground.

Jessie stared at it. This was the first real handgun she'd ever been close to. Her eyes went to the trigger. It was such a small piece of metal for such a lot of potential death. She moved closer. For a second, she felt as if she might collapse, her legs had so little strength. After a few steps, she eased herself down on a rock so she was sitting across from him. It was hard not to keep looking at the gun. She pulled her attention away from it and looked at Dan. His eyes were huge, his face anguished.

"I've screwed up, Jessie. Bigger than you could ever imagine."

She nodded. "I think I know." The pits of his eyes filled with pain. "I don't know the how of it," she said. "And I don't know the why of it, but I think all this sickness that's going around has something to do with the water. And something to do with you."

He put his head in his hands. "I didn't mean for anyone to get sick. You've got to know that."

She shook her head. "I do know that. You're not that kind of man."

He yanked his body to the side as if to avoid the rope

of her compassion. When he spoke, he almost shouted. "People might die because of me. Die!" His voice cracked.

"You feel responsible," Jessie said, cringing. It was a stupid thing to say. This wasn't someone in her office! This was someone about to kill himself!

"I *was* responsible! When the sewage lagoon broke at Carlingview, it was the middle of the night, and I thought if I flushed the system, I could fix it. But I couldn't fix it. I couldn't, I…"

His eyes were wild.

Jessie scrambled to put the pieces together. The spill had been at Carlingview. That was how Sonny had become sick. And the contaminated water had probably sluiced down into the lake and somehow entered the treatment plant. Dan had tried to cover up by flushing the bad water out. Which he'd done, but not before some unlucky people had turned on their taps that night for a drink of water. Elfy had been one of them.

"We thought we'd hosed everything down at Carlingview, but Sonny must have been playing up there and—" Dan threw his face into his hands, shaking his head from side to side. "I never knew it would be so bad."

"No."

"I risked people's lives."

Jessie felt anger rise in her like a pointed finger. People were sick because of this man. Sonny and Elfy and others. Maybe even Harley. She yanked her mind away from that thought. It frightened her too much. If Dan had reported the spill to the Medical Officer of Health, a boil water order would have been issued, health officers might even have been dispatched to go door-to-door.

Would that have prevented Elfy from getting sick?

Jessie doubted it. By the time the warning could have gone out, most of the people who were now sick had already been contaminated. Sonny, on the other hand, was a different story. If the medical officers had been informed, Carlingview would have been shut down, and Sonny would have been taken to another location. The boy would be playing with his toys right now.

Jessie sighed. Hurting a child, especially a child you loved, was an awful thing. She could understand why Dan wanted to die. Living with that kind of pain would be horrific.

The pages on Dan's notepad fluttered in his lap. "I wrote it all out."

Jessie nodded. "Would you let me read it?"

He shrugged but passed the notepad.

She accepted it into her hands as if it were a fragile thing. She'd never actually held a suicide letter before.

The pages felt so thin, far too thin for the weight of the suffering he had scrawled upon them. The lettering was big and very black, so there was little white space. Some of the words were pressed into the paper so hard, they indented the fabric of the pages. This must be how Dan feels, she thought: the blackness pressing in on him, obliterating any space or light.

Over her years as a psychotherapist, she'd listened to many clients talk about their wishes to die. Some had even confessed their plans for dying, but so far, not one had ever taken his or her life. Thank God. But she had counselled many survivors of suicide—the wives, husbands, children of people who had found their loved ones asphyxiated by carbon monoxide or decapitated by shotguns. Sometimes it took years to get those survivors to trust again. Suicide had slashed the wrists of their belief in others. Oddly enough, however, statistics revealed that the children of parents who had killed themselves were more likely also to kill themselves, despite knowing the horror of it.

Jessie read Dan's pages slowly, carefully, as if looking for instructions on how to deactivate a ticking bomb.

"Every detail in there is true," he told her.

She nodded. She, more than anyone, knew how difficult it was for Dan to be honest, but in the pages she was reading, he had poured out everything, describing in detail what had happened, and what he had done. And not done. His last act was going to be a truthful one.

The pages mentioned several people by name: Megan, Sonny, his parents. A little further along, she read her own name as he wrote about his appreciation for the work they had done together. She felt sad reading this part. Yes, she had helped him to tell the truth, but what good was that if he couldn't stand by that truth? If she'd only had a few more months with him. What he was facing was devastating, but she had helped clients through devastating situations before. She'd had clients who had hit people with their cars, clients who had slapped their children, clients who had beaten up their spouses. People sometimes did bad things. But life could go on. Dan's life could go on. She could help him to manage the pain. But if he killed himself, the pain would simply get passed on to everyone else in his life. That was the horrible thing about suicide. It left the mess for others to clean up. And just as it was no easy job washing a loved one's brains off the wall, it was even more difficult to clean up the psychological splatter.

"Dan, you made a mistake, a bad mistake, but—"

A burst of air came out of his mouth. He shook his head, "Don't!"

A flood of emotions filled her chest. "Dan, killing yourself will hurt a lot of people. And there's been enough hurt."

He snorted again. "Killing myself isn't going to hurt anyone. They'll all say 'Good riddance to bad rubbish'."

She made herself take a breath. "Yes, people will be angry when they hear what you did. I'm angry at what you did. A friend of mine is in the hospital fighting for her life..." She paused and pulled in some air. "But that doesn't mean I want you to die."

She watched Dan drop his head into his hands. He looked as compressed as a fist. The intensity of his suffering made her speak again. This time her voice was no more than a whisper.

"I'd be sad if you died. Very sad."

He covered his head with his arms as if to block her words. He choked and tried to swallow down his feelings, but they were too great for him to hold back. An anguished sound escaped from him, and he began to sob.

Jessie got up and put the palm of her hand on his back, just touching him lightly so he knew someone was with him. She was glad he was crying. If anything could soften the iron grip of his self-hatred, it would be tears.

When he was quiet, she sat back on the rock.

"I almost killed someone once," she said.

Dan pulled his head up and looked at her. His face was bloated, and his eyes were red, but there was something looser about him now.

"It was a child, too. Almost a child, anyway. A teenager. But unlike you, I wanted to hurt him, I'm ashamed to say.

And I might have, if he hadn't managed to harm himself first." She looked out over the water. "He was just a kid with a loud boat, but he just about drove me crazy, driving up and down and up and down in front of our place." She frowned. "I won't go into all the details, but there was an accident. And the boy ended up being in a coma. For a few weeks. Which, of course, felt like months. Meanwhile, everyone treated me as if I had hurt him. The police took me into custody, the whole bit."

He stared at her, trying to read it for what had happened. "Did the boy live?"

Jessie nodded. "Yes, he did. He completely recovered in the end. And, strangely enough, he and I became friends. He still writes me from time to time." She leaned forward. "But when he was in the coma, I felt like someone had pushed me into a hole and covered me with mud. Which is how I'm guessing you're feeling."

Dan didn't answer, but she had his attention, so she carried on.

"You've done an important thing in this letter, Dan. You've told the truth. Don't back away from it."

"But Sonny—"

From the way he kept coming back to the grim possibility of Sonny dying, she knew this was the pivotal point for him. She decided to face it directly.

"Yes, Sonny may die. And if he does, that will be a tragedy. But tragedy can be faced."

Dan shook his head violently. "I can't. I can't. My life is over, Jessie. Over!"

"Yes, the life you lived is over. But there may be another one waiting for you." She lifted the pad of paper. "You've already started. You've told the truth here. That's the beginning. Stand behind that truth now. Accept the consequences of what you did and go forward. That's the only way out."

"They'll put me in jail."

"Yes, they might. But even if they do, it's possible to live a meaningful life in jail. Some people actually find who they are in jail. They go back to school or study a new profession. They come to terms with what they have done and forgive themselves. When they get out, they move to a new town and start all over again."

Dan stared at her as if she'd just showed him the outline of a door in a rock wall.

Chapter 35

Dan sat in the corner of the cabin, a thin blanket wrapped around his shoulders. It was cool this morning, and there was a wispy mist on the surface of the lake that reminded him of autumn. It was hard to imagine that in a few months, this lake would be frozen. Would he be in jail then?

He had been alone here now for two days. No one had called. No one had come to see him. He wasn't surprised. Yesterday, he'd gone with Jessie to give a statement to the police, so everyone knew now what he'd done. Jessie had called a lawyer, so he'd had legal representation as the officers questioned him. She'd also stayed with him while he called his parents. And Wayne. Then she'd driven him back to Meat's and made him promise not to make any more attempts on his life.

She had told him she'd be back again soon, but she hadn't come. Was something wrong? Maybe the old woman she'd told him about was now sicker. Or maybe Jessie herself was sick.. He knew he could probably find out by turning on the radio. Last night he'd almost managed it. Pushed by his need to find out how Sonny was, he'd gone over to the radio, stood beside it, even touched the "on" button with his fingers, but he couldn't get himself to switch it on.

Drops of water fell from his eyes to the blanket. He hadn't cried in over thirty years, but now that's all he was doing. He felt spongy with tears, sodden with grief. Even when he slept he cried, sometimes so desperately, the sound of it woke him up. In the morning, there were salt crystals all over his pillow. They felt like tiny balls of gritty remorse.

He was grateful that he could sleep. It was the only time when he felt any relief. Besides, there wasn't much else to do. He'd been fired from his job, so he didn't have that responsibility any more. Despite the fact that there was no food in the cabin, he didn't dare go into town. He could barely face himself, let alone anyone else. Besides, the thought of food made him sick.

He wished now he hadn't promised Jessie he wouldn't kill himself. Of course, he didn't have his gun any more. Jessie had given it to the police, but there were other ways to die. If he wanted, he could take his truck and drive it off the end of some dock in Port Carling. He grimaced. Given his luck so far, someone would be there to pull him out. At five in the morning? That didn't seem likely, but then neither had it been likely that Jessie would show up in time to stop him from putting a bullet through his brain. Maybe it just wasn't his time to die.

Through the window, he could see the first rays of the morning sun dappling through the trees. Yearning for the feel of the sun's warmth, he pulled himself up and went outside. He was intending to go down to the lake but decided not to risk it. What if there were people out on the lake and they pointed at him and shouted obscenities? He cowered into a corner of the porch and sat in one of the old wicker chairs.

A light breeze was coming across the water, and he

moved so that he could feel the sun on his face. It was as warm as a hand, and he felt himself calm.

When he opened his eyes, he saw a daddy-long legs spider making its way up his ankle. With its long, hair-thin legs, it looked like a spider on stilts. He crouched and gently moved his hand under it. The spider had no weight at all.

A year ago, maybe even a month ago, he would have tossed this spider away, maybe even hurt it with inadvertent force. He looked down at it now and was struck by the fact that what he was holding was a living organism. Somewhere in its Rice Crispy shaped body, it too had eyes and a heart. He imagined how he must look to the spider—huge, hulking, dangerous. Is that why it wasn't moving, because it was too afraid?

Gently, Dan eased the spider down to a window ledge. Slowly, moving leg by elegant leg, the spider walked away. Dan thought it beautiful.

He wished Sonny were here to see the spider. Sonny had liked looking at insects and snakes and things like that. He'd had an innate curiosity about all living things. It was unfair, that he, Dan, who was so undeserving, should be here, sitting in the sun, when Sonny was fighting for his life in a dark hospital room.

But life wasn't fair. Jessie had often said that in their sessions, and it was true.

His right hand throbbed. It always did this when he had an impulse to draw. Maybe he would draw a cartoon for Sonny. He remembered the first day that he'd met the boy and how the two of them had drawn dinosaurs in the sand. If he drew a special cartoon for Sonny, would Megan let him see it? Would the boy even be conscious enough to see it? Dan picked up some paper and a pen anyway.

He found himself drawing frames, liked he used to in his old cartoon days. Almost immediately, InkBoy swooped into the first frame, standing strong and tall, his muscular arms akimbo and ready for action. He stared out at Dan, awaiting orders.

A surge of warmth went down Dan's body. It felt so good to be drawing again. His hand moved forward to the second frame, and he drew a large sound bubble. It filled with the cries of a sick child.

InkBoy leapt into action. Drawing himself a pair of huge wings, InkBoy flew off in search of him. He found the boy in a small white room, with tubes going in and out of his body. One of the tubes was coming from a clear bag of fluid hanging from a metal tree that stood on wheels beside the bed. Another was connected to a dialysis machine.

With his X-ray eyes, InkBoy began to scan the boy's body. It was so silent. There was no drumbeat of life force pounding through the boy's veins, nothing proclaiming an insistence on living, only a weak pulsing that seemed to be getting slower and slower like the beats of a song just before it came to an end.

Quickly, InkBoy scanned other areas of Sonny's body. It wasn't difficult to see the devastation the E. coli had caused. The lining of the boy's bowels had been hit hard, but his kidneys had suffered the most damage.

InkBoy hung his head. The boy was going to die. And he, with all his superhuman powers, could do nothing.

No, wait. There was something he could do.

Very slowly and with great care, he drew a great white dinosaur. And as gently as if he were lifting a bird fallen from its nest, he placed the boy's body on cushions on the dinosaurs back. The boy opened his eyes and smiled at him.

When the dinosaur disappeared into the clouds, the pen dropped from Dan's hand. Inside him, he could feel InkBoy, in all his dark grandeur, weeping.

Chapter 36

The day after Jessie had accompanied Dan to the police station to make his confession, she visited Elfy in the hospital and was relieved that the old woman seemed better. Harley still wasn't feeling great, but he'd been all right when she'd left that morning. While at the hospital, she heard that some of the sick people were even well enough to leave the hospital and that there'd been no new cases. Jessie allowed herself to think the worst was over.

Although Jessie hadn't heard how Sonny was doing, at least everyone knew now what had happened and what the problem was. Once the town knew what it was dealing with, the general level of alarm diminished. Most of the people in Port Carling were drinking bottled water, and a thorough investigation had been started.

Dan had been suspended from his work, but at least he hadn't killed himself and made the tragedy that much worse. And the heat wave seemed to be over. Today was decidedly cooler.

As Jessie returned home and walked through the garden, she noticed a pile of what looked like old blankets out by the trees near the water. She was wondering how they had gotten there, when the pile of blankets moved. And Harley's booted foot jutted out from under the heap.

She went to him immediately, gently peeling back the

husk of blanket to find his head. His back was at her chest and, leaning towards his ear, she said his name. Frightened at his lack of response, she said his name louder.

"Harley!"

He jerked back, his eyes opening, then, as if his eyelids were too great a weight, he let his eyes fall closed.

"It's like I have a porcupine in my belly," he said, wincing in pain.

Jessie curled into him, wondering what to do. In all her years of knowing him, Harley had never been sick—not really sick. Sure, from time to time, he had a touch of the flu or a cold, but his strong physiology had always allowed him to carry on. Nothing had ever brought him down. Not like this, sprawled on a blanket, teeth biting back the pain.

Like most other people in Muskoka, she now knew more than she ever wanted to know about E. coli, and there was no question in her mind that Harley was suffering from it.

"It's eating me alive," he said, holding his belly.

Elfy had endured abdominal pain, too. Elfy, however, was in the hospital. She had doctors looking after her. Even though Jessie knew the doctors couldn't do much, she felt better knowing the old woman was getting expert medical care. As far as she could see, that was paying off—Elfy was slowly improving.

"I want you to go to the doctor," she said to him.

"Don't have a doctor," he said, not opening his eyes.

"I'll get Peter to look at you. You know Peter. He's the one who comes to pick up Marjorie."

"Give me a few days," he finally said.

Jessie groaned. She wanted to call the doctor now. She

rearranged the blanket around his shoulders. At the very least, she wanted to get him inside. The fact that he wanted to be outside, near his beloved Mother Earth and not in his comfortable bed, told her how very sick he was.

Harley seemed to drop down into sleep, and Jessie tried to figure out what to do. It relieved her to think that Elfy was getting better. Perhaps Sonny was getting better too. She hadn't heard anything to the contrary, and no news was good news, wasn't it? If a young boy and an old woman could beat E. coli, surely Harley, with his strong body, could as well.

She decided to give him twenty-four hours. She brought her sleeping bag out and stayed with him, rearranging the blankets to keep him warm, feeding him vegetable broth and washing the film of sweat from his skin.

The next day at dawn, she stared into the tentative early morning light and looked worriedly at the sky. It looked as if it might start raining at any moment. What would she do then?

Agitated, she strode up to the house. As she approached the porch, she saw some willow branches piled at the far end of the veranda. Alex had brought them yesterday. Alex, Jake, the Grannies, everyone was being so kind, chipping in to visit Elfy, helping with the bird refuge. Stories of people helping each other were all over town. Funny how difficult times could bring out the best in people. It was just as Harley said: one extreme begged another.

When Jessie entered the kitchen, its familiar shapes and colours comforted her. Opening the fridge, she poured herself a small glass of orange juice from a carton and turned on the radio. The tone of the newscaster's voice made her immediately nervous. She stiffened as she caught the end of his sentence.

"—Port Carling's first casualty."

She backed against the counter. The newscaster carried on.

"Sonny Walker, aged five, died this morning at The Hospital for Sick Children in Toronto. Memorial services will be—"

Jessie felt her knees buckle, and her back slipped down the long cupboard. Sonny had died? Died? That meant Elfy might die. Harley…

With sudden energy, she got to her feet and went back outside to Harley. Using the tree to steady herself, she eased down beside him. Sonny had died. Died. She kept repeating the word, turning it in her mind as if trying to find the right way to insert it into her brain. But her brain kept rejecting it.

She thought about Megan. The poor woman. She would be in her own personal hell right now. As would Dan. She thought about calling him but knew she didn't have the energy.

Harley had curled into himself like a caterpillar fallen to the road. He was still sleeping, and she wrapped her arms around him and pressed her mouth into his back. His heart was just a few inches from her lips.

"Don't die," she said silently, her lips brushing against his shirt. She couldn't imagine life without Harley, couldn't imagine even wanting life without Harley. He was so intricately intertwined with all that was valuable to her, so interwoven with everything she loved.

She was shaking now and weeping. A hand reached up and touched her face. With great effort, Harley pulled himself around so he was facing her.

His eyes fluttered and opened It frightened her how little of him she found there.

"Harley, we have to get help."

Slowly, he moved his tongue to moisten his lips. His mouth moved slightly, but no words came out. He closed his eyes again.

Unable to hold back her desperation, she shook him. "Harley, I'm calling the doctor. You have to see someone…I can't just watch you…"

I can't just watch you die. Those were the words she would have spoken, and they shocked her so much she put her head on his chest and began crying again.

Harley spoke a word into her ear. It was as soft as a whisper.

"*Nokomis.*"

Jessie sat up. *Nokomis* was the Ojibway word for grandmother. Of course! She could call One Eye, Harley's grandmother. One Eye would know people on the reserve who did healing. Maybe there was even a native doctor she could call.

"I'll be right back." She rushed into the house.

She was dialling One Eye's phone number when Aggie came in. Aggie was a substantial woman who always had an air of authority, but this morning she walked tentatively as if she weren't quite sure the ground would hold her up.

"I brought some vegetable juice for Harley," she said, holding up a jar. Jessie nodded, but the phone was ringing now, and she turned away so she could give it her full attention. She willed One Eye to answer. If there was anyone who could help Harley, One Eye would know. Jessie counted the rings. On the fourth ring, someone picked up.

"Hello."

At the sound of One Eye's voice, words swollen with fear tumbled out of Jessie's mouth.

One Eye listened, then said, "Noah Song Maker. I'll get him." And she hung up.

Chapter 37

Jessie put the phone down and pressed her hands together, index fingers touching her lips. She felt drenched with relief. Help was on its way.

Aggie brought a glass of the vegetable juice and handed it to Jessie. "Is Harley worse?"

"It's okay," Jessie said quickly. "Someone, a healer, is coming. From the reserve…"

Aggie arched an eyebrow. "Someone from the reserve?"

Jessie ignored the innuendo and sipped the juice. It was thick and tasted of peppers and tomatoes. "I'll need tobacco," she said, thinking aloud.

"Tobacco? What in Heaven's name for?"

"In the Anishinaabe tradition, tobacco is used as part of their ceremonies." She was about to add that the smoke from tobacco was what carried people's prayers to the Spirits, but the look on Aggie's face made her reconsider. She'd said enough.

"And I suppose you want me to go and get it for you?"

Jessie looked up. "Would you? I don't want to leave Harley. Even for a little."

Muttering, Aggie picked up her purse and went to the door.

"Thanks," Jessie called. Feeling buoyed by this sudden turn of events, she poured a second glass of the vegetable juice and took it out to Harley. As he propped himself up to sip it, she told him One Eye was coming. "And she's bringing someone. Noah Song Maker."

One of Harley's eyebrows lifted, but he said nothing. He finished the juice and collapsed back down into his blankets.

When Aggie returned, the two of them waited for One Eye. By mid afternoon, One Eye had not arrived, and Aggie left to visit Elfy. Jessie continued to stare at the driveway. What was taking the old woman so long? Worried that she was lost, Jessie went back up to the house and turned up the ringer on the phone.

Hour after hour passed. By dinnertime, her worry had turned to anger. Had One Eye misunderstood the urgency of Harley's situation?

The light was dimming when an old brown Oldsmobile nosed up the lane. It was full of people. Jessie thought it was some lost tourists and expected the car to turn around, but it stopped, and One Eye got out of the passenger seat.

Jessie wanted to shout, "Where have you been?" But relief that help had come washed her frustration away.

With her long, gun-grey hair tied behind her, One Eye nodded a hello to Jessie. As always, Jessie found her focus going to the old woman's bad eye, which looked as if it were rolled up somehow, perhaps in an attempt to see out the top of her head. The old woman's other eye, the "good" one, was a rich, damp-earth brown and had the intensity of both eyes together. This eye grabbed Jessie's face then searched beyond it for Harley. When she saw him, she went to him immediately. For a woman of girth, she moved quickly.

Jessie didn't know Ojibway, but she could tell that

One Eye was asking him questions.

"*Aanimizi*," she called over her shoulder to the others still in the car.

Jessie moved close to Harley. She felt frightened by the sharpness of One Eye's tone. "What did you say?"

One Eye pulled herself up. "I'm saying he's sick. Very sick." She went back to the car.

Jessie followed with her eyes and saw that the man who'd been driving was now standing by the side of the car. He stood absolutely still and was looking into the woods. He was young, in his twenties, Jessie guessed, and small bodied. The features of his face were sharp, hawk-like. Was this Song Maker? She didn't think so.

"Vernon," One Eye said by way of introduction. She pulled a basket from the car. "He's our fire-keeper."

Jessie watched Vernon disappear into the woods and returned her gaze to the car. Someone large and bulky was moving around in the backseat. Jessie tried to get a clearer view, but because of the shade and the way the car was parked, she wasn't able to see very well into its interior.

The back door of the car opened, and a bear-sized man got out. His face was huge, and the skin on his cheeks was pockmarked and scarred. One scar looked like the mark the heel of a boot makes in mud. He wore jeans and a sleeveless blue jean jacket. His arms were a rich deep brown, but they were marked with various white scar squiggles as well.

Jessie watched as he threw a cigarette to the ground and stomped on it with his beaten-up running shoe.

Was this man Song Maker? The man who was supposed to be healing Harley? As the question formed in her mind, his eyes caught hers, and he nodded.

Feeling more anxious than ever, Jessie looked away. She wished now that she'd insisted Harley see Peter. Peter was a doctor. He would have been able to give the best advice the profession had to offer. What could this man possibly do? He looked like someone who'd just stepped out of a rehab centre.

Song Maker reached back into the car and brought out something rolled in an animal skin. He walked over to Harley and laid the bundle carefully on the ground.

Vernon reappeared from the woods and dropped an armful of dead branches near the bundle, then arranged the wood to make a fire. When he was done, Song Maker unfurled the animal hide and laid out its contents.

Jessie turned to Vernon and whispered, "What is that?"

"His medicine bundle," Vernon said.

He brought out some sage, a smudge bowl, a hawk feather, something made out of bone that looked as if it could have been a whistle and a few small packets.

When the contents of the skin were all laid out, Song Maker took the hide and draped it over Harley. Vernon moved in front of the unlit fire and began talking in Ojibway.

Jessie guessed from other rituals she had done with Harley that Vernon was talking to the Four Directions and asking for their blessings.

Vernon's voice was trance-like, and as he spoke, he lit the fire and sprinkled tobacco over the flames.

Song Maker then stood up and offered more tobacco to the fire. He put some of the dried sage in his smudge bowl and lit it. Aromatic white smoke curled into the air. He passed the bowl to Vernon, who used his feather to usher the smoke around his entire body. After he had smudged himself, he took the bowl to each person in turn.

When Vernon came to Harley, he was careful to make sure the smoke touched all areas of Harley's body. Weakly, Harley used his hands to help Vernon sweep some of the smoke towards his chest. It consoled her to see the sanctity Harley was bringing to the ritual. He had told her once that the Spirits would only come to the pure of heart. If that were so, he was preparing himself fully.

Song Maker came over to Harley now, and the two of them spoke in low tones for several minutes. Jessie had heard Harley speak a few words in Ojibway before, but never as fluently as this. She reminded herself that Ojibway was his mother tongue, the language he'd first heard in his mother's womb, so the sound of it would have flowed through his body like blood. And with it would have come all the memories a language holds within it. The Anishinaabe called this blood memory. The truth of the ancestors.

Song Maker moved away from Harley now and began to talk in a low, private way. He was still speaking in Ojibway, so Jessie couldn't discern the actual words, but she knew he was praying. It sounded intimate and hushed, as if he were talking to his best friend about something of great importance.

He began to sing. The song was full of calling. It was a prayer of calling. Jessie could almost feel it shooting up to the spirit world. She closed her eyes. The song stopped. The whistle sounded four times. Then all was silent.

The silence may have been empty of sound, but it felt charged with energy. So much so that Jessie felt squeezed, as if her entire body were surrounded by a blood pressure cuff being pumped to full swell.

"*Majimanidoo.*"

One Eye jerked her eyes to Song Maker, and Jessie gripped her arm. "What's he saying?"

"Bad spirit."

Jessie's anxiety rose. Over the years, Harley had told her about a variety of native practices, and she had accepted their validity with a certain amount of psychological largesse. But now that it was Harley whose life was at stake, she didn't feel so emotionally generous. In fact, she felt protective of him and worried.

Song Maker was talking faster now, and One Eye was talking too. Jessie listened hard, then whispered to One Eye, "What are they talking about?"

If One Eye heard her, she gave no indication. Feeling desperate to know what was going on, Jessie was about to ask again, when she heard the name Morris. That was Harley's father's name. Another name was spoken too, but it was an Ojibway name. Seeing the emotion the name evoked from One Eye, Jessie thought they must be talking about One Eye's daughter. Harley's mother.

Harley was sick, terribly sick, and they were talking about his family? In the Ojibway tradition, illness was considered part of the person's entire social context, but wasn't that a discussion for after Harley was well?

Jessie shoved her hands under her legs. It was all she could do not to pull Harley up and drag him off to the doctor. The air around her seemed to get tighter and tighter.

Song Maker began to talk faster now, almost shrieking up to the heavens. His speech was loud and impassioned.

Jessie turned to Vernon, who was standing as calmly as if he were in a grocery line. "What's he saying?"

Vernon spoke matter-of-factly. "Song Maker says the water poison wouldn't have come into Harley's body if the waters inside him hadn't already been sick. From his family."

Jessie was well aware of the terrible hurt Harley had endured because of his father's abuse and his mother's suicide, but to talk about all that now seemed crazy to her. Harley was physically sick.

"Now Song Maker's going to doctor him," Vernon said.

The word "doctor" alarmed her. What did that mean?

Harley writhed as another cramp seized him. Jessie squeezed his hand in both of hers.

Song Maker reached over and touched her hand. She knew he wanted her to move her hand away from Harley.

"No," she said. She needed to keep her grip on him. At all costs.

Song Maker turned the fullness of his face towards her, and she looked into his eyes. She was expecting reprimand, but there was only compassion. He took her hands in his. The palms and fingers were huge, like paws, but they emanated unutterable peace.

When he let her hands go, she nodded to him.

Song Maker laid his giant hands on Harley now. He held them there for a long time. Slowly, Harley's body, which had been contorted with pain, began to relax. After a while, he took a huge breath and lay perfectly still.

"*Zoongizi,*" Song Maker said.

Jessie was about to ask for a translation when she saw One Eye nod up to the heavens in deep gratitude.

Song Maker stood up, walked over to the car and lit a cigarette.

"Is that it?" Jessie was so surprised by the abrupt end to things, that she wasn't even sure she spoke the question aloud.

Chapter 38

Dan packed all his clothes, leaving out a fresh shirt and a pair of underwear. He closed the cardboard flaps on the box, took it out to the porch and stacked it on top of the others. He stared out across the lake. On the other side of the bay, there was a flag of bright red leaves on one of the maple trees. Tomorrow was the first day of September, and he was relieved the summer was over.

First thing tomorrow, he was moving to his new place in Orillia. It was just a room, but it would do until the court case was over, and he went to jail. He wished he could skip the court appearance and go directly to jail as in a Monopoly game. He was dreading the trial. He couldn't see the point of it. He was guilty and was going to plead guilty, and as far as he was concerned, the sooner his punishment started, the better.

But, as Jessie had reminded him the other day, all he had to do at the trial was tell the truth. It wasn't like he had to fabricate some complicated story and then remember what he'd said to which person. He wasn't doing that any more.

When he and Wayne had been charged with criminal negligence, his lawyer had said they would both get off with a hefty fine as long as no one died. But Sonny had died. Dan knew he was lucky that others hadn't died as well, but for him, the loss was as great as if half the town had perished.

When the stack of boxes became unsteady from the height, he began carrying them out to the car. What would he do with all this crap when he went to jail? He'd give it away, that's what he'd do. It had no meaning to him now. He would be wearing regulation clothing where he was going anyway. He would also be given a number to identify himself. He didn't mind. It would be a relief not to be reminded about who he was.

Until he went to jail, he would need his clothes. He had to get a job, for one thing. Once he'd settled himself into his room in Orillia, he planned to start looking for something, anything—leaf raking, fence fixing. As long as the job allowed him to work outside and alone, he would be grateful.

"You're not a leper, you know," Jessie had said to him the other day when she'd telephoned. He was so grateful they were talking again. He still hadn't seen her because, as she'd explained, she'd been taking care of people who were sick, a fact which made him all the more appreciative of her calls.

"You're someone who made an awful mistake," she told him. "You won't be the first person who's made one, and you won't be the last."

He knew that, but only in his head. Shame still burned through his bones. In yesterday's conversation, she'd made a point of telling him about other people who had, through their own "unconsciousness" as she'd put it, done something terrible: people who had caused fires, or hit someone while driving a car, people who had smashed their spouse's faces in, people who had committed war crimes. He knew she was trying to get him to understand he wasn't alone in harming others. In fact, everyone had hurt someone at some time in their lives. It was just a matter of degree.

In the stories Jessie told him, the person who had done the harm always attempted to make amends. In one story, Jessie told him about a man who had locked his daughter out of the house for coming home late, only to learn from the police that she'd been raped and murdered within an hour of his turning the bolt. According to Jessie, it had taken the man over a year to stop crying, but he'd eventually forgiven himself enough to start a life again. Since then, he'd created a hotline for kids to call at any hour of the day or night. Even now, he toured the country, talking to kids about how to be street smart. The title of his talk was "How To Be Smart When Your Parents Are Dumb".

Dan knew Jessie was telling him about such people in the hopes that it would help him think about his own life and what he might do to make amends. Right now, he couldn't imagine ever making up for what he'd done. How could he make it up to Megan? Right now his crime felt far too horrendous ever to atone for.

Dan pulled out some cleaning liquid from under the sink and began to sponge down the fridge. As he set the trays of ice cubes from the freezer into the sink to thaw, he wondered what he might tell prospective employers. He knew it would be easier if he made up a new name. He could say he'd just moved here from Alberta or something. But even the thought made him feel unclean somehow. Ugly in his heart. Lying wasn't an option any more.

He was washing the butter dish when he heard the slam of a car door out in the parking area. Meat always had people dropping by when he was at the cottage, or the visitor might be his mother. She was the only one who came regularly. And when she did come, there was a furtiveness about her visits that made him think his father didn't know she was making them. He didn't ask. He was grateful simply to see her. And even more grateful that she never said anything about what had happened. There was no point. She knew he felt awful. And he could tell she felt awful too. Words weren't going to change that. Nor were words going to change the little pink pillows under her eyes that she always got when she'd been crying.

What astounded him was that even with all his fuck-ups, she still loved him. He could feel it in the hug she gave him when she arrived. Each time she came, she cooked him some meals and cleared out the ones she'd left from the week before without saying anything. To make her happy, he tried to eat when she was there. The rest of the time he didn't bother much. He knew he'd lost weight, because he had to use a belt to hold his pants up. Jessie had suggested it was part of the way he was punishing himself. Maybe that was true. But shouldn't he be punished? Sometimes he wished he could be flogged or whipped—just to pay some sort of penalty.

Dan was rinsing the sponge when he saw Meat coming up the path to the bunkie. He entered the kitchen and stood in the doorway, an open bottle of beer held protectively to his chest. Gripping another bottle by the neck, Meat stretched his arm out towards Dan as if he were passing a relay stick.

Dan reached forward and took the beer. It felt strange in his hand, like an artefact from another world.

Meat took a long slug and said, "See the game last night?"

Dan looked at him incredulously, as if he were relating

information about another planet.

Meat lifted his beer to his mouth and eyed Dan down the long shaft of the brown bottle. "Still think you're getting a bum deal. It wasn't your fault the lagoon busted."

A slight smile crept to Dan's mouth. After all these days of mouth-slackening sadness, it felt strange to experience a smile again. But Meat's allegiance was endearing. Meat was such a guy's guy, so willing to defend a buddy against all odds.

"Want a good lawyer? I know a guy who could make the Mafia look good."

Dan looked at Meat fondly. Should he try to explain that it actually felt good not to try and squirm out of this, that there was strength to be found from owning up to what he'd done? No. Meat was a hockey player. To him, offence was the best defence, so there wasn't much point.

"Thanks," he said, "but I think I'll stick with the lawyer I have."

Meat moved his big head up and down and shifted his feet awkwardly. "If there's anything I can do."

Dan was about to let the comment go by, but an idea came into his mind. "Actually, there is something."

"Just name it, dude."

He found Meat's eyes. They were squirrel grey. Funny, he had known Meat all these years, yet had never really looked at him, at least not closely enough to know the colour of his eyes. Dan spoke into those eyes now. "You could drop the assault and trespassing charges."

Meat pulled his head back as if he'd been hit with a pie. "You want me to let those two nutbars off the hook? Why?"

A rush of emotions rose in Dan's chest. He turned away and said. "One of them got sick. From the water. The other

272 Karen Hood-Caddy

one's been helping her. And others. If you dropped the charges, it would be one less thing for them to worry about."

Dan watched as Meat took the bottle to his mouth again and swung back his head. Meat's neck was as wide as another man's thigh and looked just as powerful. The hockey player swallowed hard. As he did, his Adam's apple looked like a fist going up and down.

Setting the empty bottle on the counter, Meat said, "My mother wants me to drop the charges too."

"Your mother?"

"Yeah. She thinks it's bad publicity." He turned his palms up. "Two crazy old ladies bust a guy's balls, and they get the sympathy. Go figure."

Dan said nothing.

Meat gave him a jovial punch in the shoulder. "Well, I got a date. So—" He punched Dan again. "Take her easy." He grinned. "But take her." He waved and was gone.

Dan stood without moving and watched Meat leave. When he was alone again, he sat down on the deck and sipped the beer. He hadn't had anything to drink since the day of his attempted suicide. The beer tasted different from his memory of it. And to his surprise, it didn't taste that fantastic. He was glad. There would be no drinking in prison, so he might as well get used to going without it.

His mother had already told him she would visit, no matter how far away the prison was. Her commitment amazed him. His father, on the other hand, hadn't called or made contact with him since Dan had been charged.

"He'll never speak to me again," he'd told Jessie when they were talking about Frank one day.

"Never's a long time," Jessie had said. "He might come around one day."

Meanwhile, Dan didn't mind not talking to Frank. He didn't think he could cope with his father right now anyway.

No, if he could talk to anyone, it would be Megan. He'd imagined calling her a thousand times, imagined telling her how sorry he was, but he knew that hearing from him would cause her pain, and he didn't want to cause her any more than he already had.

"The sewage leak wasn't just your responsibility," Jessie had reminded him the other day. "Wayne played a part in it too."

Wayne. From what Dan had heard, Wayne had gone into seclusion after he had been charged and wasn't seeing anyone. So, Megan had essentially lost him as well. She'd lost Sonny, her brother, and now Carlingview was up for sale.

How could a person handle so much pain? He felt he was learning the answer to that from personal experience.

Hearing another car, he went to the window. He didn't recognize the vehicle. Was it a reporter? He tensed. There had been so many at one time.

He could see someone reaching into the back seat for something. A baseball bat? A rifle? There were lots of rednecks in this town. Maybe one was coming for him, bent on teaching him a lesson.

"Come on in," he should yell. "Put me out of my misery."

He smiled ironically. Jessie couldn't be mad at him if someone else ended his life.

Then he realized that the person who was reaching into the car was too shapely to be a man. He stretched forward to see her better. What was she getting from the back seat? When he realized who it was, he stiffened.

Carrying the squirming bundle, she approached the

cabin. "Anybody home?"

Dan stood immobilized.

"Dan, I know you're here somewhere..."

He heard the screen door open and turned. He saw the baby first and felt a thin trickle of happiness move through his chest.

"I heard you were moving," Christie said. She pulled her fingers through her shiny brown hair and away from her full face.

"Who told you?"

"Your mother. I've been calling to see how you were."

Dan stared at her. He didn't know what to say. She looked good. At ease somehow.

The baby began to squirm, and she unzipped the carrier to readjust him. "Can you take him a minute?" As she tried to lift the baby out of the carrier, one of his feet got caught, and Dan had to untangle it. When the baby was free, Christie put him in Dan's arms.

Dan scrambled to hold the baby so his head was supported. The child smelled of talcum powder.

"He's heavy, isn't he? He's got your strong body," Christie said. "Come on, let's go down to the water. I need to cool off."

Christie led the way, and Dan followed slowly, holding the baby protectively into his chest.

At the water, Christie sat down at the end of the dock, took her shoes off and dangled her feet in the water. Dan sat down beside her. He was about to give the baby back to her when she reached towards the child and began unsnapping his jumper suit.

"Poor thing, he looks so hot."

Freed of his clothes, the baby kicked happily at the air.

Dan dipped his hand in the water and trickled it on the baby's feet. The boy shrieked with delight and pumped his legs up and down.

"What are you going to call him?"

"I'm calling him Dan. Little Dan."

Dan felt a thickness in his throat and looked out over the lake. The sky was turning pink, and he could see the first evening star.

After a while, Christie began to dress the boy again. Little Dan began to fuss, and Christie lifted him up, raised her shirt to nudge a full breast into the baby's mouth. Dan didn't know what to do with his eyes, so he looked back at the sunset. The sound of happy suckling filled the still night air.

When Dan looked back at the boy, he was asleep.

Christie set their sleeping son in Dan's arms as she rearranged her blouse and bra.

Dan looked down at the baby. The boy's eyes were closed, and there was an exalted peace on his face. Dan thought about Sonny. He knew he could never change the terrible thing he'd done to the boy, but was it possible for him to make it up to the spirit of Sonny through fathering this child that he held in his arms? Little Dan made a happy chortling sound in his sleep.

Chapter 39

Jessie dipped her paddle in the lake and thrust the water back. Elfy's yellow canoe scooted forward, bright against the black-green water. As usual, the lake was a myriad of colour, dark here beside the canoe, but full of silver apostrophes where she had dipped her paddle. And, if Jessie looked ahead, beyond Elfy's crimson red sweater, the surface of the lake was winking blue and grey.

They were close to shore now, and Jessie steered the canoe around some rocks that poked their heads up just above the surface of the lake. She smiled. Rocks were so self-assured. They didn't notice their surroundings and weren't aware of their effect on their surroundings. Water, on the other hand, had an intimacy with all that it touched. Perhaps that was because water was penetrable. Even now, she could see how the lake took the sunlight into it, sucking it down into its belly. Rocks, earth, forest, they kept the light out. Not water. Water drank the light in and became luminous.

It was reassuring to know that wherever she and Harley ended up living, they would be near water. They'd already decided that. And now that they'd made up their mind to leave, Jessie was looking forward to it. As long as she was with Harley, it really didn't matter where she was.

Although he was still recovering, still taking the various

herbs and medicines Song Maker had given him, there was no question he was on the mend. And that's what mattered, not whether Song Maker had been the one to heal him.

In the front of the canoe, Elfy was sorting through mail. Jessie had wanted her to leave it until after the canoe ride, but this was Elfy's first day back from the hospital, and she was eager to catch up on things.

"Lookie, lookie," Elfy said, waving something in the air. "Tickets!"

"What kind of tickets?"

"These are worth a fortune!" She reached one hand back so Jessie could see them and raised the other in victory. "Season's tickets to the Toronto Maple Leafs. Wow! What a great homecoming present." She grinned.

"Who gave you those?"

Elfy snorted. "I was so excited, I didn't even look." Her eyes scrambled down the letter that was in her lap. "Jesus in a jump suit!" She looked up at Jessie with large eyes. "You'll never guess."

"No, I probably won't, so tell me."

"Our favourite hockey player's mother!"

"They're from Andy Malowski's mother?"

Elfy nodded vigorously and looked back down at the letter. "The tickets are for both of us. And—they're dropping the charges."

Jessie stopped paddling and smiled. How interesting. The court case had been the last thing tying her to Muskoka. And now that tie had just been snipped.

"Now you won't even have to come back for the trial," Elfy said. Her voice was not happy.

"No, now I can come back just because I want to," Jessie said.

"Sure will be weird not being able to call you up on the phone," Elfy said.

"You can call me on the cell phone any time. And that will only be until we get settled and get a regular phone."

"Yeah, but it'll be long distance."

"Call collect. I won't mind."

"It won't be the same not being able to see you whenever I want."

No, Jessie thought, it won't, and there was no point in trying to make it sound like it would.

"I'm going to miss you too," Jessie said finally. "But, remember, Harley has to keep his stores stocked, so we'll be driving through here once a month anyway. Maybe we can stay with you at the cottage sometimes. That's if you're not in Toronto at one of your hockey games."

Elfy guffawed. "The tickets were for both of us."

"I hereby bequeath my part ownership to you."

"Too bad Dan is so young, or I'd take him."

"Take him anyway. It's never too early to get a kid used to the sound of a puck whizzing into a net. After all, he is Canadian."

Elfy laughed again. "Yeah, I guess if I want someone to keep me in the lap of luxury when I get old, if I ever decide to get old, having a famous hockey player for a relative could come in handy."

Jessie smiled. It was a relief to her that Elfy had Christie and Little Dan in her life. She knew Elfy would have lots to occupy her time and heart when Jessie had gone.

Elfy stuffed the tickets back in the envelope, crossed her arms and stared ahead. "I still wish you weren't leaving."

Jessie was quiet. All the talking in the world wasn't going to make Elfy feel better. But leaving was the right thing to do, of that she was certain. The water catastrophe had shown her how precious life was. Someone you loved could be taken from you at any moment. Sonny had been taken from Megan. Harley had almost been taken from her. The fingers of death had certainly fondled his body, but death had turned away. For now.

Harley, of course, had no doubt whatsoever that his healing had come from the ceremony with Song Maker. Jessie had certainly felt the man's power. But was that power enough to heal someone? She couldn't decide. There was no need to decide either. In matters of what she called The Mystery, the mind was out of its league.

Meanwhile, what she wanted was to spend her days making sure she had as much time as possible with the man she loved.

Of course, Hope-in-Hell was going with them. Harley planned to find him a water home far away from any human intervention, a place where Hope-in-Hell would never hear the sound of dynamite again.

As yet, their destination wasn't clear. The plan was to spend the next few months poking around the north. Hopefully, by the time the snow fell, they would know where they wanted to settle. There was no rush. Although Harley was stronger every day, he wanted to be entirely well before they set off. Besides, they both felt it was important to say goodbye to Muskoka before they could say hello to somewhere else.

"I hear Carlingview is up for sale," Elfy said.

"I heard that too."

Although Jessie didn't say so, she'd heard that from Megan, who was staying in Toronto with friends. Megan was still in deep grief over the loss of Sonny, but friends and family had gathered around her, and she was coping, which was all she could be expected to do at this stage. One day she would feel like living again, but that wouldn't be for a while. Meanwhile, Jessie had given her the names of some excellent therapists in the city in case she felt she needed help. Of all the possible losses to bear, Jessie knew that losing a child was the most excruciating.

"I wonder if anyone will buy the place," Elfy said.

"Carlingview? Someone will. Eventually. People will start to forget."

"Half the town's still using bottled water."

It was true—even though the water had been tested by many qualified officials.

"That will change once the new water treatment plant opens," Jessie said.

The plant was scheduled to open in October. Town officials were boasting that the new technology would be so advanced that a situation like the one that had just happened could never happen again. Jessie couldn't imagine a system so comprehensive that it could totally compensate for human error, but she kept her opinions to herself. These days, people liked to believe that technology could save them from bad things ever happening. Jessie hoped she never allowed technology to seduce her that completely. The truth was, bad things happened sometimes. To her, the ultimate human competence was resilience, and resilience only came by facing challenges head on. That's what Dan was doing. Facing his challenges head on.

It had always amazed her what the human spirit could endure. Dan was a true example of that. And, oddly enough, his burdens seemed to be developing his emotional and spiritual muscle. It was strange, but sometimes the very act of giving up one's life allowed a person to step into it more fully.

Not so, however, with Lyn. Jessie had finally found out where Lyn was living and had gone to see her. Bill, Lyn's ex-partner, had told her where the cabin was. Despite his warnings, Jessie had been shocked. The cabin was in the woods in the middle of nowhere. Set on cinderblock, a foot off the mould-producing ground, it was no bigger than a large tool shed. A dozen large oxygen canisters were leaning against the small porch.

A sign nailed to the door of the cabin said, "Caution: Oxygen in use. No smoking. No open flames. No matches. No candles. A Chemically Sensitive, Allergic Person Lives Here. Do not come into the house if you're wearing perfume, hair spray, deodorant or dry-cleaned clothes."

Jessie had gone to the door. She could hear the thrum of the air filter even from where she was standing. She knocked, then knocked again. A very thin woman came to the window wearing an oxygen mask. Jessie only recognized her by her long, black hair. Shaking her head as if in warning, Lyn wrote something to Jessie on some paper. The big letters said: "Roads tarred yesterday. Can't risk opening door."

Jessie sighed. She didn't know what to do. She had no pen and paper to write on and didn't think her voice would be heard over the noise of the air filter. Finally, she put her arms around herself, as if in a hug and pointed to Lyn. "For you," she mouthed.

Lyn smiled. It was a small, thin smile, but it was a smile.

Jessie stood there for a minute, not knowing what else to do. Bill had told her that he dropped off supplies for her and was generally keeping an eye on things. Thank goodness for him, Jessie thought as she waved goodbye.

Now, as Jessie paddled on, she wondered what Lyn's chances were of ever getting better. According to her research, a small percentage of people with E.I. did heal, but it took a long time.

Jessie sighed. People like Lyn were like the canaries in the mineshaft, warning the rest of the world that something was seriously wrong. How many more people would have to get sick before the others woke up? Only if E.I. became more pervasive would it receive more attention. Perhaps then, more healing options would be found.

Meanwhile, Lyn had no choice but to try and survive. Jessie just wished there was more she could do to help. Song Maker's face appeared in her mind. Would he be able to help? Jessie decided she would call him when she got back. Maybe she could take him out to see Lyn before she and Harley left.

Ahead of her in the boat, Elfy shifted her weight as if she couldn't quite get comfortable.

"I wish I could stop thinking about Sonny," Elfy said. "He was so young to die. Too young to die. It should have been me."

"It wasn't your time, Elf."

"I guess not."

They both were silent. Finally, Elfy said, "I wonder what's going to happen to Dan?"

It was the question on everyone's mind. Some people in town thought his punishment should be severe. To them, there was no punishment severe enough for someone who killed a child.

The majority of the townspeople, however, were too exhausted by all that had happened to care. They knew that no punishment could bring Sonny back, nor could any punishment alleviate the stain the water disaster had put on Muskoka's history. They knew that only time could heal what had happened, and they were anxious to move on.

Because of Sonny's death, it was certain Dan would go to jail for some period of time. She knew from her various talks with him that he was prepared for this eventuality. In a way, she thought it might help him to feel as if he'd paid part of his debt.

However long he went to jail, she knew he would never get over the mistake he'd made, nor would she want him to. It was too important an experience. At the moment, he was carrying it like a huge weight and was wobbling under the pressure. At some point, she hoped he would become strong enough to carry it and still move forward with his life. There was much about Dan that was good.

Yesterday he'd told her that he'd started a new comic strip. Dan said the idea for the comic had come from InkBoy, so he was going to draw the cartoon under that pen-name. He also said that if he ever sold the idea to anyone, he would dedicate the profits to the childrens' hospital in honour of Sonny. Jessie thought that was a great idea. Such an action would be healing for all concerned.

He had also shared with her some of the conflicting feelings he had for Little Dan. As he began to care about the child, he felt as if he were being disloyal to Sonny. Jessie was able to reassure him that his feelings for Little Dan were to be nurtured and supported. She told Dan that he had an opportunity with this child to father in an entirely new way. It pleased her to think that the sins of the father might not be passed along.

The yellow canoe bumped gently against Jessie's dock.

Up at the house, Christie was turning the old bird room into a room for the baby. It made Jessie smile that Christie was moving into their house. Since Elfy's place wasn't winterized, Christie couldn't stay there much longer. So Jessie had suggested she move into their place after she and Harley had gone. It was just another small sign that they were doing the right thing.

Elfy used the curved handles of the swimming ladder to pull herself from the boat.

"I'll be up in a few minutes," Jessie said and watched Elfy head off, the hand holding the tickets pumping hard in her eagerness to get to other people for a good show and tell.

Jessie sat back in the canoe and trailed her hands in the lake. The water felt so alive that for a moment, she imagined her hands were in the body of another being, a water being that stretched itself over the entire planet.

Over the last few weeks, as she'd done her research, she'd been encouraged by the thousands of people and groups, all over the planet, who had the kind of consciousness that respected all living things. The question was, were the millions who treated the planet with respect enough to counter the many more millions who didn't? She'd once heard that it only took ten per cent of the human population to embrace an idea for it to become an accepted philosophy. How many conscious people would it take to make ten per cent? She had a feeling the world was close to that number now.

When she and Harley were settled in their new place, she planned to get in touch with some of those people and groups. Even though she was going to be nestled away in a cabin in the wilderness, she would carry on her work to raise consciousness about nature. And meanwhile, she would live in a way that was totally in tune with it. She smiled. She had a feeling nature was going to like that as much as she.

She tied up the canoe and looked out over the lake. Then, on impulse, she stripped down and dove in. The water took her into its coolness and slipped and slid around her body, washing her face, brushing her hair back, swirling around her skin. Wanting to stay immersed in it for as long as she could, she swam underwater, wiggling her way through the bright greenness. The sun filtered through the water making her arms appear golden as they made large curves in front of her. She swam on, feeling her lungs widen and stretch in search of air. When the imperative to breathe drove her up towards the silver surface, she burst through, spouting a fountain of water out her mouth. Her gums tingled, and she flipped over and arched back, spreading her arms out so she could float.

She felt as if she were lying on the belly of the great water mother. A deep peace buoyed up within her. She closed her eyes and became aware of a slight pulse in the water. It wasn't a rhythmic kind of pulsing as in the blood in a human body, it was more like a steady radiating energy, primordial and sacred. She had felt this energy before, felt it in the woods, smelled it in the wind, tasted it in the first crunch of lettuce from her garden, but here, in water, she felt as if she were closest to the centre of its heart.

No wonder water felt like home.

Slowly, she swam back to the dock. Harley was waiting for her. She reached up her hand, and he pulled her out of the water, then wrapped a towel around her shoulders. Arm in arm, they walked up the steps.

Karen Hood-Caddy was born in Toronto, Ontario, but spent all her summers at the family cottage in the Muskoka region. After years of travelling and working abroad, she returned to Muskoka, where she works as a life coach and leads workshops on a variety of topics.

Her first novel, *Tree Fever*, was published by RendezVous Press in 1997. The sequel, *Flying Lessons*, followed in 2001. The author can be contacted at:

karen@personalbest.org